I0699612

THE WEXLEY INN

RACHEL HANNA

CHAPTER 1

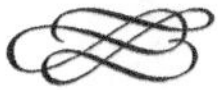

Isabella Montgomery pulled her rental car to the side of the road just before the bridge to Wexley Island, her hands trembling slightly on the steering wheel. Through the windshield, she could see the white columns and wraparound porch of The Wexley Inn rising above the marsh grass, like something from a dream - or maybe a memory that had haunted her for thirty years.

She'd been twenty-two the first time she'd seen this view, riding in Thomas Langley's beat-up pickup truck during spring break of their senior year of college. He'd brought her home to meet his daddy and show her the island where he'd grown up. "*One day,*" he'd said, pointing at the old inn across the water, "*I'm gonna restore a place just like that.*" She'd squeezed his hand and whispered, "**We will.**"

Now, at fifty-two, she was finally here - alone.

"Oh, so you're the one who bought the old inn," the guard said, looking at her over his reading glasses with great curiosity. "Haven't seen that much excitement since the Ladies Club had their big dustup over the Christmas decorations last year."

"Yes, I'm the new owner," Isabella said, smiling politely, although all she felt was impatience. "That's all the paperwork right there."

The guard studied the documents as if he were going to present a case in court, and then finally nodded.

"Well, welcome to Wexley Island, Ms. Montgomery. You can follow that main road right there until you reach our one little traffic circle. Take the second exit toward the historic district. You can't miss the inn. It's the big white building with the wraparound porch."

She nodded. "Thank you," she said, accepting the visitor's pass he handed her, along with what appeared to be a huge thick booklet full of community guidelines.

She laughed to herself when she thought about how he described how to get to the house that she now owned. She knew exactly where The Wexley Inn was. It had been her dream for a long time. Well, since the moment Thomas had pointed across the marsh toward it.

For a split second, she allowed herself to wonder about him. To wonder where he'd ended up in life. To wonder if he ever visited Wexley Island. Doubtful. Thomas was the most talented person she'd ever met. Surely he was in some big city, designing skyscrapers or houses for the rich and famous.

As the gate lifted, she felt a strange mixture of anxiety and excitement. This moment represented everything she'd worked toward since her divorce two years ago, since she'd cashed in her retirement and walked away from over twenty years of managing other people's hotels.

Most people would be sad after a divorce, but the event had barely bothered Isabella. Not a tear was shed, in fact. Her marriage had only lasted five years, and two of those years were spent apart, as Todd had lived in London, running a hotel there.

Maybe she'd thought a woman her age should finally marry. She didn't know why she'd said yes, but she knew it was the wrong decision from the moment she'd said *"I do."*

Wexley Island was meticulously maintained, and the road wound through smaller neighborhoods and elegant homes with expansive porches and perfectly manicured lawns. Sprinklers cast rainbows in the morning light as they nourished beds of camellias and azaleas. She passed the entrance to *The Palms*, where a discreet sign announced the prestigious name of The Wexley Inn. A little further down, another sign was marked *The Dunes*, where the newer and larger homes overlooked the Atlantic Ocean.

Her rental cottage was located somewhere in between, not quite grand enough for *The Palms*, but certainly respectable from the pictures she'd seen online. She would move in later in the day after she'd had a chance to walk through the inn.

She had closed on the inn without seeing it in person, which was probably a crazy idea. But it didn't matter to her. When she saw it on the market, there was never a question whether she'd buy it. It didn't matter to her whether a family of geese lived in it; she was meant to own The Wexley Inn. Once the inn was somewhat livable, she would move into it, but for now, she figured staying in a cottage was better.

She saw a small family of deer grazing peacefully near the road, completely unbothered by her car. She slowed down and watched them, a smile spreading across her face. This wasn't something she often saw, having worked in big cities for the last twenty-plus years. The guard had mentioned several things before she drove away, including the fact that the deer were protected on the island - wildlife in general, really - including raccoons, possums, and the occasional alligator.

Wexley Island was a real-life wildlife sanctuary.

As she rounded the corner to the Historic District, she saw The Wexley Inn. Her heart literally skipped a beat. The photographs she'd seen over the years certainly hadn't done it justice, and it had been a long time since she had driven by it herself, back when it was still in good repair.

Even though it was neglected, it was magnificent. A three-story white clapboard structure with black shutters, a huge wraparound porch, and gabled windows. Ancient live oak trees stood on either side of the property, as if they were sentinels, their branches creating natural archways over an oyster-shell driveway.

She parked and sat for a moment, remembering Thomas's voice: *"Look at those bones, Isabella. You can always fix up a house if the bones are good."*

"Well," she said to herself quietly, "here goes everything."

She stepped out of her car, the humid coastal air both embracing and assaulting her simultaneously. The scent of jasmine and salt water mingled in the air. She wore a simple white linen dress and comfortable black flats, practical for exploring an old property but still professional enough in case she encountered any of her new neighbors.

As Isabella climbed the steps to the porch, she noticed a few worn spots in the wooden floorboards, the peeling paint on the railings, and several missing spindles. This renovation would be extensive, but she'd budgeted for that, thankfully. What mattered to her was that the bones of the place were solid.

She unlocked the front door with the old antique key the real estate agent had given her, feeling a bit of a thrill as she turned it in the lock. The door swung open with a creak, revealing a grand entryway with a sweeping staircase. Dust danced in the air as sunlight streamed through the windows, illuminating the faded grandeur of the space.

For the next hour, she moved methodically through the inn, making notes on her tablet about every room. The fourteen guest rooms would need to be completely updated. The dining room required restoration, and the kitchen would as well. She winced as she surveyed all of the outdated appliances and worn countertops that would have to be entirely gutted, but the hardwood floors throughout could be refinished instead of being replaced. The original moldings were mostly intact.

When she finally reached the back of the house,

she found a set of French doors that led out to an overgrown garden. She pushed them open and stepped outside, surprising herself when she came face-to-face with an elderly woman sitting calmly in a worn wicker chair, sipping a glass of sweet tea.

"Oh, sorry, I didn't realize anyone was here," Isabella said, extending her hand. "I'm Isabella Montgomery, the new owner."

The woman looked at her with shrewd, dark eyes that contrasted her cloud of white hair. She wore a crisp white blouse and navy slacks and looked far more put together than one would expect for somebody who was apparently trespassing on Isabella's new property.

"Luella Washington," the woman said, accepting Isabella's handshake with a firm grip. "I was the former cook at this establishment for forty-two years, and I'm the current resident of the staff quarters." She pointed toward a small cottage partially hidden by overgrown camellia bushes at the edge of the garden. Her Southern accent was as thick as the moss hanging from the trees.

Isabella blinked in surprise. "I'm really sorry, but I didn't think anyone was living on the property. I mean, the previous owner didn't mention—"

"Mr. Harrington knew better than to try to evict me," Luella interrupted, crossing her arms over her chest. Her tone wasn't confrontational; it was just matter-of-fact, like her words were the law and that was it. "My quarters were not a part of this sale. You'll find that in the fine print if you look carefully enough."

Isabella made a mental note to call her real estate agent as soon as possible. This was a complication she hadn't anticipated or wanted.

"Okay," she said carefully. "Well, it's a pleasure to meet you, Ms. Washington."

"Luella, please." Her expression softened ever so slightly. "I should warn you, this old place has a way of choosing its owners. It's been standing here since before my grandmother was born. I've seen owners come and go, and the ones who try to change too much around here never last very long."

Before Isabella could respond to her very cryptic comment, Luella set her teacup on the table and stood.

"You'll want to check the attic. There's a leak above the third-floor guest bathroom that never got fixed properly. People like to cut corners nowadays. The wiring in the east wing also needs replacing. That's a fire hazard."

With that, she picked up her teacup again and walked with a dignified slowness toward her little cottage, leaving Isabella staring after her.

Well, that was unexpected, Isabella thought. Maybe having someone with intimate knowledge of the property would prove to be useful, assuming Luella was willing to share more practical insights and fewer mysterious warnings.

Isabella continued her inspection of the property, confirming Luella's information about the leak. She made additional notes. By midday, she had a comprehensive list of renovations that needed to be addressed immediately. The scope of it was more daunting than she ever could have thought, but it wasn't unmanageable, not with the right contractor.

Her next stop was the Wexley Island Bank to meet with Gerald Stewart. He was handling her renovation loan. The bank was located in a stately brick building right on the edge of the historic district. Inside, its interior was all polished wood and subtle luxury. The building was surrounded by live oak trees draped in Spanish moss, just like out of a picture book of the Lowcountry.

"Ms. Montgomery, welcome," Gerald said. He was a ruddy-faced man in his early sixties with a booming Southern voice that contrasted with the quiet atmosphere of the bank. He waved her into his office, where several folders were neatly arranged on his desk. "I've been looking forward to meeting you. That inn has been an eyesore for far too long. It's going to be good to see it restored to its former glory."

"Well, that's exactly my plan," Isabella said, taking a seat. "I've just come from there. The renovation is going to be extensive, a lot more than I expected seeing it in person, but I know it's worth it."

"Oh, of course," Gerald nodded enthusiastically. "That building is a part of this island's heritage. Now, I've taken the liberty of reviewing the inspection report, and I've prepared some preliminary loan options for the renovation."

They spent the next half hour discussing the financials, with Gerald explaining the intricacies of renovation loans for historic properties and all the associated details.

"So the architectural review board will need to approve any exterior changes," he said, a hint of warning in his voice. "They can be, well… let's just call it *particular*."

"I understand. I'm committed to preserving the historic character of the building. It's very important to me."

"Oh, good, good. That'll help. Now, about contractors." He shuffled through his papers. "That might be a bit tricky. Most of the major renovation companies are booked solid with projects over on *The Dunes*."

Isabella had anticipated this. "I've already reached out to several firms in Charleston who specialize in historic renovations. They're willing to commute."

Gerald looked uncomfortable. "Well, you see, the thing is, our review board favors local businesses for significant projects like this. Obtaining approval for outside contractors to work on this island is a bureaucratic nightmare. Security clearances, temporary passes, insurance requirements."

Isabella felt uneasy. "So then what do you suggest?"

"Well, there's really only one local contractor that has the expertise and capacity to handle a project of this magnitude," Gerald said. He pulled a business card from his desk drawer. "Langley Restoration. Thomas specializes in historic properties. He did the Beaumont place over in *The Palms* last year. Absolutely magnificent work. I feel sure that the committee would allow him to handle the work on The Wexley Inn."

The room seemed to tilt sideways. Isabella stared at the card Gerald held out to her, her vision tunneling.

Thomas Langley.

Not just any Thomas Langley. *Her* Thomas Langley. The man who'd held her close on this very island thirty years ago and promised they'd build a life together. The man who'd vanished without a word one day after graduation, leaving only a brief note saying he "had to go home" and "couldn't explain."

"Is something wrong?"

"No, I just…" Isabella forced herself to take the card, her fingers feeling numb. "That name sounds familiar, that's all."

"Oh, Thomas has been on this island forever. His daddy worked maintenance for several of the old estates before he passed. Then Thomas went off to college, I think for architectural engineering, and later returned to start his business. He's highly respected here, but he can be a bit particular about the projects he takes on."

Isabella nodded, but her mind was racing. What were the odds it was the same Thomas? Thomas Langley? That man who broke her heart all those years ago? He was now potentially the only person who could help her realize her dream.

"So I've set up a meeting for you with him tomorrow morning," Gerald said, oblivious to the fact that she was losing her mind and having the world's worst internal panic attack. "Nine o'clock at the inn. I hope that's okay."

"Wait, you've already contacted him?" She tried to keep her voice from sounding like a shrieking alarm bell.

"Of course." Gerald looked surprised. "Property like the inn, that's big news on a small island. He knows it's being renovated, and he's the logical choice for the job."

She took a deep breath, trying to center herself, trying desperately to remember all those meditation classes she took. It didn't seem to be helping her much right now.

She was no longer that naïve twenty-two-year-old college student whose world had been shattered when Thomas Langley had walked away without any explanation whatsoever. She was a successful businesswoman with decades of experience handling all kinds of difficult situations, and she would handle Thomas Langley.

"That's fine," she said, her voice sounding way steadier than she actually felt, "and I appreciate your help setting that up."

As she left the bank, Isabella walked straight to her car, closed the door, and blew out the most extended breath of her life.

Of all the complications she had anticipated, running into Thomas hadn't even been on the list. Why would it? What were the chances he'd still be on this small island after all these years?

She looked at the business card in her hand.

Langley Restoration.

The logo featured a little historic home with meticulous detailing, just the kind of attention to craftsmanship she remembered him displaying in their architectural projects.

Isabella started the car and was determined not to let this development derail her plans. She would meet with Thomas tomorrow and maintain strict professionalism. Who knows, maybe he wouldn't even remember her. Of course, that was unlikely given their long relationship in college.

She was determined to focus on what mattered - bringing The Wexley Inn back to life. And if he were the best contractor for the job, she'd hire him, despite their personal history. After all, it had been thirty years, and they were probably both different people now.

Whatever had been between them was long gone, relegated to the past, like the faded old photographs she had packed away decades ago. He was probably married with kids, and she had her own life going on, as well. There was no need to let the past get in the way.

By the time she arrived at her rental cottage, a charming one-bedroom bungalow closer to *The Palms* than *The Dunes*, she had convinced herself that the meeting would be nothing more than a professional discussion between two people.

She spent the evening unpacking her essentials and creating a vision board for the inn on the dining table, pinning various fabric swatches, color themes, and photographs of the historic hotel interiors that inspired her. The physical activity helped keep her mind off the impending reunion. Of course, she could do all of this online, maybe even create a Pinterest board, but Isabella was old-school.

As twilight fell, she stepped onto the small porch with a glass of sweet tea in her hand and watched as fireflies danced among the oak trees.

Despite her anxiety, she couldn't help but feel a sense of rightness about being here, finally. This was her chance to create something meaningful, something that was truly hers, and she wasn't going to let anything or anyone stand in her way, not even Thomas Langley and the ghosts of what might have been if he hadn't run away all those years ago.

She took one final sip of her tea and went inside to get ready for bed.

Tomorrow would be challenging, but she was ready, because she had to be. There was no other choice.

Thomas Langley woke before dawn, as he most always did. The last remnants of moonlight were still filtering through the plantation shutters of his bedroom window, casting striped shadows across the hardwood floors that desperately needed refinishing. It was funny how contractors could handle everybody else's work but always left their own to the end of the list.

He lay still for a moment, listening to the crickets and frogs that served as Wexley Island's natural alarm clock. The humid air drifting through his windows carried the familiar scents of jasmine and salt marsh - smells that usually comforted him but today felt heavy with the weight of impending confrontation.

He'd had trouble sleeping for most of the night,

his mind circling relentlessly around the information Gerald Stewart had shared yesterday afternoon when they were on the golf course.

"Isabella Montgomery," Gerald had said casually, lining up his putt. "That's the name of the woman who bought the old inn. Apparently, she's some retired hotel executive for one of those big luxury chains. She's meeting with you tomorrow morning to talk about renovations."

The name had hit Thomas like a physical blow, causing him to miss his own putt by several inches.

"Hey, something wrong with your swing today?" Gerald had asked, looking up from retrieving his ball.

"No, I just thought I recognized that name," he said, struggling to keep his composure, "but I must be mistaken. It's a pretty common name."

He knew he wasn't mistaken. There couldn't be two Isabella Montgomerys in the hotel industry, both with ties to South Carolina. It had to be her - the woman he had walked away from three decades ago, making what was both the most honorable and most heartbreaking decision of his life.

Thomas had watched Isabella's career growth for years, sometimes checking her out on social media or reading articles about her rapid climb through different companies in trade magazines.

Now, as the first hint of dawn lightened his bedroom, Thomas swung his legs over the side of the bed and ran his hand through his salt and pepper hair. He was going to need an extra cup of coffee this morning.

In the kitchen of his modest but meticulously restored cottage - except for the floors - Thomas ground fresh beans while the kettle heated on the stove. He made coffee every morning like it was a ritual, but today his hands weren't quite as steady.

He opened the drawer beside the sink, the one that had all the miscellaneous items that didn't belong somewhere else, and pushed aside batteries, rubber bands, and spare keys until he found the worn envelope hidden at the back. He hadn't looked at it in years, but he'd never been able to throw it away.

Inside was a photograph, its colors faded, but the memory was still as sharp as broken glass. A younger version of himself stood with his arm around Isabella, her honey-blonde hair catching the sunlight, those hazel eyes bright with dreams they'd planned to build together. They were standing in front of their senior project, a detailed architectural model of a restored antebellum home. Both wore college sweatshirts and matching expressions of pure joy. *Someday we'll do this for real,* she'd whispered that day. *'Just you and me, bringing old places back to life.'*

Funny how things turned out.

He had made the only choice he could thirty years ago, but that didn't stop him from wondering what his life might have looked like if circumstances had been different.

He carefully put the photograph back into its envelope, then placed the envelope in its hiding spot. He poured his coffee and took it out onto the back porch to watch the mist rising from the tidal creek that bordered his property.

His phone rang, disrupting the morning quiet. Emma, his daughter, always seemed to sense when something was troubling him.

"Morning, Dad," she said in a cheerful voice. "I was up early prepping for a client presentation, just thought I'd check in."

"Well, you sound chipper for someone who's never been a morning person," he said, smiling.

Emma had always been a night owl, even as a kid, a trait that had made those sleepless nights after Sarah's death harder when it was just him trying to manage bedtime routines alone.

"Well, lots of coffee and the fear of failure works every time," she said, laughing. "How are things over on the island?"

He hesitated. "Oh, you know, the usual. Gerald and I played golf yesterday, and I've got a meeting about a potential new project this morning."

"Oh, really? What is it?"

"The old Wexley Inn is being renovated. New owner wants to restore it, you know, turn it back into a functioning inn."

"Wow, that place has been empty forever," Emma said. "Well, it'll be good to see it fixed up. Who bought it? One of those investment firms that's constantly trying to buy up the island property?"

Thomas paused. He had never told Emma anything about Isabella. There'd never been a reason to talk about a relationship that ended before Emma was even born.

"Oh, it's a woman named Isabella Montgomery, I think they said. Apparently, she's retired from running luxury hotels and wants to create something of her own."

"Well, then, she came to the right place. Has she hired you?" Emma asked. "No one knows historic restoration better than my dad."

"She hasn't hired me yet. We're just meeting to discuss all the possibilities."

They chatted for a few more minutes about Emma's work in Atlanta and her plans to visit the island next month.

When they were about to hang up, Emma said, "You sound a little off, Dad. Is everything okay?"

"Oh, sure, just didn't sleep well. Good luck with your presentation."

After ending their call, Thomas finished his coffee and took a shower. An hour later, he was dressed in his usual work clothes - a well-worn but clean button-down shirt, navy today, with khaki pants and sturdy boots. He considered wearing something more formal for the meeting but chose not to. This was his island, his territory, and he would present himself just as he was.

He drove his pickup truck slowly through the island's winding roads, taking the long route to the inn to give himself a little more time to prepare mentally. A great blue heron stood motionless in the tidal creek beside the road, fishing with the patience Thomas wished he possessed. Spanish moss swayed in the breeze, and the air shimmered with heat that promised another scorching Lowcountry day.

He passed Maggie Beaumont's elegant home, where he'd spent six months restoring the original woodwork last year. Further down, he noticed Vivian Pierce's pristine garden, where every plant seemed to grow in perfect submission to her will, much like she expected the island's residents to behave.

He arrived at the inn twenty minutes early, parking his truck out of sight. He didn't want to seem too eager, even though he couldn't explain who he was trying to fool.

The morning was already warming up, promising one of those typical Lowcountry summer days where the humidity made the air feel like a damp blanket. He walked the grounds, evaluating the property professionally while he tried to calm his racing thoughts.

The gardens had given way to the Lowcountry's relentless growing season - camellias and azaleas battled for space with aggressive kudzu vines, while palmetto fronds rustled secrets in the breeze. But he could see the structure of formal design beneath the chaos, the ghost of what had once been the island's showplace.

As he rounded the corner to look at the back garden, he almost collided with Luella Washington as she was carrying a watering can toward her cottage.

"Well, mornin', Thomas," she said. "You're early."

"Morning, Luella," he nodded. "Just getting a feel for the place before the meeting. Haven't been here in a very long time."

Luella had been at the inn for as long as Thomas could remember. His father had often spoken fondly of her cooking, claiming her shrimp and grits could make a grown man cry with joy.

"She's inside, sugar. Been here since dawn, bustlin' around with her lists and measurements. Child's got more energy than a mosquito at a fish fry."

Thomas felt a flush creep up his neck. "I'm just here to talk about renovations."

"Uh-huh." Luella's expression remained neutral, but her eyes held hints of amusement. "Well, some things come full circle, don't they? Time has a way of bringing you right back."

Before Thomas could respond to her comment, Luella walked away, humming softly to herself.

He checked his watch. He was still ten minutes early. He considered waiting, but decided against it. Better to face this head-on than prolong his anxious anticipation. He climbed the steps to the back porch, noting the worrying sag in several of the floor-boards, and knocked on the door.

For a moment, there was silence, but then he heard footsteps approaching, and the door swung open.

And there she was.

Isabella Montgomery stood framed in the door-way, a clipboard in her hand, looking both familiar and yet completely different. Her honey-blonde hair was shorter now, styled in a practical bob that framed her face. Fine lines had appeared at the corners of her eyes and mouth, but didn't detract from her beauty, just spoke to the years that had passed. She wore a simple linen top and tailored pants, practical for surveying a construction site.

His chest tightened with an ache he thought he'd buried thirty years ago. Every carefully rehearsed professional greeting evaporated from his mind. For a moment, neither of them spoke.

"Thomas," she finally said. Her voice was controlled, but he thought he heard a slight tremor that only somebody who knew her well would notice. "Thank you for coming."

"Isabella," he managed to say. "It's been a long time."

That was the understatement of the year.

Her expression gave away little as she stepped back to allow him to enter. "Please come in. I've set up in what was once the inn's library."

He followed her through the familiar back hallway, noticing how she moved with the same graceful efficiency he remembered. The scent of her perfume - something with a subtle note of jasmine - briefly took him back in time to university hallways and late-night study sessions. He found himself noting details he had no business noticing - the graceful line of her neck, the way she still twisted her pen when thinking, the wedding ring that was notably absent from her left hand.

The library was just as he remembered it, though the furniture was dusty and the once-rich curtains hung faded and limp. She had set up a folding table with her laptop, various folders, and what appeared to be preliminary renovation plans.

"Would you like some coffee?" she offered, gesturing to a thermos. "I made it myself, but it's not too bad."

"Thank you," he said, accepting a cup, grateful for something to do with his hands. "So, about the inn."

She appeared to relax a bit as they shifted into professional territory.

"Yes, I made an offer on it six weeks ago and finally closed last week. I plan to restore it as a working inn with modern amenities, while respecting its historical character and significance to the island."

"It's an ambitious project," he said. "This place hasn't operated as an actual inn in at least fifteen years."

"Seventeen," Isabella corrected. "The previous owner used it as a summer home for a few years and then left it vacant. But the structure is fundamentally sound, I think, according to the inspection."

Thomas raised an eyebrow. "I would want to verify that myself. You know, these inspectors sometimes miss things in buildings this old, especially if they don't know much about historical construction methods."

"And I would expect nothing less." Isabella pulled out a folder and handed it to him. "These are my preliminary ideas and the areas that I've identified as priorities. Of course, I would value your professional assessment."

He took the folder and examined the contents. Despite the complete awkwardness of their reunion, he couldn't help but feel intrigued by the project. The Wexley Inn was an important historical building and one that deserved a proper restoration.

For the next forty-five minutes, they moved through the building together, clipboard and camera in hand, discussing structural issues, preservation concerns, and renovation priorities. Their conversation remained strictly professional. He found himself overly aware of her proximity - when she leaned over to point out details on the plans, or brushed past him in narrow doorways.

As they inspected the grand staircase, he pointed out the craftsmanship of the original banister. "This is hand-carved black walnut. You know, you don't see work like this anymore. It needs restoration, because replacing this would be a crime." As he ran his hand along the carved banister, he remembered Isabella doing the same thing during their college visits to historic homes. She'd always had an instinct for quality craftsmanship. It was one of the things that had drawn him to her.

She nodded. "Of course, I agree completely. I want to preserve all of the original elements, if possible."

"The upstairs floor will need to be reinforced to meet some modern safety codes, if you're having guests," Thomas said. "And the plumbing throughout is absolutely ancient. Complete replacement there."

"What about electrical?"

"Same. Full rewiring, I'm afraid. That can be done without damaging the plaster, if we're very careful, but it certainly won't be cheap."

They moved carefully through each room, the initial awkwardness fading into a shared professional focus. Thomas was impressed by Isabella's knowledge and the effort she clearly put into planning the renovation. She understood both the practical and aesthetic challenges of the project.

When they reached the third floor, she pointed out water damage on the ceiling. "Luella mentioned a leak that was never properly fixed."

"Oh, Luella told you about that?" Thomas asked, surprised.

"Yes, she was quite, shall we say, *informative* when I arrived yesterday." Isabella's tone was dry. "She also told me that she comes with the property, which my real estate agent conveniently failed to mention to me."

Thomas couldn't help but smile. "You know, Luella has outlasted three owners. I don't think anybody has seriously tried to make her leave since old Mr. Preston back in the nineties. That didn't end well for him."

"Oh?" Isabella said, raising an eyebrow.

"Well, let's just say Mr. Preston discovered that the health department takes anonymous complaints about restaurant code violations very seriously." Thomas smiled. "Especially when they come from someone who knows every detail of the kitchen's operation."

Isabella laughed, a genuine sound that momentarily bridged the gap of the years between them. "I suspected she might be a formidable opponent, so I'm thinking it might be wiser to just consider her an ally."

The sound of her laughter hit him like a physical blow. He'd forgotten how her laugh could light up a room, how it used to make him feel like the

luckiest man alive."You're very wise indeed,"
Thomas said.

They finished their inspection on the back porch,
where he pointed out the areas of structural
concern.

"Well, overall, I think it's in better shape than I
expected," he said, looking at his notes. "The foundation is solid. Most of the issues seem to be cosmetic,
or they are systems that would need updating
regardless. It's definitely a significant project, but
doable."

"And is it a project that you'd be interested in
taking on?" Isabella asked very directly, meeting his
eyes for perhaps the first time since he arrived.
When their eyes met, Thomas felt the familiar jolt
he'd experienced the first time he'd seen her in
Professor Martinez's architectural history class.
Thirty years, and she could still knock the breath out
of him with a single look.

He held her gaze, carefully considering his
response. Working with Isabella would mean
months of regular contact, managing not only the
complexities of this major renovation but also their
tangled personal history. The wisest choice would be
to suggest someone else, perhaps another contractor
from Charleston. However, The Wexley Inn
deserved the best restoration possible. And despite

their past, he knew he was the right person for the job.

"Yes," he said. "I'd be interested. I'd need to work up a detailed estimate, of course, and a timeline. And there are the review board approvals to consider."

"I understand," she said, nodding. "So how long will it take to prepare a proposal?"

"Two weeks should suffice. I'd want my structural engineer to come in for a thorough assessment first."

"That sounds reasonable," she said, closing her notebook. "Just to be clear, Thomas, this is a professional relationship. Whatever happened between us in the past is irrelevant to this project."

She delivered the statement calmly, but Thomas didn't miss the hint of steel beneath her words.

"Of course, agreed," he said. "The inn deserves our best work, regardless of personal history."

As he got ready to leave, they were interrupted by the sound of footsteps on the gravel drive. Through the window, he saw Vivian Pierce approaching the front door, impeccably dressed as she always was, in a cream linen suit, even though it was getting hotter by the moment.

"Seems you have another visitor," Thomas said. "Vivian Pierce. She's vice president of the

Lowcountry Ladies Club and the self-appointed guardian of anything to do with Wexley Island."

Isabella looked out the window. "Well, I've done my research on the key island residents, and she's on the architectural review board as well, right?"

"And six other committees," he said. "She'll be very interested in your plans for the inn. Very interested."

"Yeah, I'm getting the impression that that's not necessarily a good thing."

"Well, let's just say Vivian has strong opinions about how things need to be done on this island. She and I have had our, shall we say, 'professional disagreements' over the years."

Isabella straightened her shoulders. He remembered that gesture well from their university days when she was preparing to face a difficult presentation or professor.

"Well, I guess I'd better make a good impression then."

"Would you like me to leave?" Thomas offered, although he was very curious to observe their interaction.

"There's no need," she said with a small smile. "As you said, she'll be interested in my plans. Might as well see that I've already engaged the island's premier restoration specialist."

The compliment was delivered casually, but it caught Thomas off guard. Before he could respond, there was a sharp knock at the front door.

"Shall we?" Isabella gestured toward the hallway.

As they walked to the front of the inn, Thomas couldn't help but admire her composure. Facing both him and Vivian Pierce in her first twenty-four hours on the island would have intimidated a lot of people, but Isabella just moved forward with the confidence of someone accustomed to navigating challenging situations.

When she opened the front door, Vivian's perfectly composed expression registered brief surprise at seeing Thomas standing beside the inn's new owner.

"Good morning," Isabella said, trying to sound pleasant. "You must be Vivian. I'm Isabella Montgomery, the new owner of the inn. Please do come in."

Vivian stepped inside, her gaze assessing both Isabella and Thomas before settling on Isabella with a pleasant smile.

"Welcome to Wexley Island, Ms. Montgomery. I see you've already met Thomas." There was a slight emphasis on his name that carried the hint of a question.

"Yes, we were discussing renovation plans,"

Isabella replied. "Thomas comes highly recommended."

"Oh, I'm sure he does," Vivian said with honeyed poison. "Thomas and I have collaborated on numerous projects around the island over the years. His work is... *adequate...* though sometimes his interpretation of historical accuracy can be rather creative for those of us who value authentic preservation."

Thomas bit back a retort. He knew Vivian was trying to establish her dominance in the conversation. She'd opposed nearly every renovation proposal he'd submitted in the last five years, always finding some minor detail to criticize before the review board.

"I reviewed his portfolio extensively," Isabella replied with the calm confidence of someone accustomed to handling difficult people. "His ability to balance historical integrity with necessary modern functionality is exactly what this project requires. I'm not interested in creating a museum. I'm creating a working inn."

Vivian's smile tightened. "Well, I'm sure you know hotels, being from the corporate world, but Wexley Island has its own unique character and traditions." Her voice was slow and Southern. "The Lowcountry Ladies Club has a vested interest in making sure the inn's restoration respects our cherished island heritage."

"And I look forward to learning more about that heritage," Isabella replied diplomatically. "Maybe you could join me for tea one afternoon and share your insights. Of course, I value local knowledge."

The invitation was perfectly pitched, respectful without being deferential. Thomas found himself impressed with her handling of Vivian, who clearly hadn't expected such poised resistance.

"Well, that would be lovely," Vivian said. "In fact, the Ladies Club is hosting our monthly luncheon next week. We would love the opportunity for you to meet everyone who matters on the island. I'll have my assistant send you the details."

Thomas pondered her words. Only those people who mattered.

"I'll be delighted to attend," Isabella said.

After a few more minutes of carefully navigated small talk, during which Vivian managed to drop references to her family, her family's three generations on the island, and her position on the Architectural Review Board - twice - she finally left.

"It was a pleasure meeting you, Ms. Montgomery. I look forward to seeing your renovation plans in great detail." She gave a pointed look to Thomas and then added, "You'll want to be especially careful with any exterior modifications. The Review Board is quite stringent."

After Isabella closed the door behind Vivian, she turned to Thomas with a raised eyebrow.

"I'm sensing there's some history there beyond professional disagreements."

Thomas shook his head. "Vivian expected to get the Beaumont house restoration contract last year. She had recommended her nephew's firm to Maggie Beaumont, despite the fact that they have no real experience with historic properties. And then Maggie hired me instead."

"Ah, and I'm guessing Vivian isn't someone who forgets such things."

"Oh, she keeps a mental ledger with impeccable accuracy," Thomas said. "Just know that she'll be watching this project very closely, looking for any reason to raise objections to the review board."

Isabella nodded. "Good to know. I've dealt with difficult board members before, but I do appreciate the warning."

They walked back to the library to gather their notes after the morning inspection was complete. As Thomas got ready to leave, he found himself reluctant to end their meeting, despite the emotional complexity of seeing Isabella again after so many years.

"I should have my team out here tomorrow to start a more detailed assessment, if that's okay with you."

"That would be perfect," she said. "I'll be here all day."

He hesitated, then added, "Listen, Isabella, about what happened—"

She held up a hand, stopping him.

"Thomas, I meant what I said. This is a professional relationship. The past is the past."

Her tone was firm, but he could see the flash of old pain in her eyes before she looked away.

"Of course," he said quietly. "Well, then I'll see you tomorrow."

As he drove away from the inn, Thomas's hands gripped the steering wheel more tightly than necessary. Seeing Isabella again after thirty years felt like walking into a wall of memories he thought he'd put behind him. She was so strikingly familiar yet totally transformed—successful, confident, and guarded in ways the young woman he'd known never was.

He expected her to be angry, maybe even hostile. Instead, she remained coolly professional, concentrating on the project rather than their shared history. In some ways, it was harder than outright resentment.

What right did he have to feel disappointed by

her emotional distance? He was the one who walked away all those years ago. He made his choice—the honorable choice given the circumstances—but that didn't change the fact that he hurt her deeply.

He drove past the turnoff to his cottage, choosing instead to go to his workshop on the other side of the island. He needed the peace of working with his hands, focusing on the grain of the wood and the precision of his tools, rather than the complications of the past.

As he parked outside the converted boathouse that served as his workshop, he decided to follow Isabella's lead. They would keep a strictly professional relationship. He would give The Wexley Inn the restoration it deserved, and perhaps in the process, he could show her that he had become a man worthy of respect, if not forgiveness.

It was the most he could hope for, and probably more than he deserved. He'd been the one to walk away, choosing duty over love, responsibility over dreams. He'd lived with that decision every day for thirty years, telling himself it was the right thing to do. But seeing Isabella again, seeing the woman she had become without him, made him wonder if the biggest mistake of his life wasn't leaving her, but staying away so long that coming back might no longer be an option.

CHAPTER 3

Isabella stood at the entrance of the Wexley Country Club, adjusting the sleeve of her green silk blouse before pushing the ornate wooden door. The Lowcountry Ladies Club's monthly luncheon was her first official social event on the island. Despite navigating years of high-pressure corporate functions, she felt a bit nervous.

The gleaming marble foyer opened into the Blue Heron Restaurant, where floor-to-ceiling windows framed a panoramic view of the Atlantic. Spanish moss-draped oaks swayed in the salt breeze beyond the glass, and Isabella could hear the distant cry of actual blue herons fishing in the tidal marsh.

Crystal chandeliers shimmered above round tables, covered with crisp white linens, each featuring a centerpiece with a carefully arranged selection of local flowers. The room buzzed with conversations among elegantly dressed women.

"Ah, Ms. Montgomery, you found us."

Vivian Pierce walked up toward Isabella's elbow, perfectly attired in her mint green linen dress and her steel gray hair swept up into an immaculate bun.

"Let me introduce you to everybody who matters on Wexley."

There it was again - *everybody who matters.*

"Thanks for the invitation," Isabella said, noting how Vivian's smile didn't quite reach her eyes. "I've been looking forward to meeting more of the community."

"Well, bless your heart, I'm sure you have. We're very selective about our membership here, but we always make an effort to welcome... suitable newcomers."

The slight pause before the last word spoke volumes. Isabella assumed one needed money or stature to be a part of the club. She didn't have a lot of either, but she needed these connections, one way or the other.

"This way, please."

As Vivian guided her through the room, Isabella kept a professional smile—the one she had perfected during countless hotel openings and tough board meetings. She had learned to read a room within minutes, identifying the power players, the followers, and the potential allies. These skills had served her well in corporate boardrooms from Atlanta to Charleston, and they would serve her here too.

She caught fragments of little conversations that hushed momentarily as they passed.

"Buyin' that old inn without any island connections whatsoever..."

"I heard she used to be sweet on Thomas Langley back in college..."

"Corporate hotel background, probably gonna turn it into some modern monstrosity..."

Isabella kept her expression as neutral as possible. She hadn't expected her history with Thomas to come up so quickly, though she shouldn't have been surprised. Heat crept up her neck. Apparently, her private heartbreak had become public entertainment faster than kudzu overtaking a fence line. The thought of these women dissecting her past with Thomas over their mimosas made her stomach clench.

Small islands, like luxury hotels, ran on the currency of information and gossip.

"Ladies, may I present Isabella Montgomery, our newest property owner?" Vivian announced to a table of women. "Isabella, these are some of our executive committee members."

Isabella shook hands and exchanged the usual pleasantries, trying to remember any names and details. She had good experience, as she was used to recalling important clients. Most of the women stayed very calm and polite, but their curiosity showed through beneath their social masks.

"Now, this is Margaret Beaumont, our club president," Vivian said, her tone carrying the slightest edge as she introduced a striking woman who had silver-streaked dark hair and warm brown eyes.

"Maggie, please," the woman corrected, standing up to shake Isabella's hand. She seemed genuinely warm and kind. "It's so lovely to meet you, Isabella. I've been watching that beautiful old inn sit empty for far too long. I can't tell you how pleased I am that someone with your background has taken it on. Welcome to Wexley."

Something in Maggie's very direct gaze and genuine smile put Isabella at ease immediately.

"Well, thank you. It is quite a project, but I'm excited about the challenge."

"And I imagine that you've already engaged Thomas Langley for the restoration?" Maggie asked, gesturing for Isabella to take an empty seat beside her. "He did marvelous work on my home last year."

Isabella felt Vivian stiffen slightly beside her. "Yes, he's preparing a detailed proposal now."

"Well, he's an excellent choice," Maggie said. "He understands the soul of our island architecture better than anyone, and he restored the original heart pine floors in my library that three other contractors said needed replacing."

"Thomas certainly has his admirers," Vivian interjected, "though his insistence on historical preservation sometimes conflicts with today's modern safety standards." It seemed Vivian had a problem with Thomas no matter what he did. Either she was criticizing his knowledge of historical preservation or his understanding of modern conveniences.

"Well, I found his knowledge to be quite impressive," Isabella said, "but I value hearing any different perspectives during the renovation. Maybe you could advise me on which aspects of the inn are especially meaningful to the long-time islanders."

This simple invitation, acknowledging Vivian's status while gently establishing Isabella's authority over her own home and project, seemed to soften the tension somewhat. Vivian's smile became a fraction more genuine.

"Well, I'd be happy to share my insights. My grandmother used to attend social functions at the inn during its heyday. She spoke of the magnificent Christmas balls they hosted."

As lunch was served, Maggie guided the conversation, bringing out various club members to share island stories and traditions with Isabella. Gradually, the initial frost began to thaw.

"So tell us, Isabella, what made you choose Wexley Island for your project?" asked an older woman named Charlotte. She learned that Charlotte was married to Gerald Stewart from the bank.

"While I was looking for a certain type of property - something with history and character in a community that values preservation - when my real estate agent sent me the listing for the inn, something about it just spoke to me." Isabella left out the part where she had seen Wexley from afar decades ago.

"Had you visited the island before?" another woman asked.

Isabella took a sip of iced tea. "Many years ago, just briefly. I've always remembered how beautiful it was."

She sensed there was an unasked question hanging in the air - about Thomas, about their past - but no one broached it. Instead, the conversation shifted to the challenge of renovations and island building codes.

As dessert was served, which was a delicate lemon tart with local berries, Vivian steered the conversation toward the upcoming Architectural Review Board meeting.

"Now, you'll need to present your plans in great detail. The board is committed to maintaining the island's aesthetic integrity and, of course, historical accuracy," she said, being very clear. "I'm sure Thomas has explained the process."

"Yes," Isabella nodded. "It's similar to the historical preservation committees I've worked with for hotel restorations in Charleston and Savannah. I appreciate the importance of maintaining architectural consistency."

"Well, the difference is," Vivian said with a thin smile, "that our board has the final say on what proceeds and what doesn't. Even the most, let's say, enthusiastic renovators have found that they need to adjust their visions to fit Wexley's standards."

Several of the women exchanged glances, and Isabella sensed that this was a line Vivian delivered to all the newcomers. Before she could say anything, Maggie intervened.

"What Vivian means is that we value our island's unique character, but the board has always supported thoughtful restoration projects, especially for landmark buildings like the inn." She turned to Isabella with a smile. "I would be happy to review your plans before the meeting if you'd like. I served on the board for fifteen years before becoming the club president."

"Oh, that would be so helpful," Isabella said. "I'd value your perspective."

As the luncheon wrapped up, Vivian made sure to introduce Isabella to the other Ladies Club members. The exchanges were brief but revealing, exposing some subtle alliances and factions within the island's social scene. Isabella wasn't quite sure what she had gotten herself into.

When she finally made her exit, Maggie walked with her to the veranda overlooking the ocean.

"Sugar, don't let Vivian rattle you," she said softly. "She's been actin' like the queen bee of this island for so long, she's forgotten there are other flowers in the garden. But she doesn't speak for all of us, not by a long shot."

"Thank you so much for your kindness today," Isabella said. "I do get the impression I've walked into a complex social landscape."

Maggie laughed - a rich, deep, genuine sound. "Oh my dear, that's putting it mildly. Wexley is paradise in so many ways, but it's also a tiny pond with fish who've grown accustomed to their pecking order. Any newcomer with your credentials - especially with a connection to Thomas Langley - was bound to cause some ripples."

Isabella hesitated, but then decided to ask a direct question. "So everyone knows about my history with Thomas?"

"Oh, Vivian made certain of it," Maggie confirmed. "Though I suspect she doesn't know the full story, few do. But Vivian's not one to let sleeping dogs lie, especially when there might be something in it for her. Just keep that in the back of your mind."

Something in Maggie's tone made Isabella wonder precisely what the older woman knew, but before she could probe further, Maggie changed the subject.

"You know, why don't you come to my house for tea tomorrow afternoon? I'll tell you everything you need to know about navigating the Architectural Review Board, and maybe even a few things about who's really who on Wexley Island."

Isabella accepted gratefully, exchanging contact information.

As she drove back toward the historic district, she reflected on the luncheon's dynamics. It had been a while since she needed to navigate such complex social situations, but luckily, her skills hadn't faded. In the corporate world, she had always known how to quickly spot allies and obstacles, a talent that would serve her well in this setting.

She sensed undercurrents she couldn't quite

identify - subtle alliances and ancient grudges that seemed to center around the inn itself. More than one woman mentioned how much they'd missed having the island's 'heart' operational again.

She stopped at the Island Bake Shop, needing a moment to decompress before going back to the inn. The small café was pleasantly busy, with a mix of island residents and people visiting for the day; its walls were decorated with black-and-white photographs of Wexley through the decades.

As she waited for her coffee, she looked at a photograph of the inn from the 1950s with its wrap-around porch crowded with guests, all wearing summer attire. The image reinforced her vision - that this is what she wanted to restore. Not just the building, but the sense of welcome and community that it once embodied.

"That was taken during the island's golden era," a voice said beside her.

She turned to find a fit, tanned man in his early sixties smiling at her, with silver hair and designer casual wear that screamed affluent.

"I'm Grayson Williams," he said, extending his hand. "You must be Isabella Montgomery. You know, word travels fast around our little island."

Isabella shook his hand, recognizing his name from her research. Grayson Williams was a prominent developer with a diverse range of investments across the Lowcountry.

"Nice to meet you, Mr. Williams."

"Oh, Grayson, please," he said, smiling, revealing his perfect teeth. "I've been hoping to catch you since I heard about your big purchase. The inn is quite a project to take on by yourself."

"Well, I enjoy a challenge."

"Admirable, though sometimes the smartest approach to a challenge is recognizing when to bring in reinforcements." He gestured toward a quiet table in the corner. "Do you have a few minutes? I want to discuss an opportunity that might interest you."

Isabella had to admit that her curiosity was piqued, so she joined him at the table, and he wasted no time getting to his point.

"I represent a group of investors who are interested in developing premium properties on Wexley. We've had our eye on the inn's location for years, but Old Man Harrington refused to sell to us." He leaned forward slightly. "We are prepared to offer you a very attractive return on your investment. You could walk away with a tidy profit and none of the headaches of this massive restoration."

She kept her expression neutral as he continued

outlining the offer to purchase the inn and its grounds for a modern luxury resort.

"Your proposal is definitely generous," she said when he finally finished, "but I didn't buy the inn as a flip opportunity. I'm going to restore it and operate it myself."

His smile remained perfectly in place, but his eyes went cold as a January morning. Isabella had seen that look before - the expression of a man accustomed to getting his way, one way or another.

"Noble intentions, of course, but restoration costs on historic properties tend to spiral beyond all reasonable estimates. And the review board…" He paused meaningfully. "Well, they can be particularly difficult for outsiders to navigate - especially those without proper… guidance." He handed her a business card. "When the reality of this sinks in - and it will - you can give me a call. My offer still stands."

As he left with a courteous nod, she tucked the card into her purse and mentally added him to her growing map of island dynamics.

She had stepped into a quagmire she hadn't anticipated. In her mind, she was buying a charming little inn that needed fixing, and she planned to spend her days welcoming visitors to her beautiful place on the island. But with Vivian's thinly veiled opposition and now Grayson's obvious interest in her property, it was becoming clear that the inn meant more than just a building to Wexley's power players.

She finished drinking her coffee and drove to the inn, where she found several members of Thomas's crew taking measurements of the foundation. He himself was nowhere in sight, which was a relief. Their brief professional interactions over the past week had been cordial, but she could tell they were strained, each of them being careful not to reference their shared past. It was like this giant elephant in the room, and they were both just walking around it, hoping not to trip over its trunk.

Inside, Isabella found Luella in the kitchen, looking at the ancient stove with a critical eye.

"This old thing needs to go to the scrap heap," she announced without preamble, gesturing at the stove, "along with pretty much everything else in this kitchen. But I reckon you already figured that out."

"Yes, it's on the list," Isabella said, setting her bag on the counter. "Luella, can I ask you something?"

The older woman looked at her. "You can ask all you want, sugar. Whether I answer depends on what business it is of yours."

"How long have you known Thomas Langley?"

Her expression remained impassive. "Well, since he was a gangly boy about twelve years old, up in here with his daddy doing maintenance around this place. Used to sneak him leftover pie when no one was looking. He was too skinny back then."

Isabella nodded, uncertain of how to phrase her next question. Luella saved her the trouble.

"If you're wondering whether he told me why he left you all those years ago, no, he did not. Thomas keeps his sorrows to himself. But I'll tell you this much - that boy's carried a burden for years that's been eatin' at him like rust on iron. Maybe it's time some truths saw daylight." She stared at Isabella for a moment. "You know, I've been around long enough to know that most young men don't walk away from the kind of love you two had without some mighty strong reason."

Isabella felt a familiar ache at the memory. She tried to push that away. "Well, whatever his reason was, he never shared it with me. He just said he had to go home and couldn't explain. That was it."

Luella grunted. "Well, some stories aren't mine to tell. But I'll say this. Thomas Langley is a man who's always done what he thought was right, even if it cost him." She turned back to looking at the kitchen cabinets. "Now, if you're planning to serve proper meals here, we're going to need to expand the pantry area. The original layout had a better flow to the dining room."

Getting the hint that the conversation about Thomas was finished, Isabella moved on to talking about the kitchen renovations. For the next hour, she listened as Luella shared all her thoughts about the inn's operational history and the practical improvements that would help it run better if they wanted to turn it into a working business.

Later that evening, Isabella sat on the porch of her rental cottage and watched as the sunset painted the sky in spectacular pinks and oranges. She spent her day being evaluated by the Ladies Club, by Grayson Williams, and even by Luella in her own way. It was tiring but not unfamiliar. She had been assessed and judged throughout her entire corporate career by people who underestimated her abilities.

What was different this time was that the judgments weren't just professional. There were undercurrents about her past with Thomas that created a personal layer she hadn't expected to have to deal with when she moved to Wexley.

A familiar pickup truck slowly passed her cottage, and she recognized Thomas at the wheel. He raised his hand in a brief greeting before going on down the road. Her pulse quickened traitorously at the sight of him, and she found herself watching until his taillights disappeared around the bend. Damn the man for still affecting her this way. Such a simple gesture, but it sent a complicated swirl of emotions through her. Frustration, nostalgia, and a stubborn attraction she wished she could dismiss as easily as she had denied Grayson's offer.

Thomas was still devastatingly handsome - more so, actually, with silver threading his dark hair and fine lines that spoke of years spent outdoors. She'd secretly hoped thirty years would have been less kind to him, that time would have dulled the sharp attraction she'd felt. Instead, he'd aged like fine bourbon - smoother, more complex, and far more dangerous to her peace of mind.

She sighed and turned her attention to the renovation plans spread across her lap. She'd come to Wexley Island to build something meaningful, something that was completely hers for once. She couldn't allow an old heartbreak or any island politics to derail that.

Tomorrow she'd meet with Maggie, get more information about navigating the review board, and continue pressing forward.

As darkness fell, bringing with it the evening chorus of cicadas and frogs, the air grew thick with the scent of night-blooming jasmine, and somewhere in the distance, she could hear the haunting call of a screech owl. These were the sounds of her youth, of those stolen spring break days when she believed her future was written in Thomas's promises. Whatever invisible lines had been drawn in the sand today - between allies and opponents, past and present - she was determined to chart her own course through them.

The Wexley Inn would rise again, more stunning than ever. And if that meant taking on the island's power brokers, navigating Vivian's social battles, and working alongside the man who once held her heart —and then shattered it—well, she'd endured worse. She had built a career transforming rundown properties into welcoming, beautiful spaces.

This time, she was determined to do the same for herself.

CHAPTER 4

Thomas arrived at the inn before dawn, his truck loaded with equipment for the day's initial work. The sky was starting to brighten, casting soft pink hues on the old building's white clapboard. He paused briefly, appreciating the peaceful beauty of the scene. It was a grand structure silhouetted against the waking sky, and the morning mist wreathed the ancient oaks beside it.

The early hour had always been his favorite time to start a project. The world felt fresh and full of possibilities before any complications inevitably arose.

As he unloaded all his gear and tools, he noticed movement on the porch. Isabella stood by the railing, wrapped in a white cardigan to ward off the morning chill, watching him. She raised her hand to greet him but made no move to come closer, keeping a careful distance that had been part of their interactions since his first visit. He returned her gesture and kept on setting up.

She arrived earlier than he expected. Most clients wouldn't show up until at least a few hours into the workday, if at all, but Isabella had always been different. She had always fully engaged herself in whatever caught her interest at the moment, and apparently, that hadn't changed.

His crew arrived shortly afterward, parking their trucks in the gravel lot behind the inn. Five men and two women, all locals who had worked with Thomas for many years, some since he first started his company. They knew their jobs well and trusted each other.

"Morning, folks," Thomas called as they gathered around the tailgate of his truck. "Before we start, I want to introduce this project."

He pulled out the original blueprints of the inn, carefully preserved and recently retrieved from the county archives.

"This is The Wexley Inn, built in 1872 by Charleston merchant Henry Wexley as a summer retreat. What we're looking at today isn't just a building. This is a piece of the island's history."

He traced his finger along the lines of the structure on the paper.

"Heart pine floors. Hand-carved black walnut banisters. Plaster walls with horsehair reinforcement. This is craftsmanship you rarely see nowadays, so our job is to preserve what can be saved and restore what cannot, while bringing all of the systems up to modern code."

He looked around at his team. They all appeared interested, as usual. Most of them had lived on or near the island their entire lives, so the building was important to the community as a whole.

"So there's a right way and a wrong way to approach a project like this," he continued. "Some contractors would come in here, gut it, and start fresh. Obviously, that's faster and cheaper, but you know that's not how we work. We want to respect the bones of this building, the intention of the original artisans. This inn deserves our very best work."

Wade Collins, Thomas's foreman for the past decade, nodded. "You know, my granddaddy used to tell stories about the grand dances they held here back in the day. Said the whole island would turn out. Folks in their finest clothes, music spillin' out onto the veranda. Even the service staff would sneak peeks from the kitchen windows."

"I had my first date here when it was still operating," added Eliza Wright. She was the crew's master carpenter. "Senior prom, dinner, 1985. Bobby Crawford in his daddy's borrowed tuxedo, me in a dress I'd saved three months of babysittin' money to buy. Fancy white tablecloths, crystal goblets, felt like we were movie stars for one night. It's been closed for so long, some people forget what it means to the community."

Thomas nodded, glad they understood the project's significance. "Well, today we're going to do the preliminary assessment - foundation, structural integrity, systems. We need to know exactly what we're working with before we finalize our plans."

He assigned tasks to each member, and they dispersed to their respective work areas. Then Thomas headed toward the foundation access point and noticed Isabella had moved to the garden where she was talking with Luella.

The morning sun caught her honey-blonde hair, igniting it with golden highlights, and for a moment, he was transported back to their college days. Isabella leaned over drafting tables, passionately explaining her design ideas, her hair flowing like silk across her face until she impatiently tucked it behind her ear, a gesture so painfully familiar it made his chest tighten. Even now, thirty years later, she moved with the same graceful efficiency that first captivated him in Professor Martinez's class.

He pulled his attention back to the present. Foundation. He needed to focus on the foundation.

For the next several hours, he immersed himself in all the technical aspects of the inn's structural systems. The foundation was primarily composed of brick piers, with a later addition of concrete infill, a typical feature of buildings from this era in the Lowcountry. To his relief, the brick was in remarkably good condition, although the mortar would need repointing in certain areas.

Around mid-morning, as he was examining the crawl space under the east wing, he heard a voice call down to him.

"How does it look?"

He came out to find Isabella standing nearby, dressed in practical jeans and a simple blue button-down shirt, with her hair pulled back, holding a clipboard in her hand.

"Better than I expected," he said, dusting off his hands. As he spoke, he noticed how the morning light played across her face, highlighting the determined set of her jaw he remembered so well. She was close enough that he caught the subtle scent of her perfume - different from what she'd worn in college, more sophisticated now, but it still made his pulse quicken in ways he had no business noticing. "Foundation is solid overall. There's some water damage in the southeast corner where the downspouts have been misdirected, but nothing structural. The floor joists under the main parlor have some termite damage, but it's localized."

"Well, that sounds promising," she said, making notes. "What about the wiring?"

"Well, that's where things get complicated. The inn has been rewired at least three times over the years, and each new system was layered over the old one instead of being properly replaced. It's a fire hazard, so we're going to need to strip it all out and start fresh."

She nodded. "I figured as much. And plumbing is the same?"

"Afraid so. The good news is we can access most of it without damaging the original plaster, if we're really careful. Bad news is we're going to add significant time and cost to the project."

"Well, I'd rather do it right than cut corners." She looked up from her notes. "I want this place to last another one hundred fifty years."

Thomas felt a surge of respect for her. Too many property owners prioritized speed and cost over quality and longevity.

"Then we're on the same page, I suppose," he said.

"I'll have my structural engineer come out tomorrow to verify my assessment, but I'm pretty confident we can restore the building to its full glory without compromising its historical integrity."

A small genuine smile curved Isabella's lips, the first real one he'd seen directed at him since her arrival on the island. For a moment, she looked exactly like the girl who used to light up when he'd share his ideas about historic preservation. The sight hit him like a physical blow, reminding him of everything he'd given up thirty years ago.

"Great. That's exactly what I wanted to hear."

The moment was interrupted by a shout from in front of the building.

"Dad? Are you here?"

Thomas recognized his daughter's voice immediately. "Oh, that's Emma. My daughter. I wasn't expecting her today."

Isabella's expression shifted slightly. A flicker of something. Discomfort? Curiosity? It crossed her face before her professional mask returned.

"Oh. Well, you should greet her. I'll check in with Luella about the kitchen assessment."

Before he could respond, she turned and walked toward the back of the house with her movements brisk and purposeful.

Thomas found Emma on the front porch, dressed

in what was her everyday business casual attire - a pair of tailored pants and a silky blouse that probably had some designer name he couldn't pronounce.

"Emma," he hugged her. "What brings you here in the middle of the week? I thought you had that big client presentation."

"Finished it yesterday," she said, stepping back and surveying him with a critical eye. "You're filthy. Have you been in the crawlspace?"

"Oh, you know me too well," he smiled. "Want to see what I'm working on?"

"That's why I'm here. Ever since you mentioned you'd landed the inn renovation, I was curious to see the inside." She looked over the building. "It's spectacular, even in its current condition. Tell me again about the new owner."

Thomas hesitated, unsure how to navigate this unexpected complication. "Her name is Isabella Montgomery. She retired from the hotel industry, and she wants to restore the inn and use it as a functioning business." He'd already told her this on the phone, but Emma was a curious person. Actually, she should've been a detective in one of those dark rooms with a single light hanging above a table.

Something in his tone must have alerted Emma.

She studied him with narrowed eyes. "What are you not telling me?"

Before Thomas could respond, the front door opened and Isabella emerged. There was a moment of silent assessment between the two women from different chapters of his life.

"You must be Emma," Isabella said, extending her hand. "I'm Isabella Montgomery. Your father's doing a great job assessing the renovation needs here."

Emma shook her hand, her expression politely neutral. "Nice to meet you, Ms. Montgomery. The inn is a big project to take on."

"Please, call me Isabella. And yes, it is. That's what makes it so exciting." She looked between Thomas and Emma. "I'm going to leave you two to catch up, but Thomas, if you need me, I'll be reviewing the upstairs floor plans."

As Isabella disappeared back into the house, Emma turned to her father with a raised eyebrow. "So that's the new owner you've been so vague about when we talk."

Thomas sighed. "Let's take a walk around the grounds. I need to check the exterior drainage anyway."

As they circled the property, Thomas explained all the technical aspects of the renovation and pointed out architectural features. Emma listened, but he could sense her waiting for the information he was avoiding.

"Dad," she finally said, stopping beneath one of the old oaks. "Why do I get the feeling there's something important about this Isabella that you're not telling me?"

He ran a hand through his hair. "Isabella and I… well, we knew each other a long time ago, before I met your mother."

"Knew each other," she repeated.

"As in we were in college together," he admitted. "It was serious."

"How serious?"

"Very." He looked away, focusing on the marsh in the distance. "She was the first person I ever loved."

Emma was silent for a moment. "And now she's back, hiring you for a major project? That's quite a coincidence."

"No, it wasn't planned, at least not on my part. And she had no idea I was still on the island when she bought the inn." He turned back to his daughter. "Look, it's strictly professional between us now. It's been thirty years, Emma. We're different people."

"Well, maybe so," she said, "but I've never heard you mention her before. Not even once in all these years."

"Well, some chapters of life are better left closed."

"And yet here she is, reopening that chapter, whether you wanted it or not." She had a protective worry on her face. "What happened between you two? Why did it end?"

He hesitated. He'd never discussed the circumstances of his breakup with Isabella, not even with Sarah during their marriage. It was a private pain, a choice he made that changed the course of his life.

"It's complicated, Emma. I made a difficult decision that hurt her deeply." He met his daughter's eyes. "But she's my client now, and I'm going to give this project my best work, regardless of our history."

She studied his face, clearly sensing there was something more to the story, but she knew him well enough to recognize he wouldn't be pushed further.

"Just be careful, Dad," she said. "I don't want to see you get hurt."

He smiled slightly. "Isn't that supposed to be my line? I'm the parent here."

"And I'm the only one of us who inherited Mom's common sense," she said. "Speaking of which, I should probably meet this Isabella properly, since you're going to be working with her for months."

Before he could object, she started striding back toward the inn. He hurried to catch up, wondering how this unexpected collision of past and present would unfold.

They found Isabella in the main parlor, discussing molding restoration with Eliza. She looked up, her professional smile firmly in place.

"Emma wanted a proper tour," Thomas explained. "She has a great eye for design and might have some insights to offer."

"I'd be glad to show you around," Isabella said. "Though I should warn you, it's very much a work in progress."

As Isabella guided them through the first floor and explained her vision for each space, Thomas watched the interactions between the two women with a mix of fascination and anxiety. Emma was politely reserved but asked intelligent questions while studying Isabella. For her part, Isabella simply maintained her usual warm professionalism, neither too familiar nor too defensive.

When they finally reached the dining room, Isabella outlined her plans for restoring it to its original grandeur.

"The proportions of this room are remarkable," she said, gesturing toward the high ceilings with their ornate plaster medallions. "We're going to finish these original floors and restore the wainscoting. I hope to find a period-appropriate light fixture to replace this current lighting."

"What about the wall?" Emma asked, pointing to

a section that separated the dining room from a smaller sitting area. "It kind of interrupts the flow."

"That's actually not original to the building," Thomas said. "It was added during the 1940s restoration, probably to create a private dining space for the owner."

Isabella nodded. "Yeah, I've been debating whether to remove it. On one hand, it would restore the original layout and bring more light to this section, but on the other hand, two distinct spaces offer more flexibility when we're hosting events."

"What does the historical record show?" Emma asked.

"I actually found an old photograph from 1910 that shows the original layout," Isabella replied. She reached for a folder on a nearby table and pulled out the sepia-toned image that depicted the dining room in its early setup.

"That's beautiful," Emma said, studying the photograph. "More elegant than this current arrangement, though I understand there are some practical considerations."

"Exactly my dilemma," Isabella said, sighing. "Your father's structural assessment will help determine if the wall is load-bearing, and that might just settle the question."

"It's not," Thomas said. "Purely decorative. You

could take it off without compromising the building's integrity."

Isabella looked happy. "Well, that's helpful to know. I'm leaning toward restoring the original open concept, then using furniture arrangement to create the distinct areas when needed."

"That's a good compromise," Emma said.

The tour continued to the kitchen, where they found Luella making notes about storage requirements. The older woman greeted Emma, having known her since childhood.

"Well, look at you, all grown up and proper," Luella said. "Your mama would be proud."

"Thanks, Miss Luella. Hey, are you still making the best peach cobbler on the Eastern Seaboard?"

"You know it, although this kitchen needs a complete overhaul before I can do my best work." Luella turned to Isabella. "Now, I've made you a proper list of what this kitchen needs to pass health department inspection. Lord knows they're pickier than a preacher at a potluck dinner, but we'll get it right."

"I appreciate that," Isabella said. "Your expertise here will be invaluable for designing a functional space."

As they continued through the inn, Thomas became more and more aware of the surprising development that Emma was warming up to Isabella. His daughter had a well-honed ability to assess character, a skill that had served her well in her marketing career, but she was genuinely engaging with Isabella, more than just being polite.

Their tour ended in the garden, where Luella had begun clearing decades of overgrowth from what had once been a formal herb and flower garden. As they walked through the overgrown pathways, Thomas found himself hyperaware of Isabella's presence beside him - the way she paused to examine particular plants, the graceful way she moved through the tangled garden, how the dappled sunlight played across her features.

"The landscaping will be in phase two," Isabella said. "After all the structural work is complete. But these gardens were once the highlight of the property. I'd love to restore them, maybe even with an emphasis on native plants."

"You know, there's a landscape architect in Charleston who specializes in restoring historic gardens," Emma said. "Jessica Oakes. I know, pun intended, I guess. She did the Middleton Place refurbishment. I can introduce you if you'd like."

Thomas tried to hide the surprise at his daughter's offer of assistance.

"Oh, that would be wonderful, thank you."

As they said their goodbyes, Emma's demeanor toward Isabella was noticeably warmer.

"It was great meeting you, Isabella. Your vision for the inn is awe-inspiring, and I can't wait to see how it progresses. You're in good hands with my dad."

"The pleasure was mine," Isabella said, "and you've offered some wonderful insight today. Feel free to visit anytime you're here on the island."

After Emma left, promising to meet Thomas for dinner later, there was an awkward silence between him and Isabella.

"Your daughter is wonderful," Isabella finally said. "She certainly has your eye for structural integrity, but also has a distinct perspective all her own."

"Thanks," Thomas replied, feeling a swell of pride. "She surprises me every day."

Isabella nodded. "She's protective of you. That's nice to see."

Before Thomas could respond, Wade Collins approached with an urgent question about the electrical assessment, and the moment passed. Isabella excused herself to review the notes, leaving Thomas to address the technical issue.

The rest of the day passed with lots of productivity. Thomas and his team completed their preliminary assessment of the inn's structural systems. By late afternoon, he had a comprehensive overview of the building's condition. It was better than he feared in some areas and worse in others, but overall, a great restoration project.

As the crew packed up for the day, he found Isabella on the front porch looking at their findings.

"We'll have a detailed proposal to you within a week," he said. "My structural engineer will verify everything tomorrow, but I'm pretty confident in our overall assessment."

"That's excellent news," she said. "I appreciate how thorough you and your team have been."

A warm breeze stirred the Spanish moss hanging from nearby oaks, carrying the sweet scent of jasmine from the overgrown garden. For a moment, the years between them seemed to compress. It brought Thomas back to similar evenings where they spent their time discussing design concepts on university benches, their heads bent together over sketches, the world full of possibilities.

"Isabella," he began, uncertain of exactly what he wanted to say, but feeling the need to acknowledge it. "About Emma."

"She's lovely," Isabella interrupted. "You've done a great job raising her, and you should be proud."

"Well, I am," he said. "Thanks for being so

gracious with her. She can be a little overprotective of me."

"As she should be." Isabella's expression was completely unreadable. "Family looks out for each other, and that's how it should be."

Something in her tone, a slight wistfulness perhaps, reminded him that she'd never had any children of her own. According to discreet inquiries around the island, she'd been married to another hotel executive, but that relationship had ended in divorce two years ago.

"Will you be at the architectural review board meeting next week?" he asked.

"Yes, although Vivian has warned me not to expect immediate approval. Apparently, the board prefers to 'thoroughly consider' all proposals, especially from newcomers like me."

He smiled. "That's Vivian-speak for 'we're going to make you jump through hoops because you're not a third-generation islander.' However, don't worry; your plans are very solid, and the historical accuracy will likely satisfy the board's concerns. Well, most of them."

"Most?"

"Grayson Williams sits on the board. He has his own ideas about the island's future development, and they do not align with historical preservation."

"Yes, I met him yesterday. He made a generous offer to buy the inn from me."

Thomas felt a surprising surge of alarm. "Wait, he did? What did you tell him?"

"I told him I didn't buy the inn to flip it. I came here to create something meaningful, not make a quick profit."

Relief washed over Thomas. The idea of the inn falling into Grayson's hands and being demolished for one of his modern resort complexes was deeply unsettling.

"Well, I'm glad to hear that," Thomas said. "Grayson has been trying to get his hands on this property for years. He sees the historic district as prime real estate for development rather than preservation."

"So I gathered," Isabella said, "and he wasn't exactly subtle about his intentions."

The last of Thomas's crew waved goodbye and then left, leaving Thomas and Isabella alone on the porch. The late afternoon light filtered through the oak trees, casting dappled shadows across the weathered floorboards.

"I'd better go," Thomas said, knowing he needed to meet Emma for dinner.

"We've made good progress today," Isabella nodded. "Thanks, and please thank your crew as well. They're remarkably knowledgeable and have been so respectful of the property."

Her professional mask was firmly back in place.

"They understand what this place means to the island. Most of them have personal connections to the inn when it was operational."

A comfortable silence settled between them, filled with the evening chorus of birds settling in for the night and the distant whisper of waves hitting the shore. The air between them felt charged with unspoken memories and careful boundaries. Thomas found himself wanting to say something more, to bridge the careful distance they kept, but the weight of thirty years and too many regrets kept him silent.

"Good night, Isabella," he said, descending the porch steps.

"Good night, Thomas," she replied softly.

As he drove away, Thomas glanced in his rearview mirror to see Isabella still standing on the porch, her figure silhouetted against the white clapboard of the inn. She looked both perfectly at home there and impossibly distant, like a dream he'd once thought he could hold onto, now just close enough to remember what he'd lost, but too far away to ever reclaim.

CHAPTER 5

Thomas found his daughter waiting for him at The Blue Marlin, a casual seafood restaurant overlooking the marina. She had secured a table on the deck with a view of the marina, where ceiling fans stirred the thick evening air that carried the scent of salt marsh and fried seafood. Strands of white lights twinkled overhead like landlocked stars, and the gentle lapping of boats against the dock provided a soothing rhythmic background.

"Sorry, I'm late," he said, sitting down across from her. "I was wrapping things up at the inn."

She studied him over the rim of her wine glass. "So, Isabella Montgomery."

He sighed and reached for the water the server had already placed on the table. "Yes. I was wondering how long it was going to take you to bring that back up again."

"Oh, I showed remarkable restraint," she said with a grin. "I waited a whole five minutes after you sat down, didn't I?"

Despite his discomfort with the topic, he laughed. "Yes, so very considerate of you."

"She's not what I expected."

"Well, what did you expect?"

"I'm not sure," she said, shrugging. "When you said she was your first love, I guess I pictured someone… I don't know, different. More dramatic, maybe? She's very composed and professional."

"She always was," he said. "Even in college. She approached everything with precision and focus, but there was this passion underneath that polished exterior - about architecture, about history, about creating spaces that brought people together."

Emma watched her father's face carefully. "You never mentioned her. All these years, not a word."

He looked out over the water, where boats gently rocked at their moorings. "Well, some wounds are better left undisturbed."

"Did you love Mom?"

The question was asked gently, but directly, in typical Emma fashion.

He turned back to his daughter, surprised. "Of

course I did. Your mother was an extraordinary woman - kind, intelligent, courageous. Our marriage wasn't perfect, but we built a good life together, and I have never regretted that for one minute."

"But Isabella was first," Emma said, an observation more than a question.

"Yes. She was first."

The server arrived to take their orders, providing a welcome interruption. After picking their meals - grilled snapper for Thomas and shrimp and grits for Emma - they fell silent until they were alone again.

"Why did you leave her?" Emma finally asked. "If she was your first love, what happened?"

Thomas hesitated. He'd never discussed this kind of thing with anyone, let alone his daughter. He'd carried the weight of his decision alone all these years.

"Life happened," he said carefully. "My father's business was failing - bad investments, medical bills from an accident. We were facing bankruptcy, losing everything. Your mom's family had money, old Lowcountry wealth, and when I called them desperately asking for a loan..." He paused. "They agreed, but only if I came home immediately after graduation and married Sarah. They said she'd never gotten over our high school relationship."

Her eyes widened. "They blackmailed you. My grandparents literally blackmailed you?"

Emma had been close to Sarah's parents, especially after she passed. Thomas hadn't told her what they had done because she needed all the love she could get as a child. He wasn't going to rob her of that.

"I thought I was being noble," Thomas said quietly. "Saving my father, giving Sarah what she wanted, letting Isabella pursue her career without being dragged down by my family's problems. I couldn't tell Isabella the truth. She would have insisted on helping somehow, and I couldn't let her sacrifice her future for my family's mistakes."

She was silent for a moment, processing her thoughts. "Does Isabella know that was the reason you broke things off with her?"

"No. I couldn't bring myself to tell her the truth. I thought a clean break would be easier for her, allowing her to focus on her career without complications or obligations to me. I told her I had to go home in a note, and that was it."

"Oh, Dad," Emma said softly, her expression sympathetic rather than judgmental. "You were trying to protect everyone, but you ended up hurting yourself the most, didn't you?"

"At the time, I thought I was sparing her unnecessary pain. She was brilliant, had so many opportunities that I couldn't match. The last thing she needed was to feel tied to a man with problems."

Thomas hated telling his daughter all of this, but she was an adult now and old enough to understand. He'd loved Sarah when he first met her in high school, but what did kids know about real, abiding love? He'd been way too immature to choose a life mate at that age. Isabella had been his true love.

Their food arrived, steam rising from the plates. Neither of them immediately began eating.

"And now she's here on your island, hiring you for a major project…" Emma trailed off. "Boy, the universe sure has a twisted sense of humor."

"So it seems," Thomas said, picking up his fork.

"What are you going to do? Will you tell her the truth now?"

He hesitated. "I don't know. It's been thirty years, Emma. Does it even matter anymore why I left? We're both different people now."

"It matters because secrets have a way of surfacing, especially on this island, and it always happens when you least expect it, Dad. From what little bit I saw today, Isabella doesn't strike me as someone who appreciates being kept in the dark."

They ate in silence for a few minutes.

"There's something about her," Emma said thoughtfully. "The way she handles problems without falling apart. I don't remember Mom as clearly as I wish I did, but I remember that about her - how she stayed calm even when things got scary. I can see why you'd be drawn to someone like that."

Thomas nodded. "They would have been either the best of friends or the most formidable opponents, and probably both at different times."

Emma smiled. "I like her, Dad. Despite myself, despite knowing she was important to you, I like her. She's very straightforward and very passionate about the inn."

"She is." Isabella's vision for the inn aligned perfectly with his own values about historic preservation, a fact that pleased and complicated his feelings about the project.

They finished their meal, and Emma reached across the table to touch his hand.

"Maybe it's time to tell her the truth, Dad. Thirty years is long enough to carry that kind of burden alone. And from what I saw today, I don't think the feelings are as buried as either of you pretends they are."

He squeezed her hand, thankful for her concern and wisdom.

"When did you get so insightful about relationships?"

"Oh, I learned from watching the best," she said. "You and Mom may not have had a grand passion, but you showed me what respect and commitment looked like, and that's worth more than any fairy tale romance."

Later that night, after he drove Emma back to his cottage, where she'd been staying during her visit, Thomas stood on his back deck overlooking a tidal creek. The moon cast silver light across the tidal creek, turning the marsh grass into a sea of liquid silk and making the still water look like hammered pewter. Night birds called from the darkness, their voices weaving through the humid air.

He kept thinking back over his conversation with Emma. It had unearthed memories and emotions he'd kept buried for such a long time. Seeing Isabella again was disorienting, for sure, but having his daughter meet her? Well, those two worlds colliding added layers of complexity he hadn't anticipated.

The young man who'd made that choice had believed he was protecting everyone. Now, watching Isabella move through his world with such grace and determination, he wondered if he'd been too proud to let her choose her own path.

Now, time had brought Isabella back into his life,

and the question was whether this unexpected reunion would heal old wounds or create new ones. Either way, he was committed to the inn's restoration, and he would give Isabella's project his best work - not because of their past, but because that building deserved nothing less, and Isabella's vision for its renewal aligned with his own so perfectly.

Whether their personal past could, or should, be addressed remained to be seen. He'd spent decades convincing himself he'd made the right choice. But seeing Isabella again, working beside her, remembering what they'd once meant to each other, it was becoming harder to believe that protecting her from his family's crisis had been worth the cost to both their hearts.

An afternoon thunderstorm had been forecast all day, and the thick gray clouds hanging over Wexley Island proved it. Isabella stood in the sweltering inn kitchen beside Luella, watching her measure ingredients with practiced precision despite the ancient stove that made the room feel like a furnace. Afternoon light slanted through the windows, illuminating motes of flour dust dancing in the air.

"Now, you need to pay attention," Luella said, her hands moving confidently as she mixed a bowl of shrimp and grits. "This recipe has been in my family for generations, and the secret is in the timing. You add that cheese too early, and it becomes stringy, but you add it too late, and it won't melt properly."

Isabella observed, making notes in a small, leather-bound journal. When she had impulsively asked Luella to teach her some traditional Lowcountry recipes that they might feature on the inn's menu, she hadn't expected such a culinary education. Luella approached cooking with the same meticulous attention to detail that Thomas brought to the historic restoration.

"Okay, now you try," Luella said, stepping back from the counter and gesturing for Isabella to take her place.

Slightly intimidated, Isabella took the wooden spoon and started stirring the creamy mixture, trying to match Luella's rhythm and pressure.

"Quit being so hesitant," Luella said. "Grits sense fear just like horses. You gotta be confident."

Isabella laughed, unsure if Luella was making a joke or being serious. "You know, I never thought cooking had so much in common with corporate leadership, but you might be onto something there."

"Mmm-hmm," Luella hummed, watching her

closely. "Leadership, cooking, renovation - all of it's about knowing when to be firm and when to be gentle." She gestured toward the window where Thomas could be seen directing his crew as they secured exterior materials against the approaching storm. "Some folks understand the balance better than others."

Isabella followed Luella's gaze and watched as Thomas pointed out something on a blueprint to one of his workers. Over the past few weeks, since the architectural review board had finally approved the preliminary plans for the renovation, he and his crew had made impressive progress on reinforcing the inn's structure. Each day, Isabella observed his careful approach, preserving original elements when possible and replacing only what couldn't be salvaged, always with an eye toward maintaining historical accuracy.

"He's very good at what he does," Isabella said, turning back to her cooking task.

"Oh, he always has been," Luella said. "Even as a little boy, he had a gift for seeing how things fit together and what made them strong."

Isabella hesitated for a moment but then asked the question that had been on her mind since her conversation with Luella weeks ago. "You said before that Thomas always did what he thought was right, even if it cost him. What did you mean by that?"

Luella was quiet for a moment, staring into the bowl. "Not my story to tell," she finally said, "but I will say this. Thomas Langley carries more weight than most people will ever realize, and he has since he was barely more than a boy himself."

Before Isabella could probe any further, the kitchen door swung open and Thomas entered, a concerned expression on his face.

"Sorry to interrupt, ladies," he said, nodding to greet both of them. "Storm's movin' in faster than we expected. We're going to secure the site, but you might want to move your car to higher ground, Isabella. That driveway tends to flood in heavy rain."

A low rumble of thunder rolled across the marsh like a warning, and the Spanish moss outside the windows began dancing in the rising wind.

"There's a parking area behind my cottage that never floods," Luella said. "You can leave it there till the storm passes."

"Thank you, I'll do that shortly," Isabella said, wiping her hands on a kitchen towel.

"I've got the crew moving materials inside and covering what can't be moved," Thomas said. "The roof patch we installed yesterday should hold, but I'd like to stick around a little while to make sure there are no leaks in any of the areas we're working on."

Isabella nodded, appreciating his thoroughness. "Well, of course. I was planning to stay to review the dining room plans anyway."

Luella gave them both a knowing look before turning to remove her pot from the stove.

"Well, there ain't no sense in letting this food go to waste. You two might as well eat it while you wait out the storm." She started transferring the shrimp and grits into serving dishes. "Thomas, make yourself useful and set the table in the small parlor. The dining room's still too dusty for civilized eating."

He raised an eyebrow but didn't argue, taking plates from the cabinet with the ease of someone who knew Luella's kitchen as well as she did. Isabella watched his movements, noticing how comfortable he seemed in this domestic setting. For a moment, she could imagine what their life might have looked like—sharing meals, working together, building something lasting.

Isabella moved to help, gathering silverware and napkins and trying to ignore the weird domesticity of the moment. When she couldn't handle not staring at Thomas anymore, she ran outside to move her car.

Twenty minutes later, the three of them sat in the small parlor as rain began pattering against the windows. The candlelight flickered across Thomas's face, and Isabella found herself stealing glances at him when she thought he wasn't looking.

Luella had set up a surprisingly elegant display on an antique side table she'd pulled into use, complete with candles 'in case the power went out'," she said. She mentioned it would probably go out on this island if a squirrel so much as sneezed at a power line.

The meal was delicious, the shrimp and grits creamy and perfectly seasoned with subtle heat. Isabella savored the authentic flavors, already envisioning this dish being featured on the inn's future menu.

"This is absolutely wonderful, Luella," she said. "I can see why your cooking has been legendary here."

"Still is," Thomas said with a smile. "Luella's catering is the most requested on the island, even with all those fancy Charleston chefs coming in."

Luella waved away the compliments, although Isabella detected a pleased look in her eyes. "It's just good, honest cooking. Nothing fancy about knowing how to treat your ingredients right."

The rain intensified, drumming against the windows and roof. A flash of lightning illuminated the room, followed almost immediately by a crack of thunder that rattled the old windows.

"Wow, that was close," Isabella said, trying to mask her slight unease. She'd never been entirely comfortable during thunderstorms, a childhood fear she'd mostly outgrown but that still came up occasionally.

"Just a typical summer squall," Luella said calmly. "Comes on fast, raises holy hell, then moves on through, unlike some storms that settle in and won't budge." She gave Thomas a meaningful look.

The conversation turned to the inn's history, with Luella sharing stories about notable guests and island events that had taken place over the decades. Isabella listened because she wanted to mentally catalog all the details that she could incorporate into the marketing materials once the inn reopened.

"You know, we had Kennedy folk stay here once," Luella said. "Not the president himself, mind you, but his sister and her husband. Gracious as you please, those two, and they knew how to treat the help proper."

"I didn't realize the inn had such distinguished guests," Isabella said.

"Oh, in its heyday, this place was the go-to spot for what they call 'discreet luxury,'" Luella said, using air quotes. "Politicians, business magnates, even some Hollywood types. They came because they could relax here without all the usual fuss. Island residents have always been respectful of people's privacy. Well, until we got the Lowcountry Ladies Club. Those ladies don't respect anybody's privacy. I suspect Vivian Pierce has been keeping a close eye on how much time Thomas's truck spends parked here. That woman's got a nose for gossip sharper than a bloodhound's."

Thomas chuckled under his breath.

Another lightning flash and thunderclap - this one so loud it made Isabella jump. Seconds later, the lights flickered and went out, plunging the room into gray dimness, relieved only by the candles Luella had lit.

"Right on schedule," Luella said, not sounding the least bit surprised. "Island power's about as reliable as a chocolate teapot. I'd better check my backup generator. Thomas, there are more candles in that kitchen drawer if you need them."

As Luella walked out to go to her cottage, clutching a small flashlight, Isabella and Thomas were left alone in the candlelit parlor. The sudden intimacy of the setting was unmistakable, shadows dancing on the walls and rain creating a private cocoon of sound.

Thomas cleared his throat. "You know, Luella is always prepared."

"I see that," Isabella said, taking a sip of her water. "She's been invaluable, giving me all of her knowledge of the inn and its operations."

"Luella sees everything that happens on this island," Thomas said. "Always has. She probably knows more about island secrets than the rest of us combined. Sometimes I think she's just waiting for folks to figure out what she already knows."

A particularly violent gust of wind rattled the windows. Isabella couldn't suppress another small start of surprise.

"Still don't like storms much, do you?" Thomas said gently, and Isabella realized he'd remembered this detail about her from so many years ago. The recognition in his voice was oddly comforting.

She smiled slightly. "Childhood thing. We had this huge old oak tree fall on our house during a storm when I was eight years old. No one got hurt, but the sound… I guess I've never quite forgotten it."

Thomas nodded. "That's legitimate fear then, not irrational at all."

"Well, that's nice of you to say, but I'm a grown woman now. I shouldn't still be jumping every time I hear thunder."

"Fear doesn't always listen to logic," Thomas

said, his voice carrying the weight of experience. "Sometimes it just settles into your bones and stays there, reminding you what you can't afford to lose. You know, after Sarah, my wife, was diagnosed, I developed this paralyzing fear of hospitals, not for myself, but for Emma. Every doctor's appointment, every mention of not feeling well, and I'd be right back in that oncology waiting room, watching Sarah fade away and knowing I couldn't fix it."

The personal confession surprised Isabella. He'd been so professional since they'd begun working together and rarely offered glimpses of his private thoughts or feelings.

"I'm sorry about your wife," Isabella said quietly. "That must have been really hard for both you and Emma. I can't even imagine."

He looked down at his plate. "It was. Sarah fought for seven years, from when Emma was six until she was thirteen. Those were hard years, watching Sarah decline while trying to keep things normal for Emma. By the end, I was doing most of the parenting while Sarah was in and out of hospitals. Emma was old enough to understand what was happening, but too young to really process losing her mother."

Against her better judgment, Isabella couldn't

help but ask the question. "How did you move forward from something like that?"

"One day at a time," Thomas said. "You know, you just have to focus on what's in front of you. And Emma needed me to be steady. My clients needed their projects completed, and the business needed someone to direct it. Having a purpose helped; it took my mind off it. I still had my moments, though."

Isabella nodded. When her own brief marriage had ended, she'd thrown herself into her career with such an intensity that she started having panic attacks. But work had always been her anchor during personal storms.

Another lightning flash lit up Thomas's face. The strong lines and the kind eyes that once looked at her with so much love now carried a mix of hard-earned wisdom and guarded emotion. For a brief moment, Isabella let herself wonder how different their lives might have been if he hadn't ended things so suddenly all those years ago, for reasons she still didn't understand.

The question that had been in Isabella's mind for years must have shone on her face because Thomas's expression became questioning.

"Isabella—"

There was a sudden crash from upstairs that

shattered the moment. It was the distinctive sound of something very heavy falling to the ground.

"That came from the third floor," Isabella said, already up on her feet.

Thomas grabbed one of the candles. "It's probably just the temporary support in the bathroom. Maybe the storm shifted something."

They ran upstairs, Thomas leading the way with the candle, casting shadows ahead of them. The old staircase creaked beneath their feet as the storm's fury became more pronounced on the upper floors, where the wind whistled through small gaps in the window frames.

In the third-floor bathroom, they found the source of the noise. A section of the ceiling had given way, dumping water, plaster, and insulation onto the floor. Rain poured through the new opening, already creating a puddle on the wooden floorboards.

"Oh gosh, we need to contain this before it damages the floor," Thomas said. "There are tarps in my truck. I'll be right back."

"Okay, I'll start cleaning up what I can," Isabella said, looking around for something to collect all the debris.

Thomas hesitated for a moment. "Wait for me to

get back. That ceiling is unstable. I don't want you getting hurt if more of it comes down."

The concern in his voice was professional, but it carried an underlying note of personal care that Isabella found both comforting and unsettling.

"I'll be careful," she said. "But we have to minimize this water damage."

Thomas nodded reluctantly before rushing downstairs.

Isabella listened to his footsteps recede and then went to find buckets or containers to try to catch the water that was still falling through the hole. She found a plastic bin in a nearby storage closet and placed it under the worst of the leak, then searched for towels to soak up the water already spreading across the floor.

By the time Thomas came back, soaking wet from his dash to the truck and back, Isabella had created a containment system of bins and towels.

"Good thinking," he said, dropping a bundle of tarps and a rope on a dry section of the floor. "Now let's get something over that hole before the whole ceiling comes down on us."

They worked together in the candlelight, rigging a temporary cover for the opening and securing the tarp to exposed beams with rope. They created a channel to direct water into the containers below. It was very awkward to work in dim light, requiring them to stand very close together, occasionally steadying each other as they reached up to secure the top.

At one moment, Thomas slightly lost his footing on the wet floor, and Isabella instinctively grabbed his arm to steady him, her hand wrapping around his bicep. She could feel the solid strength of his arm beneath the damp cotton, and suddenly she was twenty-two again, remembering how safe she'd always felt around him. The scent of his cologne mixed with rain and sawdust was painfully familiar. For a brief moment, they were pressed close, his damp shirt cool against her arm, his breath warm against her cheek.

"Oh, sorry," he said softly, regaining his balance but not immediately moving away. "Slippery."

"That's okay," Isabella said.

She was suddenly acutely aware of how close they stood, how the candlelight softened his features, and how familiar yet different it felt to have him beside her after all these years.

For a suspended moment, neither of them moved. Isabella could feel her heart pounding too fast, and it wasn't from the effort of their repairs. In the flickering candlelight, with rain pounding against the windows, it felt like they were the only two people in the world. His eyes searched her face with an intensity that made her breath catch.

She stepped back deliberately, even though every instinct urged her to move closer. The loss of his warmth felt immediate and sharp. "We should probably check the other rooms," she said, her professional tone back in place. "You know, make sure there aren't other leaks."

Thomas nodded, the moment broken. "Oh, you're right, of course. We need to split up, though, to cover more ground. You take the east wing, I'll check the west. Call me if you find anything serious."

They separated, each of them taking a candle to light the way. Isabella was happy for the task, for the necessity of focusing on something practical rather than the complicated emotions that had surfaced during their brief physical proximity.

After thoroughly inspecting the house, they found no other major leaks and regrouped in the second-floor hallway. The storm was starting to slow down, the thunder now more distant, the rain less intense.

"Everything seems secure," Isabella said. "I saw a few minor leaks in the east bedroom, but nothing serious."

"Yeah, same on my side," Thomas said. "The temporary roof patches are holding well, but once the storm passes, we'll have to properly address that bathroom ceiling. The tarp should contain things until then."

They made their way back downstairs, the awkwardness of the earlier moment hanging between them. In the parlor, they found Luella had returned and was calmly collecting the dishes from their interrupted meal.

"Roof problems?" she asked, eyeing their damp clothing.

"A section of the ceiling came down in the third-floor bathroom," Thomas said, "but we've got it contained now."

Luella nodded, unsurprised. "Oh, that bathroom's been a problem since the seventies. Previous owners attempted to fix it on a budget, but it never worked out in the long run. When will people ever learn?"

Isabella smiled at her matter-of-fact assessment. "Well, you were right about the power outage, too."

"Oh, I've seen a pattern or two in my years here," Luella said, stacking dishes. "Storm's passing now, but the power won't be back till morning, if I know this island's infrastructure."

As if to confirm her prediction, Isabella's phone chimed with a text message.

"It's from Maggie Beaumont," she said. "Island-wide power outage. Restoration crews won't be out until morning because of flooded roads."

Thomas sighed. "Well, that tracks. After the summer storms, the causeway often floods for a few hours at high tide."

"Well, you two might as well make yourselves comfortable," Luella said, picking up the stack of dishes. "I'm gonna head back to my cottage. I got a generator for my medical equipment. There are more candles in the pantry and plenty of flashlights in the emergency kit under the kitchen sink."

After Luella left, Isabella and Thomas stood there in the parlor, both uncertain about what to do next. The storm had created this unexpected intimacy, forcing them to work closely together and share a meal and conversation beyond their everyday professional interactions.

"You know, I'd better check the tarps one more time before I go," Thomas said finally.

"Oh, of course," Isabella said, nodding. "And I appreciate you staying to help with that leak. You didn't have to do that."

"Well, it's my project too," Thomas replied. "I wouldn't leave anyone to deal with that alone."

Something in his tone - perhaps the emphasis on *alone* - made Isabella wonder if he was referring to more than just a ceiling leak. But before she could analyze it further, her phone chimed again with another text.

"It's Daphne Chen," she explained. "The interior designer I'm interviewing tomorrow. She's asking if we can reschedule due to the storm damage."

"Is she local?"

"Charleston. She was planning to drive over in the morning."

"Oh, the causeway will be clear by then, but she might have trouble getting a visitor's pass if the guard station power is still out. They can be sticklers about procedure."

Isabella typed a quick reply suggesting they keep the appointment, but have a backup plan to meet in Charleston if access to the island was difficult.

"She comes highly recommended for historic properties. I hope she'll be a good fit for the project."

"I've seen her work," Thomas said. "She did the Dillon House renovation in Charleston last year. Beautiful balance of period-appropriate details with modern functionality."

"Well, that's exactly what I'm looking for. The inn needs to honor the history, but without feeling like a museum. Guests do expect some modern comforts."

"It's a delicate balance," Thomas agreed, "but when it's done right, it creates something special.

You know, a place visitors connect with history but also meets their contemporary needs."

Their shared vision reminded Isabella why they connected so deeply in college. They had complementary perspectives on architecture, preservation, and the excitement of reimagining spaces while respecting their origins. Despite everything that had happened between them, they still shared a compatibility in their professional outlooks that remained unchanged.

The lights suddenly flickered once, twice, and then remained on; the power was unexpectedly restored.

"Well, that's a pleasant surprise," Isabella said.

"Oh, don't get too excited," Thomas warned. "Island power is notoriously fickle after storms. It could go right back out again."

As if on cue, the lights flickered again and went dark once more.

"Well, you called that one," Isabella said, laughing.

He joined her in laughter, and the moment of shared amusement temporarily bridged the careful distance they'd maintained.

"You know, some things about island life never change. Power companies improved over the years, but the storms still tax the system."

"I should probably head back to my cottage

before the roads flood again," Isabella said, although she felt slightly reluctant to end their time together.

"Good idea. Do you have any candles or flashlights there?"

"Oh yeah, I stocked up after Maggie warned me about how the island's electrical system often worked."

"That's a smart woman, Maggie," Thomas said, reaching for his jacket. "She doesn't miss much."

They walked to the front door together, listening to the rain. It was now more of a trickle. The storm had passed its peak, and there was a steady drizzle without the dramatic lightning and thunder of earlier.

"Thanks again for your help with the ceiling," Isabella said as they stepped onto the porch. "I'm not sure what I would have done on my own."

"Oh, you would have figured it out. You were always resourceful."

The use of *always*, a reference to their shared past, hung between them in the air. It was the closest either of them had come to directly acknowledging their history outside of that first very awkward meeting. Isabella didn't know how to respond, so she nodded and moved toward the steps.

"Good night, Thomas."

"Good night," he said. "Drive carefully. There could be branches down on the road."

As she made her way to the car parked behind Luella's cottage, she found herself thinking about the unexpected turn the evening had taken. What had begun as a simple cooking lesson had evolved into a shared crisis, revealing glimpses of the Thomas she had once known so well.

The question that had been hovering at the edges of their minds since she discovered his presence on the island now resurfaced. Why had he really ended things with them? What had changed so suddenly that summer to turn a passionate love for each other into an abrupt goodbye?

Luella's cryptic comment about Thomas always doing what he thought was right, even at his own personal cost, suggested there was more to the story.

After all these years, did it even matter? They were different people now. They had separate lives and experiences that had shaped them.

Yet, as she drove carefully through the rain-slicked streets toward her cottage, Isabella couldn't shake the memory of that moment in the bathroom - standing so close to Thomas in the candlelight, feeling like no time had passed at all. The careful professional distance they maintained felt more fragile with each passing day.

Luella was right about some storms lingering while others passed through quickly. Isabella was beginning to suspect that what lay between her and Thomas wasn't the kind of storm that would simply blow over. Some tempests, once stirred up, demanded to be weathered completely before there could be any real peace.

For now, she had an inn to restore and a ceiling to repair. But increasingly, she wondered if healing the old building might also require healing the old wounds.

CHAPTER 6

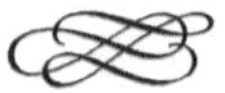

Thomas had been awake for hours as sleep proved elusive. The memories of the past and present-day concerns tangled up in his mind as the morning light filtered through the trees outside his bedroom window.

Today marked fifteen years since Sarah's passing, and it was a date he always approached with quiet reflection rather than outwardly mourning. He dressed in a clean button-down shirt and khakis, nothing formal but respectful of his annual visit to the small island cemetery, and he moved through his morning routine, automatically brewing coffee and toasting a slice of sourdough bread that Emma had brought from her favorite Atlanta bakery.

Emma.

He looked at the clock, wondering if his daughter would remember the day. She almost always did, though they rarely discussed it directly. Their shared grief had changed over the years into a more gentle remembrance, focused on honoring Sarah's life rather than dwelling on her absence.

As he sipped his coffee on the back deck and watched the morning mist rise from the tidal creek, he found his thoughts drifting to Isabella and their unexpected connection during yesterday's storm. The moment when she'd steadied him, her hand so warm on his arm, her face so close to his in the candlelight - it had brought back feelings he thought were long dormant.

The sound of his phone ringing pulled him from the reflection, and he saw Emma's name flashing on the screen.

"Morning, sweetheart," he answered as he moved back inside.

"Hey, Dad." Her voice was warm but definitely held a note of sadness. "I just wanted to check in, you know, see how you're doing today. I wish I could…"

So she had remembered.

"I'm okay," he said, trying to reassure her. "I'm going to visit the cemetery this morning."

"I wish I could be there," she said, "but this client meeting was scheduled months ago, or I would have come down for the whole weekend."

"Don't worry about it. Your mom would be the first to tell you business comes first on a day like this. You know how practical she was."

Emma laughed softly. "You know, she really was. Remember when she made us all go to that Chamber of Commerce dinner on the night after her second chemo treatment? She'd said she felt awful either way, so she might as well be productive and support local businesses."

"Oh, she was stubborn that way," Thomas said, smiling at the memory. "So how are you doing today?"

"I'm all right. It gets a little easier each year, doesn't it? I mean, not forgetting. You just… I think the sharp edges smooth out somewhat."

"I guess that's a good way to put it," Thomas said.

They talked for a few more minutes about Emma's upcoming meeting and her plans to visit the island again soon. As they were about to hang up, Emma paused for a moment and then asked, "Have you seen much of Isabella since I left? With the renovation?"

"Yes, of course," he replied. "There was a minor

crisis during yesterday's storm. Part of the ceiling gave way in one of the bathrooms, but we worked together to contain the damage as best we could."

"Oh, so just the two of you?" Emma's tone was neutral, but he could hear a little bit of concern beneath the question.

"Luella was there, too. Well, for part of it," he said. "Emma, it was strictly professional. We're colleagues working on a project together."

"Uh-huh," she said. "Well, just be careful, Dad. I like her, surprisingly, but there's still a lot of stuff unresolved between you."

"I know," Thomas said. "You go focus on your meeting today. Don't worry about me."

After they hung up, he got his keys and a small bundle of flowers he picked from his garden early that morning. White camellias. They were Sarah's favorites.

The cemetery sat on the far side of the island, a peaceful patch of hallowed ground overlooking the salt marsh. Ancient live oaks draped in Spanish moss stood sentinel over generations of islanders, their gnarled branches creating a natural cathedral against the morning sky.

As he drove, he thought about the timing of Isabella's return to his life and how curious it was, coinciding so closely with this significant anniversary.

Fifteen years since Sarah's passing. Thirty years since he'd left Isabella. These markers of his personal history seemed to be converging in ways he would have never anticipated.

The cemetery was empty when he arrived, which suited his mood. Thomas made his way along the oyster shell path to her grave, a simple little marble marker beneath a spreading oak tree. He put the camellias carefully against the stone, then stood quietly, his hands in his pockets.

"Mornin', Sarah," he said quietly, still feeling a bit self-conscious about talking to a headstone after all these years. He'd created a habit during his first year of widowhood, finding comfort in one-sided conversations. "Fifteen years. Hard to believe sometimes."

The gentle breeze stirred the Spanish moss overhead.

"Emma's doing well - crushing it at work, as she'd say. Still single, still married to her career, but she's happy."

He paused, thinking about his next words.

"You know, I've taken on a new project - the old Wexley Inn. It's a little complicated. Isabella Montgomery owns it."

He fell silent, trying to imagine what Sarah might say if she were here. She'd known about Isabella, of course, early in their marriage when they were still finding their way as a couple. He had told her about his college sweetheart, though not the full circumstances of its ending. Sarah, practical and direct as always, had just nodded and said, "Well, her loss was my gain, wasn't it?"

"Things were simple with you," he continued. "Not always easy, you know - towards the end, it wasn't - but simple. We understood each other."

He sighed and looked over the marshland.

"I never told her the truth, Sarah, about why I left, and now she's here and I don't know if I should dredge up ancient history or just let it be. I know I also didn't tell you in life, but I've confessed it to you almost every year since you died. I guess that makes me a coward. But what do I do? Do I tell her the real truth? The one I couldn't even tell you when you were alive?"

The question hung in the air, unanswered. He stood in silence for several more minutes, remembering his wife - her strength during her illness, her unwavering support of his business when they were just starting out, her fierce love for Emma.

Although their marriage had started with a lie and blackmail, it hadn't been a terrible marriage.

Sarah was his high school sweetheart, so there was affection between them. It was a good partnership for a long time. Passionate? Not really. Were they soulmates? No. But Thomas valued loyalty above much else, and he'd been loyal to her once the commitment was made.

"I miss your advice. You always knew how to cut through the noise and get to what mattered."

The sound of footsteps on the oyster shell path alerted him that someone was approaching, and he turned to see Emma making her way toward him with a small bouquet in her hand.

"Emma, what in the world? What about your meeting?"

She smiled, and she looked so much like Sarah in that moment that it tugged at his heart.

"Postponed. The client's flight got canceled due to weather, so I rescheduled for tomorrow and caught the first flight I could. I was already here when we spoke on the phone. I wanted to surprise you."

She joined him at the grave, putting her flowers beside his. Thomas pulled her into a tight hug, and then they stood together in comfortable silence for a few moments.

"I was just telling your mom about the inn renovation."

"And Isabella?"

"Well, that too."

"And what would Mom say about all this, do you think?"

Thomas considered the question. "Probably something practical and direct. You know, 'Do what needs doing and stop overthinking it.'"

Emma laughed softly, looping her arm through her father's. "That sounds exactly like her. You know what struck me about Isabella? She actually listens when you talk about the work, not just nodding along, but really understanding what you're saying about the building. Most clients just want to know when it'll be done and how much it'll cost. But she gets excited about the same details that light you up. That's... that's pretty special, Dad."

"She's a very intelligent woman. Always has been. My interests are the same as hers," Thomas said.

They went silent again, both of them lost in their private thoughts. Finally, Emma spoke.

"You should tell her the truth, Dad, about why you left. She deserves to know, and you deserve to be free of carrying that secret."

He sighed. "It's been three decades, Emma. Does it really even matter anymore?"

"Dad, you're standing at Mom's grave on the anniversary of her death, asking if the truth matters, while the woman you never explained yourself to is three miles away bringing your dream project to life. I think the universe is practically shouting that it matters."

He couldn't argue with her logic. They said their final goodbyes and walked back to their separate cars.

"I think I'll head to the inn to take some measurements I forgot yesterday," he said as they reached the parking area. "What are your plans?"

"You know, I was thinking of stopping by the Wexley Country Club for lunch. Maggie Beaumont invited me last time I was here, and I might take her up on it."

He raised an eyebrow. "Maggie Beaumont? Since when are you two lunch buddies?"

Emma shrugged. "I don't know, maybe I reached out to her about some historical information for a client project. She suggested lunch to discuss it."

"Uh-huh," Thomas echoed. "And this has nothing to do with the fact that Maggie is now Isabella's closest friend on this island?"

"It's pure coincidence," Emma said. "Just being sociable."

She wasn't even trying to hide her matchmaking scheme, and honestly, he wasn't sure whether to be annoyed or grateful for her interference.

He shook his head but couldn't help but smile. "You know you should be careful. Maggie sees everything and forgets nothing. She's the island's unofficial information broker and has been for decades."

"Oh, I'm counting on it," Emma replied, smiling. "See you back at your place later? We can grill those steaks in your freezer."

"That sounds good," Thomas said. "And don't believe everything Maggie tells you."

"Oh, only the interesting parts," she promised, getting into her rental car with a wave.

Thomas's attic was stifling, despite the early hour; the humid Lowcountry air trapped beneath the tin roof made the space feel like a sauna. Dust motes floated in the slanted sunlight that streamed through the small dormer window.

He'd come home from the cemetery hoping to distract himself with some practical tasks, remembering that he needed the original blueprint samples for the inn's windows. The specialist window restorer was coming tomorrow, and Thomas wanted to be prepared with all of the accurate historical specifications.

His father had been the unofficial historian for the island for as long as he could remember. After his parents died, Thomas carefully preserved and organized this archive, storing it in acid-free boxes in his climate-controlled attic.

He pulled down the box labeled *Wexley Inn Original Elements* and hoped to find the details for the windows that he needed. As he sorted through the papers, there was a smaller unmarked box that caught his attention. It had been pushed to the back of a shelf, half-hidden behind his father's collection of island maps. He didn't recognize it immediately, which was strange because he'd been methodical about cataloging everything when he had organized the space years ago.

Curious, he set the blueprint box aside and reached for the mystery container. It was a little wooden box with a hinged lid, dusty with age but still solid. As he lifted the lid, something caught in his breath.

Inside were letters - dozens of them - along with photographs and little mementos he hadn't seen in decades.

Isabella's letters.

After their breakup, he had packed everything away connected to their relationship because he couldn't discard the pieces of his heart, but he was too pained to keep them out in plain sight. And then when he married Sarah, he'd put the box at his parents' house for safekeeping, unwilling to dishonor his wife with a physical reminder of his first love. When his parents died, he must have unconsciously stored the box in the attic along with his father's archives and then mentally erased it from existence.

He sat heavily on an old trunk with the box in his hands. He knew he should have put it away and continued his search for the blueprints. He should have left the past undisturbed. Instead, he found himself lifting out the first letter, carefully unfolding the now yellowed paper.

Thomas,

It's only been three days since I got to New York for this internship, and I'm already missing you something fierce. It's pretty ridiculous. The city is everything that we both imagined. It's overwhelming, exciting, and endlessly fascinating. But I keep turning to tell my observations to you, only to find that you're not there beside me.

The firm is amazing. Yesterday, they even let me sit in on a client meeting for the historical library renovation project. The lead architect's approach is to preserve the original ceiling details while pulling in modern lighting solutions. It was brilliant. I took all kinds of notes to share with you once I get back.

Only eight more weeks until I'm home with you again, and it feels like forever.

All my love,

Isabella

He swallowed hard, remembering exactly when that letter had arrived. He had already talked to Sarah's parents at that point, and her father had made the demand that he marry her if he wanted to save his dad. Reading her words about the future together - their future together - and knowing what decision awaited him had been torture.

He set the letter aside and pulled out another one. This one was dated just days before he had written the note he would leave her to end their relationship.

Thomas,

I can't believe I'll be home in only two weeks. This internship has been such an incredible opportunity, but I'm so ready to be back with you. My supervisor hinted that they might offer me a position after graduation, which would be perfect timing for your graduate program in Charleston.

We could find ourselves a little apartment halfway between the two cities and make it work until we figure out our next steps.

I sketched out some ideas for that weekend cabin that we always talk about building someday. Nothing fancy, you know - just a simple retreat where we can escape when city life gets a little overwhelming.

I've enclosed a rough design. Let me know your thoughts.

Counting the days,

Isabella

Enclosed in the letter was a detailed sketch of a cabin that had Isabella's precise architectural style evident in every part. He unfolded it carefully, looking at the features they'd once discussed during late-night conversations about their future. A wide front porch overlooking the water, large windows to bring nature inside, and a big stone fireplace that would serve as the heart of the home.

He traced his fingers over the delicate lines of her drawing, recalling the late night when she had first sketched it at their favorite coffee shop, her face illuminated with dreams of their future together. 'Someday we'll build this,' she had whispered, 'and fill it with books, babies, and Sunday morning coffee.' The memory was vivid enough to take his breath away.

He'd kept every letter, every sketch, every photograph, unable to let go of these pieces of their shared past, but too guilty to keep them where Sarah might see them. Even after Sarah's death, he'd left them hidden, as if honoring his wife's memory meant keeping his first love buried. Now, with Isabella back in his life, the weight of all those unspoken truths felt heavier than ever.

After a while, he carefully placed the letters back in the box, but he hesitated over the cabin sketch. On impulse, he slipped it into the folder with the blueprints of the inn. Maybe it was time to stop hiding from these memories and to acknowledge their place in his life. The young man who had written those thoughtful responses to her letters believed he was protecting everyone. But reading her hopeful words now, seeing the future she had imagined for them, he wondered if his silence had been the cruelest cut of all.

As he moved forward, the sound of his phone interrupted his thoughts - a text from his foreman. They'd uncovered an unexpected structural issue with one of the inn's main support beams that required Thomas's immediate attention.

Grateful to have the distraction, he closed the attic and headed for his truck.

The past would have to wait. The present demanded his expertise.

When Thomas got to the inn, he found his crew carefully removing plaster around the support beam. Isabella was standing nearby, watching the process with concern evident on her face. She was calm as usual, but he knew she was worried.

"Morning," Thomas greeted her, trying to sound like everything was normal despite the emotional turbulence from the cemetery visit and then the attic discovery. "So, I understand we have found a challenge?"

She turned to him. "Yes. They were fixing the ceiling yesterday because of the leak when they noticed this." She pointed to the exposed beam, where the dark patches showed serious water damage.

He moved closer and carefully examined the wood. Isabella stepped beside him for a better look, and he caught a faint scent of her perfume mixed with sawdust and morning air. Standing so near, he noticed the fine lines of concentration around her eyes as she studied the damage.

The beam was originally part of the building, a hand-hewn heart pine that had supported the structure for over a century. The water damage occurred gradually over the decades, weakening the wood from the inside out.

"We're going to need to replace this section," he said after a thorough inspection. "The good news is I think we can sister in a new support beam without removing the original one completely, preserving what we can of the historic material but ensuring structural integrity."

She nodded. "So, what does that mean for our timeline and budget?"

"Oh, just minor adjustments to both," he said. "We'll need some specialty lumber to match the original dimensions, and it's going to be more labor-intensive than the standard replacement. I think we'll probably add three days to the schedule and maybe about four thousand to the budget."

He watched her process that information and admired the practical way she approached the setback. Many clients would have been frustrated or sought cheaper alternatives.

"Do it right," she said without hesitation. "This building has survived storms, wars, and decades of neglect. I didn't come this far to cut corners now. She deserves to stand for another century and a half."

He nodded. He appreciated her commitment to the quality. It was one of the things that had drawn him to her in college - her unwillingness to compromise on her standards and her understanding that some things were worth doing properly, even at a greater cost.

"I'll have the lumber sourced by tomorrow," he said. "We can begin the structural work as soon as it arrives."

Their conversation was interrupted by the arrival of a stylish Asian woman in her mid-thirties carrying a portfolio case and looking curiously around the construction site.

"Daphne." Isabella moved forward to greet her. "I'm so glad you made it through despite the storm aftermath."

"Oh, the causeway was clear, though I had to sweet-talk a guard into giving me a pass because I didn't have a formal appointment confirmation," she said, smiling. "Apparently, their computer system is down due to the power outage."

"Thomas, this is Daphne Chen, the interior designer I mentioned," Isabella introduced them. "Daphne, Thomas Langley is our restoration specialist and general contractor."

"It's my pleasure," Thomas said, shaking her hand. "I admired your work on the Dillon House in Charleston."

Her face lit up. "Thank you. That was a very special project. Those owners truly understood the value of preserving historical elements while creating a beautiful, livable space."

"Well, that's exactly what we're aiming for here," Isabella said. "Would you like a tour before we talk about specifics? Thomas's team has been uncovering some fascinating original elements."

As they walked through the inn, Thomas found himself very impressed with Daphne's questions and observations. She clearly understood historic preservation principles and asked insightful questions about the original materials and construction techniques. Most importantly, she seemed to grasp Isabella's vision for the space, offering suggestions that helped rather than conflicted with the building's character.

When they reached the hidden room that had been discovered during early demolition work, Daphne's excitement was palpable.

"Wow, this is extraordinary," she said, looking at the small space that had apparently been sealed off during a 1920s renovation. "Have you documented any of the artifacts?"

"Well, we photographed and cataloged everything," Isabella said, showing her the ledgers and personal items that they had carefully preserved. "I'm hoping to create a small display area for guests to learn about the inn's history."

"That's perfect," Daphne said. "We could incorporate a glass cabinet here, lighting the highlights without damaging the artifacts." She sketched quickly in her notebook as she spoke.

Thomas watched the two women collaborate, their ideas building on each other in a creative flow that reminded him of his early design sessions with Isabella in college. They shared a similar aesthetic sensibility and practical approach, focusing on solutions and respecting the building's heritage.

As the tour wrapped up in what would become the inn's main sitting room, Thomas found himself saying, "I think you two are going to work well together. You both have the same vision for this space, it seems."

Isabella looked pleased. "Well, that's my feeling as well. Daphne, if you're interested in the project, I would love to move forward with your services."

"I'm definitely interested," Daphne said enthusiastically. "This inn has immense potential, and I love your approach."

They discussed some practical details, such as the timeline, costs, and expectations, while Thomas excused himself to check on his crew's progress with the damaged beam.

When he returned, Isabella and Daphne were

reviewing fabric samples and talking about color palettes for the guest rooms.

"We'll want to distinguish each room while maintaining a cohesive feel throughout the property," Daphne said. "Maybe draw some inspiration from different eras of the inn's history."

"Oh, I love that idea," Isabella said, nodding. "It creates a narrative through the design, letting the guests experience all the different periods."

Thomas hesitated at the doorway, not wanting to interrupt their discussion. Isabella noticed him and gestured for him to join them.

"Thomas, Daphne has some questions about the original window treatments. The photographs we found show what might be plantation shutters in the main parlor, but it's hard to be certain."

"Actually, they were a custom design," Thomas said, recalling the blueprints he'd been searching for that morning. "My father salvaged one during the 1980s renovation. I think I have the original specs in my archives if you want to see them."

"That'd be great," Daphne said.

"I need to head back to oversee the beam work, but I can email you the images of the specs later today."

"Perfect," Daphne said. "And while I have you both here, I want to mention that I'm dating a local -

Jake Cooper. He runs the fishing charters in the marina. So if you hear island gossip about me seeing a local boy, that's who it is."

Isabella laughed. "Noted. I'm quickly learning that Wexley Island runs on a currency of information."

"Nothing happens here without everybody knowing about it within hours," Daphne said, rolling her eyes. "Jake warned me that I would be thoroughly investigated once word got out that I was working on this inn project."

"Well, consider yourself officially welcomed to the Wexley rumor mill," Thomas said. "Though, as a newcomer taking on this inn restoration, I think Isabella still holds the top spot for island curiosity."

"Oh, lucky me," Isabella said dryly.

As Thomas excused himself to return to the crew, he found himself thinking about the easy rapport developing between Isabella and her team. She'd always had a gift for bringing talented people together and fostering collaboration.

The rest of the day passed as Thomas focused on his work and watched his crew develop a detailed plan for reinforcing the damaged beam. By late afternoon, they had stabilized the area and were preparing for the lumber's arrival. Isabella and

Daphne continued their design discussions, occasionally asking Thomas structural questions.

When the workday wound down, Thomas found himself alone with Isabella in what would become the inn's library. Daphne had left, promising to send the initial design concepts within a week, and the construction crew had departed for the day.

"You know, Daphne's a great choice," Thomas said, gathering his tools. "She understands what you're trying to create here."

Isabella nodded. "I think so, too. She respects the history, but she's not afraid to incorporate some modern elements when they're appropriate."

"Exactly the balance this place needs," Thomas said. "You're building a very strong team."

"Well, that's the idea," Isabella said. "The inn's success will depend on having the right people involved at every level."

The silence between them felt comfortable yet tense, reminiscent of their younger days when words weren't always needed. Golden afternoon light slanted through the windows, and he found himself studying how it played across her face, hesitant to break the spell.

"I should go," he finally said, but made no immediate move toward the door. "Emma's back on the island unexpectedly, so we're having dinner together tonight."

"Oh, I thought she had meetings in Atlanta."

"Postponed due to some issues with her client."

Isabella nodded. "How is Emma? She seemed a little more comfortable with me by the end of her visit."

He smiled. "She was. Emma forms her own opinions about people, no matter what she's heard. She mentioned she liked you, actually."

Something in Isabella's expression softened. "Well, I'm glad. She's clearly very important to you."

"She's my whole world," he said, letting the honest words escape before he could consider them.

Her gaze was thoughtful as she studied him. "You've done a great job with her. She's impressive. Intelligent, kind, confident. Those qualities don't develop by accident."

"Thank you. That means a lot."

Another silence fell. This one more charged than the last. He wanted to say more—about Emma, about their past, about the letters he'd discovered that morning—but the moment didn't seem right.

"Good night, Isabella," he finally said, gathering the rest of his things.

"Good night, Thomas," she said.

As he drove home, he found himself thinking

about Emma's advice at the cemetery. Maybe it was time to tell Isabella the truth about why he had ended their relationship so suddenly - not to rekindle what had been lost, because too much time had passed for that - but to finally close that chapter that had been left painfully open.

The question was whether opening old wounds would bring healing or simply fresh pain for both of them - and whether, after thirty years, Isabella would even want to hear his explanation.

CHAPTER 7

So many thoughts occupied his mind as he prepared for dinner with Emma. Their conversation flowed easily around everyday topics, but it wasn't until they were clearing dishes that his daughter decided to return to the subject of their cemetery discussion.

"So, did you see Isabella today?" she asked a little too casually.

He nodded and loaded plates into the dishwasher. "She was at the inn meeting with an interior designer she hired. Why?"

Emma shrugged. "I was just curious. I had lunch with Maggie Beaumont."

"And how was that?" Thomas asked, raising an eyebrow.

"Very enlightening," Emma replied with a

knowing smile. "That woman has more intel than the CIA."

"And I warned you about that," Thomas said. "Maggie knows everybody's business and remembers every single detail."

"Which is exactly why she's so fascinating to talk with," Emma said as she wiped down the counter. "Did you know that she and Isabella have become quite close friends? Apparently, Maggie's taken Isabella under her wing to help her navigate island politics."

"Yes, I've heard that," Thomas said. "Maggie's a valuable ally. The Lowcountry Ladies Club respects her, even if some, like Vivian Pierce, don't particularly like her straightforward approach."

Emma nodded. "Maggie said something interesting about Isabella. She said she's never seen somebody work so hard to build something that isn't just for herself - that the end project is about creating a legacy, a place that belongs to the island as much as to her personally."

Thomas found truth in that. "Yes, that aligns with what I've seen. Isabella could certainly have chosen an easier path - you know, buy an existing hotel, build something new. Instead, she's pouring everything into preserving this piece of island history. Most developers would have demolished the place."

"It's admirable," Emma said. "Very much in line with your own values about preservation."

He gave his daughter a knowing look. "Is there a point you're working toward, Emma?"

She grinned. "Just observing that you and Isabella seem to have kept this core compatibility in your values, even though you've spent thirty years living separate lives."

"Well, professional compatibility doesn't erase a complicated history."

"No," Emma agreed, "but maybe it provides a foundation. Which brings me back to what I said this morning."

He sighed and turned to face his daughter. "You think I should tell her everything about why I left?"

"I do. Not because I'm trying to play matchmaker—"

"Aren't you?" Thomas interrupted.

Emma smiled. "Not primarily, anyway. I think you should tell her because carrying secrets is exhausting, Dad. And because she deserves to know that you didn't just arbitrarily decide you didn't want her anymore."

He thought about his daughter's words carefully. "And what if knowing hurts her all over again? Or what if she resents the choice I made without giving her any say in the matter?"

"Well, those are legitimate risks. But isn't continuing to withhold the truth just making that choice for her all over again? You decided she was better off not knowing thirty years ago. Maybe you should let her decide what to do with the information."

He had no immediate answer to the perspective. Emma's insight often surprised him. She could see situations from angles he hadn't considered.

Emma's words hit harder because they echoed thoughts he'd been trying to suppress. Every day he worked alongside Isabella, watching her pour her heart into restoring the inn, he felt the weight of that old deception growing heavier.

Later that night, after she had gone to bed, he found himself on his back porch again, listening to the sounds of the marsh at night and thinking about her advice. The cabin sketch Isabella had drawn so long ago sat on a table beside him, lit by the porch light.

Whatever he decided about revealing the past to Isabella, one thing was becoming very clear. The careful boundaries he'd built up over the years were weakening a little more each day. Every shared glance, every moment of professional cooperation, and every glimpse of the passionate, determined woman she'd become was eroding his resolve to keep the past buried.

I sabella stood in the center of what was going to become the inn's grand dining room and watched as Thomas's crew carefully removed the non-original wall that had divided the space since the 1940s.

"It's even more beautiful than I imagined," she said to Daphne, who stood beside her with a note-book full of swatches and sketches.

"Look at how the light moves through the space now. It's so much brighter, and the proportions are absolutely perfect," Daphne said, making a quick note. "You know, with the original wainscoting restored and the period-appropriate lighting, this will be spectacular. I'm thinking we could do a deep blue for the upper walls - not a navy, but something with more depth. It would complement the original wood tones beautifully."

Isabella nodded, already envisioning the completed space. "I trust your judgment. The samples you showed me yesterday were exactly what I had in mind."

Over the past three weeks, the renovation had been progressing steadily. There were occasional setbacks, of course. The damaged support beam was successfully reinforced. The roof had been repaired, and the electrical system was being fully rewired to meet modern standards. Isabella had fallen into a comfortable routine in her new space, spending her days at the inn overseeing various aspects of the project. Her evenings were spent researching historical details or reviewing design plans.

She was about to ask Daphne about table configurations when she heard a familiar voice calling her from the front hall.

"Isabella, are you here?"

"In the dining room, Maggie," she called back, smiling as her friend appeared in the doorway.

Maggie Beaumont looked elegant, as always, in a simple pink cotton dress and pearls, but her expression was way more serious than usual.

"Good morning, ladies. My, this room is turning into a beautiful space." She looked around with appreciation before turning to Isabella. "I hate to interrupt your work, but I need to talk to you about something important. Do you have a minute?"

"Of course," Isabella replied. "Daphne, could you excuse us?"

"Oh, of course. I'll go measure the upstairs hallway for the runner we talked about," she said tactfully, gathering her materials.

Once they were alone, Maggie didn't hesitate. "I've just come from a quite revealing coffee with

Vivian Pierce. It seems she's trying to gather opposition to your renovation plans for the upcoming Architectural Review Board meeting."

Isabella frowned. "But they already approved our preliminary plans. We're following everything exactly as submitted."

"I understand, but this is about the next phase. It's specifically about your plans to upgrade the kitchen to commercial standards and add modern bathrooms to each guest room. Vivian's claiming these changes will 'destroy the soul of our island's most treasured landmark.' She's even threatening to petition the state historical commission if the local board approves your plans."

"Well, that's just ridiculous," Isabella said, frustrated. "We're maintaining every historical element possible. The kitchen and bathrooms need to meet modern health codes. If this is going to work as an actual inn—"

"You and I both know that, dear. But Vivian is playing to the fears of the island's old guard. You know, she's particularly focused on the fact that you're bringing in an 'outside designer' rather than using local talent." Her expression was sympathetic but very concerned. "I just thought you should know before the whispering campaign gains too much momentum."

Isabella took a deep breath and tried to process the information. Of course, she had expected resistance to her plans. That was part of renovating a beloved historical property in a close-knit community. But she hadn't anticipated such a deliberate opposition.

"Well, thanks for the warning. What do you suggest I do?"

"A good old-fashioned charm offensive," Maggie replied with steel in her smile. "Sometimes you gotta kill 'em with kindness before they know what hit 'em. I'm hosting my annual garden party next weekend—it's where the real island business gets done, over mint juleps and petits fours. I'd like you to be my honored guest, showcasing what you're creating here. Bring your plans, your designer, and that incredible knowledge of historical preservation that you have. Then let the influential ladies of Wexley see firsthand what you're creating here."

She considered this suggestion. Public relations had been a significant part of her corporate role. She knew the value of getting ahead of a potential opposition.

"That sounds like a great approach, though I doubt Vivian will be swayed."

"Oh, Vivian is a lost cause," Maggie said, waving her

hand. "This isn't about convincing Vivian. That ship sailed years ago. It's about making sure she doesn't convince Charlotte Stewart, whose husband controls the renovation loans, or Helen Morrison, whose family founded the island. We need those votes, Isabella."

As they discussed the strategy for the garden party, Isabella found herself once again grateful for Maggie's friendship. The older woman had become an unexpected ally, offering island insights and social connections that would have taken Isabella years to develop on her own.

Their conversation was interrupted by the arrival of Luella, who carried a large wicker basket.

"Figured y'all might be gettin' a little peckish," she announced as she set the basket down. "Can't fight island politics on an empty stomach. Fresh biscuits, fruit, and that chicken salad you liked so much yesterday, Isabella."

"Oh, Luella, you're a treasure," Isabella said. "Please join us. Maggie was just telling me about Vivian's latest efforts to derail our renovation."

Luella snorted. "Honey, that woman's been tryin' to run this island since she was knee-high to a cricket. Some folks just can't help themselves."

Maggie laughed. "Well put, Luella. I've been suggesting Isabella join my garden party next weekend to win over some of the Ladies Club members before the review board meeting."

"That's a good plan," Luella said. "You should have Thomas there, too. Some of these ladies have known him since he was a little boy. They trust his judgment on these historical matters, whether Vivian likes it or not."

Isabella hesitated. "I'm not sure if Thomas would want to get involved in social politics like this."

"Nonsense," Luella said firmly. "This is his project, too. He knows how these island games are played better than most."

Before Isabella could respond, they heard the sound of Thomas's truck pulling up outside. Moments later, he was in the doorway, looking kind of surprised to find the three women in conversation.

"Morning, ladies," he greeted them. "Am I interrupting something?"

"Not at all," Maggie replied. "In fact, we were just discussing you."

He raised an eyebrow, looking between them. "Should I be worried?"

"Probably," Luella said. "Maggie's recruiting forces for battle with Vivian Pierce."

Isabella quickly explained the situation while

Thomas listened, his expression growing more serious.

"I'm not surprised," he said. "Vivian's never forgiven me for convincing the board to approve composite roofing materials on the Palmetto Street renovations last year. She was dead set on requiring historically accurate wooden shingles, even though they were a fire hazard and had serious maintenance issues."

"Well, then you understand why your presence at my garden party would be valuable," Maggie said. "Your expertise lends credibility to Isabella's vision."

He glanced over at Isabella. "If you think it would help, I'm happy to attend."

"I think it would," she admitted. "Your knowledge of the island's architectural history is far more extensive than mine. And as Luella pointed out, many of these women have known you for many years."

"Well, then it's settled," Maggie said. "Saturday at two o'clock, semi-formal garden attire. Thomas, you know where I live." She checked her watch. "Oh, I should be going. I have a foundation board meeting at eleven."

After Maggie and Luella departed, Isabella and Thomas found themselves alone in the quiet dining room. Sunlight continued to stream through the windows. Isabella found herself acutely aware of his presence in the large space, the way he moved with quiet confidence, the familiar cadence of his voice, the way afternoon light caught the silver threading through his dark hair.

"You don't have to attend the garden party if you'd rather not," Isabella said, feeling like she should give him an out. "I know these social events can be boring. They're not really my thing either."

He smiled slightly. "Oh, I've survived my share of island functions over the years. Besides, I'm very invested in this project, just like you are."

She nodded. "Well, thank you. I have to admit, I didn't quite anticipate this level of opposition when I bought the inn."

"Wexley Island resists change by default," he said as he walked over to examine the newly exposed crown molding along the dining room ceiling. "It's not personal, although Vivian certainly makes it feel that way. She opposed my parents when they bought their house back in the '70s because they weren't 'established island families'."

"And yet your family has been here for what, over fifty years now?" she asked, following his gaze as he looked at the plasterwork overhead.

"My father moved us here when I was four. He took a job as a caretaker at the Harrington Estate, which included the inn at that time. We lived in the groundskeeper's cottage until I was in high school."

This glimpse into Thomas's childhood fascinated Isabella. Despite their history and current professional relationship, she realized just how little she knew about his life before college or after their breakup. Their conversations had always remained focused on renovations and very few personal details.

"Is that how you developed an interest in historical restoration, growing up around these old buildings?"

He nodded. "My dad taught me to respect the craftsmanship in these structures. He could run his hand along a piece of molding and tell you not just when it was carved, but which craftsman did the work, what tools he used, and probably even what he had for breakfast that morning. Said every piece of wood holds the story of the hands that shaped it. He believed these buildings held the island's stories, and preserving them was preserving history itself."

"Well, he sounds like he was a remarkable man."

"Oh, he was." He turned to face her directly. "He would have approved of what you're doing here, Isabella. Not just restoring the building, but honoring its purpose as a gathering place and a part of community life."

The unexpected personal comment and the warmth in his voice when he said her name caught Isabella completely off guard. For a moment, the professional distance they'd carefully maintained broke down, and she glimpsed the young man who had once shared his dreams with her under Carolina stars.

"That means a lot to me," she said, trying to keep it professional.

They stood silently for a moment, the air heavy with unspoken thoughts and thirty years of careful distance. Thomas's eyes searched her face with intensity that made her pulse race, and for a dangerous second, she thought he might say something that would change everything. Instead, as if by mutual understanding, they both stepped back from the edge.

"You know, I'd better check on the electrical work upstairs," Thomas said, pointing toward the hallway. "The inspector's coming tomorrow, and I want to make sure everything is up to code."

"Of course," she said, nodding. "I need to review the kitchen plans with Daphne before we meet with the health department next week."

As Thomas left, Isabella found herself thinking about their brief personal exchange. Despite their best efforts to maintain strictly professional boundaries, moments like these continued to occur - small windows into the man Thomas had become over the years. So familiar, yet so different.

These glimpses both intrigued and unsettled her, despite her determination to keep emotional distance. The Thomas she was discovering - weathered by loss, deepened by responsibility, yet still possessing that fundamental integrity she'd fallen for - was somehow even more appealing than the young man she'd once loved.

She shook her head and refocused on the renovation plans spread across the makeshift table. The inn was her priority and her future. Whatever history was between her and Thomas belonged firmly in the past, and she wasn't going to complicate the present that she was working so hard to build. Yet even as she made this resolution, Isabella couldn't shake the feeling that the past and future were becoming increasingly complex to keep separate. Some foundations, once disturbed, refuse to return to their original positions.

CHAPTER 8

The day of Maggie's garden party arrived, and there was perfect weather. It was sunny but not too hot or muggy, with a gentle breeze carrying the scent of blooming camellias and jasmine.

Isabella chose her outfit carefully. She wore a pale blue dress that was elegant without being flashy, paired with simple pearl earrings and low heels suitable for garden paths.

Daphne arrived early at Isabella's cottage to review their presentation plan. She brought carefully arranged design boards to display the renovation ideas, focusing on how the modern updates would enhance rather than overshadow the inn's historic features.

"Now remember, we're not trying to defend our

design choices," Daphne said as they drove to Maggie's estate. "We're inviting these women to feel like they're a part of the inn's revival. Everybody wants to be associated with a successful restoration of an island landmark like this."

Isabella had nodded. In the weeks they'd worked together, she'd come to value not just the designer's aesthetic sense, but her understanding of the social dynamics involved in high-profile projects.

Maggie's home was the crown jewel of *The Palms* neighborhood - an elegant Lowcountry mansion with wraparound verandas that seemed to float above perfectly manicured gardens so lush they looked like something from Southern Living maga-zine. Brick pathways wound through azaleas and towering camellias, while a magnificent oak-lined alley led to the front entrance. When they pulled into the circular driveway, Isabella noticed several luxury vehicles already parked, indicating that many of the guests had already arrived.

"Are you ready for this?" Daphne asked with an encouraging smile.

"As I'll ever be," Isabella replied. She gathered her portfolio of plans and historical documents.

They were greeted at the door by Maggie herself, wearing a green dress that perfectly complemented her silver hair. "Isabella, Daphne, welcome, dears. Everyone is out in the garden. We've set up a display area for your materials on the east terrace, as we discussed." She leaned closer, lowering her voice. "Vivian arrived early with her three closest allies, but I seated them as far from your presentation area as humanly possible."

"Thanks so much for arranging this," Isabella said. "Your support means more than I can express."

"Oh, nonsense." Maggie waved away the thanks. "I've been waiting years for someone to properly restore that inn, and I'm not about to let Vivian's petty power plays interfere now that we finally have the right person for the job."

She led them through the house to the back gardens, where approximately thirty women were gathered in elegant little groups, sipping champagne and nibbling on canapés served by the staff. Isabella recognized many of the faces from the Lowcountry Ladies Club luncheon, though there were several new women as well.

As they moved through the garden, Isabella recognized the intricate social dance at play - alliances as clearly marked as battle lines, with some women asserting dominance. Meanwhile, others acted as diplomatic messengers between groups. It was corporate politics played out with tea glasses and pearls, but politics nonetheless. Vivian held court near a stunning rose trellis, her perfectly styled hair and designer dress cementing her status as one of the fashion leaders at the garden party.

"Thomas hasn't arrived yet," Maggie said, "but he texted that he's on his way. Charlotte Stewart is by the fountain. She's Gerald's wife and sits on the Historical Society Board. You want to speak with her first, for sure."

For the next hour, Isabella mingled with the guests alongside Daphne, discussing their renovation plans and responding to questions about the inn's future. To her pleasant surprise, most of the women appeared genuinely interested and supportive, asking about historical accuracy and preservation techniques.

"My grandmother used to attend dinner dances at the inn back in the fifties," one elderly woman said. "She always said the ballroom had the best acoustics on the island. Are you going to preserve that space?"

"Oh, absolutely," Isabella assured her. "The original ballroom is going to be fully restored, including that sprung dance floor. We found photographs from the era that show the crystal chandeliers and wall sconces, and we're having those reproduced by a historical lighting specialist."

The woman beamed with approval. "Wonderful. I do hope you'll revive those dinner dances. They were quite the social highlight of the season."

This pattern repeated with many guests, as each shared their personal connection to the inn's history and showed their excitement for the restoration. Isabella started to realize that the inn wasn't just a building to these women - it was a store of their memories, their courtships, their celebrations. Every room told stories that linked generations, and she wasn't just restoring the architecture; she was bringing back the soul of their community.

She was deep in conversation with Charlotte Stewart about kitchen designs when she suddenly sensed a subtle shift in the garden's atmosphere. Looking up, she saw Thomas arriving and heading toward them. He looked different outside the construction site, more polished in his pressed khakis and blue button-down shirt that highlighted the color of his eyes. His hair was neatly combed, though a rebellious strand had already fallen across his forehead, which Isabella found both familiar and disarming.

She caught herself marveling at details she shouldn't have noticed - how the afternoon light highlighted the silver in his hair, how his smile changed his entire face when he greeted the ladies, and the confident way he navigated through the social scene she was still trying to learn.

"Thomas, dear," Charlotte greeted him warmly. "I was just telling Isabella about how impressed Gerald is with the structural work you've done at the inn. He says it's some of your finest restoration to date."

"Well, that's high praise coming from Gerald," Thomas said, smiling. "He's never been one to offer compliments lightly."

"Isabella was showing me the kitchen plans," she continued, "such a thoughtful balance of modern functionality and historical aesthetics."

"Well, that's been our approach all along," Thomas said. "Isabella understands that preservation isn't about freezing a building in time but allowing it to serve a purpose with appropriate updates."

Isabella didn't want to admit how much his unwavering support affected her - how it felt like having an anchor in unfamiliar waters, how his confidence in her vision made her believe in it even more fiercely. It was dangerous territory, this gratitude that felt suspiciously like something more profound. She noticed how Thomas effortlessly navigated a conversation with Charlotte, addressing any practical considerations along the way.

When Charlotte moved on to greet other guests,

he turned to Isabella with a slight smile. "So how's it going so far?"

"Better than I expected," she said. "There seems to be actual support for the project among many of the women here."

"Well, don't let that surprise you too much," he said. "Despite Vivian's influence, most of the islanders have wanted to see that inn restored for years. They just needed someone with the right vision and commitment to make it happen."

She was about to respond to the unexpected compliment when she was interrupted by Vivian Pierce, approaching with a tight smile.

"Isabella, Thomas, how lovely to see you both," she said. Her tone suggested the opposite of what she was saying. "I've been hearing quite a lot about your renovation plans today."

"I hope you've had a chance to review our detailed presentations," Isabella said, trying to sound pleasant. "Daphne has done a wonderful job showing how the modern updates will complement all of the historical elements."

"Oh yes, your designer has a contemporary perspective," Vivian said, her slight hesitation revealing her clear disapproval. "Although one does wonder if someone with deeper roots in our island's heritage might have made more... traditional choices. We do have such a distinctive aesthetic here."

Thomas stepped in. "Actually, Vivian, Daphne's approach aligns perfectly with the guidelines established by the National Trust for Historic Preservation. Her work on the Dillon House in Charleston won recognition from the South Carolina Historical Society just last year."

Vivian's smile tightened. "Well, Charleston isn't Wexley Island, is it? We have our own standards here."

"Standards that our own Architectural Review Board established using nationally recognized preservation principles," he said firmly. "The same proven methods that have successfully restored buildings throughout the historic South."

Isabella watched the exchange with fascination, impressed by Thomas's calm but unyielding defense. He understood the island's political dynamics intimately. That much was clear. He knew exactly how to counter Vivian's objections without appearing to be confrontational.

"I understand your concern for maintaining the island's character, Vivian," Isabella said. "It's something we all value. But that's why I've been so careful to document and preserve any original elements when possible."

"Yes. Well, we've learned from experience that good intentions don't always lead to the right results, haven't we?" Vivian's sharp look at Thomas carried the weight of past conflicts. "Some projects that seemed promising at first have turned out to be… problematic for our island's character."

Before either could respond to this thinly veiled criticism, Maggie appeared at Isabella's elbow. "Vivian, darling, Eloise Whitaker is looking for you. Something about the hospital fundraiser committee meeting."

With a final tight smile, Vivian excused herself and left Isabella feeling like she had just survived a minor skirmish in an ongoing war.

"Oh, don't let her rattle you," Maggie said softly. "Vivian's influence isn't what it used to be, even though she believes it is. This is especially true since I became president of the Ladies' Club."

"Well, she seems really determined to oppose this renovation," Isabella said.

Thomas and Maggie exchanged a knowing look.

"It's not just about the inn," Thomas said. "Vivian had her eye on the Ladies' Club presidency for years before Maggie was elected, and before that, she lost the Historical Society chairmanship to my mom."

"Oh, that's ancient history," Maggie waved dismissively. "The point is, her opposition is more about maintaining her perceived authority than any actual concern about your renovation plans."

"Well, that doesn't make her any less dangerous to the project," Isabella said.

"True enough," Thomas agreed, "but you're making the right moves right now, today. I've spoken with all the board members I could get to, and they all seem impressed by your commitment to historical accuracy."

The garden party went on as Isabella and Daphne displayed their formal design boards to an attentive crowd. Thomas stayed nearby, offering technical insights when needed and adding credibility to their plans. When guests began their gracious Southern farewells - including air kisses and promises to 'do lunch soon' - Isabella felt cautiously optimistic. She'd won hearts and minds today, and in a community where personal relationships matter more than policy positions, that could be decisive.

"You were magnificent," Maggie declared. "Knowledgeable, passionate, gracious, even when Vivian tried to provoke you. I'd say you've won over at least two-thirds of the influential ladies here today."

"Well, I couldn't have done it without your support," Isabella said. "Or Thomas's," she added, glancing at him.

"Well, I'll call today a success," Maggie said with satisfaction. "Now, why don't you all stay for a more relaxed drink on the veranda? After managing Vivian and her cronies, you deserve a moment of peace."

Daphne declined, explaining she had dinner plans with Jake, but Isabella and Thomas accepted the invitation. Soon, they were settled in comfortable wicker chairs on Maggie's veranda, gin and tonics in hand, watching the late afternoon sun cast a golden light across the carefully tended gardens.

"I've always loved this view," Thomas said, looking relaxed for the first time that day. "Your parents had the best garden parties on the island, Maggie."

"Oh, Mother did love her entertaining," Maggie agreed with a fond smile, "though I do think she enjoyed the planning more than the actual events. She was always the happiest when orchestrating social maneuvers."

"Like mother, like daughter," Thomas teased.

Maggie laughed. "Guilty as charged, although I like to think my orchestrations serve a greater purpose than just social status."

Isabella watched the friendly exchange with interest, understanding there was a depth of history between Thomas and Maggie that she hadn't fully appreciated.

"How long have you two known each other?"

"Oh, forever," Maggie said. "Thomas's mama, Mary, was my dearest friend and my partner in crime on every committee this island ever invented. When she passed, I promised her I'd keep an eye on this boy of hers. Though I suspect she'd be mighty pleased with how he turned out."

"Maggie stepped in when I needed guidance the most," Thomas said, his voice thick with gratitude. "After my mom died, and years later my dad passed away, when I was trying to figure out how to raise Emma and keep the business going... well, let's just say I wouldn't have made it without her wisdom."

Something in his tone - a hint of deeper meaning - made Isabella wonder if those "difficult times" included the period after they broke up. Before she could think any further about it, Maggie changed the subject.

"Speaking of navigating difficulties, Isabella, have you given any thought to the inn's opening celebration? I know it may seem premature, but those events take planning, especially if you want to make the right impression on the island."

"I want to honor everyone who's loved this place - from the original builders to the families who celebrated here, to the island residents who've watched over it during the empty years. An event that bridges past and future, showing how preservation can breathe new life into cherished spaces."

"Perfect," Maggie nodded. "And the timing? I assume you're aiming for the holiday season?"

"Well, that's the goal. Though with renovation timelines, it's always subject to change."

"Well, we're slightly ahead of schedule on the structural work," Thomas said. "Barring any major surprises, a holiday opening is realistic."

"Wonderful!" Maggie clapped her hands together. "A Christmas grand opening is going to be so ideal. The inn was always known for its holiday celebrations in the past."

As they talked about potential themes and guest lists for the opening event, Isabella found herself enjoying the conversation. It felt good to look beyond the immediate challenges of renovation to the inn's future as a functioning business and community gathering place. She'd hardly let herself think of that so far. She was so focused on all of the renovations that needed to be done.

The sun began to set when they finally said their goodbyes to Maggie. As they walked to their vehicles, Thomas paused beside Isabella's car.

"You handled everything beautifully today," he said. "Vivian didn't know what hit her."

She laughed softly. "Well, I've dealt with difficult people before. Corporate hotel chains have their own version of Vivian Pierce."

"Still, navigating island politics isn't easy for newcomers, and you've adapted remarkably well." He hesitated and then added, "You know, you've always had that gift - seeing the heart of the situation and finding a way through it."

The unexpected intimacy of the moment took Isabella by surprise. His voice carried the same warmth she remembered from those late college nights when they worked side by side on challenging design problems, when his praise meant everything to her young heart. Thirty years later, it still had the power to quicken her pulse.

The familiar warmth in his voice sent a warning through her chest. This was exactly how it had started before - the easy collaboration, the shared vision, the feeling that they were perfect partners. And then one day, without warning or explanation, it had all disappeared. She couldn't let herself forget that pain, no matter how natural it felt to fall back into their old rhythm.

"Thank you," she said, not sure what else to say.

Thomas seemed to realize he'd crossed their

carefully maintained professional boundaries, his eyes searching her face as if wondering whether she'd noticed the shift in his tone, the way 'always' linked their past to their present. "Well, I guess I should get going. Early start tomorrow with the window restoration team."

"Of course. I'll see you there at the inn."

As she drove back to her cottage, she found herself thinking about the day's events. The garden party had been a professional success and may have secured crucial support for the renovation. Still, she'd also revealed new dimensions of her relationship with Thomas—not just as contractor and client, but as two people with a complex shared history.

For the first time since arriving on the island, Isabella allowed herself to acknowledge what she'd been fighting - the growing attraction that felt both thrilling and terrifying. But with that acknowledgment came a sharp reminder: Thomas had walked away from her once without explanation. What guarantee did she have that he wouldn't do it again? The careful professional distance wasn't just protection for her heart - it was a lesson learned the hard way.

It was a possibility she'd forbidden herself to consider until now. Though it frightened her, she couldn't deny the relief that came with simply acknowledging what had been growing between them. The inn was revealing more than architectural treasures - it was excavating feelings she'd thought were safely buried.

Thomas knelt in the crawlspace under the inn's east wing with his flashlight in his hand. He examined the ancient plumbing system that had been uncovered during the morning work. What had started as a routine inspection had revealed an unexpected complication. The original pipes were embedded in the foundation in a manner not depicted on any of the blueprints.

"Pass me the camera, would you, Wade?" he called to his foreman.

Wade handed down a digital camera that they used to document discoveries.

"How bad is it?"

"Not catastrophic, but definitely a redesign," he said, carefully photographing the pipe configuration from multiple angles. "We're going to need to reroute the new plumbing instead of running it where we planned."

After taking sufficient documentation, Thomas made his way back to the access point, emerging dusty but relieved that they had caught the issue before proceeding with the installation.

"Let's get these images to Isabella and the plumbing contractor," he said. "We're going to need to revise those plans before tomorrow's work begins."

Wade headed off with the photos, and Thomas brushed the worst of the dirt from his clothes before making his way to the makeshift office Isabella had set up in what would become the inn's library. Eventually, he found her deep in conversation with Luella, looking over menus for the inn's future restaurant.

"Sorry to interrupt," he said, "but we found something you should know about."

She looked up, her expression shifting from annoyance at the interruption to concern when she saw his dirt-smudged appearance.

"Oh no, what happened? Is it serious?"

"Not serious, but it does require attention," he said. "The original plumbing is configured differently from what the blueprints indicated. We'll need to revise our installation plans."

Luella chuckled. "I told you those old blueprints weren't reliable. The east wing was renovated in 1926 without any proper documentation. My grandma used to complain about the plumbers cursing under the floorboards for weeks."

He couldn't help but smile. "Your institutional memory continues to be our secret weapon, Luella."

"Well, it's no secret," the old woman replied with a hint of pride.

"Isabella has been picking my brain about everything from kitchen layouts to staff quarters and learning more than any blueprint could tell me," Luella said. She looked back at Thomas. "What do we need to do about the plumbing issue?"

"Wade's uploading the photos now. I'll have to revise the plans for you before tomorrow morning, but it's going to add some cost and maybe even a few days to the schedule."

Isabella nodded. "Okay, well, let me know the specifics when you have them. If we need to adjust the budget, I'd rather know sooner than later."

He appreciated her practical approach to setbacks. Some clients would have freaked out or tried to cut corners to maintain their original budget or timeline, but she always prioritized doing things right over doing things quickly or cheaply.

"We're still in good shape overall," he said. "The window restoration is ahead of schedule, and the electrical work passed inspection yesterday."

"That's great news." Isabella smiled, some of the

tension slowly leaving her shoulders. "We need a few wins to balance out the challenges."

Luella gathered her notes and rose from the chair with a deliberate movement, as if her joints didn't cooperate as easily as they once did. "Now, Isabella, you study those menu ideas I gave you real good. Shrimp and grits'll do fine for breakfast, but folks expectin' dinner are gonna want somethin' with a little more flair to it."

As Luella left, Thomas took the seat she'd vacated, pulling out his notebook to show Isabella some preliminary sketches for the plumbing.

"The main issue is here," he explained, pointing at a rough diagram. "The original pipes run through the foundation instead of alongside it, which means we can't simply replace them in the same location without compromising structural integrity."

She examined the drawing. "What's your recommended solution?"

"Reroute the new plumbing through this section." He indicated a different path on his sketch. "It's a longer run, which means more materials and labor, but it avoids disturbing the foundation."

"Well, that makes sense," she agreed. "Do what needs to be done. I trust your judgment on this."

The simple act of trust struck Thomas unexpectedly hard. Over his years of restoration work, he had become used to justifying every decision and explaining every choice to clients who questioned his expertise. Isabella's complete confidence in his judgment felt like a gift - one that reminded him why he had fallen for her analytical mind and decisive nature thirty years earlier.

"There's something else I want to discuss with you," he said, closing his notebook. "I've been thinking about that conversation you had with Maggie, about the inn's opening celebration."

She looked up. "Yeah?"

"Well, there's a place on the island I think you should see, somewhere that might inspire some ideas for the event. If you have time this afternoon, I'd love to show you."

She looked curious. "What kind of place?"

"Well, it's difficult to describe," he said with a small smile. "Better experienced than explained. It's nothing formal, just part of the island that most visitors never see."

She hesitated for a moment and then nodded. "Okay, I'm intrigued. When would we go?"

"How about after lunch? The tide will be right then."

"The tide?" She raised an eyebrow.

"Trust me," he said, standing up. "Wear comfortable shoes and clothes you don't mind getting a little damp."

Thomas would take her to a mysterious place that required precise tide timing and comfortable shoes. Whatever he wanted to show her, Isabella suspected it would be another step away from the safe professional distance they'd maintained.

The question was whether she was ready to follow where he led - and what truths might be waiting in the places most visitors never saw.

CHAPTER 9

At two o'clock, Thomas met Isabella at the small dock behind the inn. He'd brought two kayaks - the stable, sit-on-top models - suitable for navigating the island's tidal creeks.

"We're going kayaking?" Isabella asked, eyeing the boats with a mixture of apprehension and interest. "It's been a long time since I've done this."

"Oh, it's like riding a bike," Thomas said, handing her a life vest. "And these are designed for stability, not speed. The water is calm in these creeks, and we won't go far from shore, I promise."

She put on the life vest without further objection and watched carefully as Thomas demonstrated how to board the kayak and use the paddle. Even though she was initially hesitant, she managed the process with her characteristic determination, settling into the seat with growing confidence.

"The place I want to show you is about twenty minutes from here," Thomas said as they pushed off from the dock. "We'll follow this creek behind the inn and then branch off into a smaller waterway that leads to a hidden cove."

As they paddled, the developed portion of the island gradually gave way to pristine salt marshes. Tall spartina grass waved in the breeze, creating a golden-green landscape that stretched toward the horizon. Great blue herons stood sentinel in the shallows, while osprey circled overhead, scanning the water for fish.

"This is beautiful," Isabella said, pausing to take in the view. "I had no idea this was back here so close to the inn."

"Yeah, most people don't," Thomas said, maneuvering his kayak next to hers. "The developed part of Wexley Island is just a small fraction of the total land. The rest is protected marsh and maritime forest."

"Who owns it?" Isabella asked, gesturing toward the undeveloped expanse.

"A combination of the Island Conservation Trust and the State Wildlife Department. It can never be developed, and that's one of the few things almost everyone on Wexley agrees on."

They continued paddling. He occasionally pointed out wildlife or explained aspects of the marsh ecosystem. Isabella proved a quick study with the kayak, matching his pace with smooth, confident strokes.

"Turn here," Thomas said as they reached a narrow opening in the marsh grass that would have been easy to miss without his guidance. "This creek gets a bit windy, but it opens up to something special."

The channel narrowed as they proceeded, tall grass creating a natural corridor that blocked views of anything beyond their immediate surroundings. The water grew shallow enough in places that their paddles brushed the muddy bottom.

"Just go ahead," Thomas said, leading the way around the final bend.

As they emerged from the narrow passage, the creek suddenly widened into a secluded cove, surrounded by giant ancient live oaks draped in Spanish moss. The trees formed a natural amphitheater around the water, their massive branches creating a cathedral-like canopy overhead.

Isabella gasped. "Oh, Thomas, this is magical."

The wonder in her voice surprised her. When had she stopped noticing beauty like this? More unsettling—when had sharing it with someone started to matter so much? She pushed the dangerous thought aside, focusing on the acoustics rather than the man who'd brought her here.

"Wait," he said with a smile. "There's more."

He paddled into the center of the cove and stopped, motioning for her to bring her kayak next to his. When both boats were stationary, he cupped his hands around his mouth and called out a simple hello.

The sound echoed perfectly around the cove, bouncing off the natural curve of the trees and returning with clarity.

"The acoustics," she said. "It's a natural echo chamber."

"Try it," Thomas encouraged.

Isabella hesitated only a moment before she called out her own greeting. Her voice returned to her in waves, the echo clear and musical.

"This is incredible," she said. "How did you ever find this place?"

"My dad showed me when I was little," Thomas said. "He called it the Whispering Cove, said the old-timers believed it was a place you could speak to the island itself and sometimes hear it answer back."

She trailed her fingers through the water, watching the ripples spread outward. "I can understand why they think that. There's something other-worldly about it."

"I've always found it's a good place to think through difficult problems," Thomas said.

They sat in silence for a few minutes, absorbing the peaceful atmosphere of the hidden cove. A pair of wood ducks paddled nearby, looking at their human visitors with mild curiosity before continuing on their way.

"I can see why you thought this might inspire ideas for the opening celebration," she said. "There's a sense of calmness and discovery here, like you found something precious that's been here all along, just waiting to be appreciated again."

He nodded. "That's exactly what you're doing with the inn - revealing something valuable that was hidden beneath years of neglect."

"I've been thinking about a theme that honors the past and the future," she said. "What if we structured the opening as a journey through the inn's history, with each room representing a different era, culminating in its vision of a new beginning?"

"That could work beautifully," he said. "We have photographs from different periods, and Luella has all the stories we need from at least the last seventy years."

"We can incorporate music from each era - maybe local musicians performing in different spaces throughout the building," Isabella said, "and the menu could feature traditional Lowcountry dishes with modern interpretations."

Thomas found himself captivated as he watched her work through her ideas, her eyes bright with the same passionate creativity that had first taken his breath thirty years ago. She gestured as she spoke, unconsciously leaning forward, and he had to resist the urge to reach out and tuck a strand of honey-blonde hair behind her ear the way he used to. This was dangerous territory, remembering how perfectly they'd once collaborated, how their minds had moved in sync.

"What do you think?" she finally asked, pausing for a breath.

"I think it's perfect. It captures exactly what makes the inn special - its connection to the island's past and its place in the future."

She smiled, clearly pleased by his approval. "Thank you for bringing me here. It really does inspire me."

"Well, there's something else I wanted to show

you while we're out," he said, checking his watch. "If you're up for a bit more paddling?"

"Absolutely," she said.

They navigated back through the narrow channel into the main creek and then followed a different branch that led toward the ocean side of the island. After about fifteen minutes, they rounded the bend and were facing a small, secluded beach accessible only by water.

"Another hidden gem," she said as they beached their kayaks on the pristine white sand.

"This one's a bit more widely known among islanders," he explained. "Local teenagers have been coming here for bonfires for generations, despite it technically being against island regulations."

"Rebellious island youth," Isabella laughed. "Every paradise needs a forbidden fruit."

They walked along the shoreline where the receding tide had left behind perfect sand dollars and delicate whelk shells. The beach was sheltered by dunes covered with sea oats that swayed gently in the ocean breeze.

Isabella became acutely aware of Thomas beside her - the way he moved easily across the sand, how he automatically adjusted his longer stride to match hers, and how he pointed out interesting shells with the same enthusiasm he'd once shown for architectural details. It felt dangerously like old times, before everything had gone wrong.

"I thought this could be a good location for a staff appreciation event before the inn opens," he suggested. "You know, something casual to thank everybody who's worked on the renovation before the formal celebration."

"That's a wonderful idea," she agreed immediately. "Something simple but meaningful, you know, a beach bonfire, good food, maybe some music."

"Exactly - the construction crew, Daphne and her team, the staff you're hiring - bringing everybody together to celebrate what they've accomplished."

"I love it," Isabella said, smiling, "and I appreciate you thinking of it. The success of the inn will depend on the people who create it, not just the building itself."

They continued walking, collecting interesting shells, and discussing logistics for the event and the grand opening.

"So what made you decide to leave corporate hotels?" Thomas asked when they paused to watch a pod of dolphins playing in the distance. "You were at the top of your field, from what I understand."

She paused for a moment, her gaze still fixed on the horizon. "I had achieved everything I set out to accomplish professionally - regional director by forty, oversight of some of the most prestigious properties in the company's portfolio, the respect of my colleagues and the board." She looked directly at him. "But I felt like I was slowly fading into other people's expectations. Every day was about maintaining someone else's vision, meeting someone else's benchmarks, and building someone else's legacy. I woke up one morning and realized I couldn't remember the last time I had created something that was truly mine. Although now I'm finding that the idea of something being, 'completely mine' is a little bit of an illusion. The inn belongs to history, to the island, and to the people who will bring it back to life - like you and your crew, Daphne, Luella."

"The best projects are always collaborative," he said. "Though it takes a strong central vision to guide them, and that's what you bring."

"What about you?" she asked after a moment. "Did you always plan on returning to the island after college to focus on restoration work?"

It was a natural question, but it brushed against the edges of their shared history. He tried to figure out how to answer without going into territory neither of them had explicitly agreed to discuss.

"Not at first," he said. "I had offers from architectural firms in Charleston and Savannah after graduation, but circumstances, well, they changed. So coming back to the island made sense at that time, and I realized I had a knack for restoration work. I guess it was my father's influence."

She nodded, recognizing the subtle deflection for what it was. Thomas had always been private about difficult topics, but there was something in his tone - a weight that suggested those 'changed circumstances' had been more significant than he was letting on. "Do you ever regret not pursuing traditional architecture? You were so talented."

"Sometimes," he admitted, "especially in those early years. But there's something deeply satisfying about bringing historic buildings back to life, about preserving that craftsmanship that would otherwise be lost." He pointed toward the horizon. "And I can't imagine raising Emma anywhere else. The island has its limitations, but it sure is a special place to grow up."

"She's remarkable," Isabella said. "You did an amazing job with her, especially, you know, after your wife passed."

The careful way she referenced Sarah suggested Emma had shared at least some details of their family history during her visit. He felt a mix of emotion - appreciation for Isabella's sensitivity, sadness at the mention of Sarah, and a strange relief that this part of his life wasn't entirely unknown to Isabella.

"Thank you," he said. "It wasn't always easy, but Emma made it worthwhile. She's the very best thing in my life."

They walked in companionable silence for a while, each lost in their own private thoughts.

"We should head back soon," Thomas said reluctantly. "The tide will start coming in, and it's easier to navigate these creeks before dusk."

As they returned to their kayaks, Isabella stopped and looked over the peaceful beach one more time. "Thank you for showing me these places, Thomas. I feel like I understand the island better now, and why it means so very much to you."

"It was my pleasure," he said. "Sometimes the most important parts of a place are the ones that don't appear on any map."

As they paddled back, it was peaceful, both of them pointing out wildlife and interesting features of the landscape. As they approached the dock behind the inn, Thomas noticed a familiar figure waiting for them - Grayson Williams. Impeccably dressed, as always, in casual designer wear that probably cost more than most people's formal attire.

"Uh-oh, looks like you have a visitor," Thomas said, nodding toward the dock.

She followed his gaze, her expression shifting from relaxed to professional in an instant. "Ugh, Grayson. I wonder what brings him by without an appointment."

"Nothing good, if history is any indication," Thomas said dryly.

They beached their kayaks near the dock, and Thomas helped Isabella secure hers before they approached Grayson. He looked impatient.

"Isabella," he greeted her with practiced charm, deliberately ignoring Thomas. "I've been trying to reach you. Your phone appears to be off."

"I was showing Isabella some of the island's natural features," Thomas said. "Cell reception is spotty in the creeks."

"Well, how… rustic," Grayson said with a thin smile, turning his attention back to Isabella. "I want to discuss the architectural review board meeting scheduled for next week. There are some concerns about your plans, and I thought we might address them privately."

She maintained her composure, though Thomas could see the exhaustion in her eyes. "I appreciate your interest, Grayson, but my plans have been thoroughly prepared following all preservation guidelines, and Thomas and I will be presenting them together at the meeting."

"Yeah, well, that's exactly what I want to discuss," he persisted. "There's a feeling among the board members that the proposed changes to the kitchen and bathroom facilities might be excessive. I think maybe we can find a compromise before the formal meeting."

Thomas recognized this strategy immediately - divide and conquer. Get Isabella to agree to modifications without her technical advisor present.

"Any concerns can be addressed at the meeting itself," Isabella said firmly. "That's what it's for, after all. Our plans include detailed explanations for all elements."

Grayson's expression hardened. "I'm only trying to help, Isabella. The board can be difficult with newcomers, especially when they're linked to contractors who have a history of challenging our island's traditions."

The pointed look he gave Thomas made the personal nature of the comment unmistakable, but Thomas kept his expression neutral, refusing to take the bait.

"I appreciate your concern," Isabella said, her tone cool. "But I'm confident in our plans and Thomas's expertise. If there are technical questions, we're happy to address them now with you as a board member."

This direct challenge, calling Grayson's bluff about having actual concerns rather than simply trying to undermine their position, was masterfully executed. Thomas had to push back a smile as Grayson backpedaled.

"Oh, no, no, nothing specific right now, just a general sense among some members that the scope might be a little ambitious." He glanced at his expensive watch. "I should be going. I have a dinner engagement at the club. We'll continue this conversation at the meeting, I guess."

After he left, Isabella turned to Thomas with a raised eyebrow. "Well, what was that really about?"

"Grayson's been circling the historic district like a shark for years, snapping up properties when owners get overwhelmed by renovation costs or regulatory hurdles. The inn would be his ultimate prize - tear it down, build some modern monstrosity, and call it 'respectful development.'"

"As I mentioned before, he made me an offer shortly after I arrived, quite generous financially, but completely at odds with my vision for the property."

"Well, that explains his persistence," Thomas nodded. "If he can't buy it outright, the next best thing is to control what you can do with it through the review board."

She sighed, some of the day's peaceful mood evaporating. "Just when I was starting to feel like I was making progress with the island community."

"You are," he assured her. "Grayson represents a particular faction, but not the majority. Your work at Maggie's garden party did exactly what it needed to do: build support among the influential residents."

She nodded, though concern still showed on her face. "I should prepare more documents for the review board meeting. If Grayson is already working behind the scenes, we need to be completely prepared." A shadow passed over her face. "I can't afford to lose this project, Thomas. I've invested everything in it."

"Good strategy," Thomas said. "I'll have my team compile photographs of similar historical renovations that were approved in Savannah and Charleston as precedents."

They walked back toward the inn. At the entrance, Isabella paused. "Thank you again for today," she said, looking him in the eye. "Not just for showing me those beautiful places, but for helping me navigate Grayson and all these island politics. I'm not sure I could manage this project without your insight."

"You would find a way," he said with a smile, "but I'm glad to help. The inn deserves the best chance at proper restoration."

As she headed inside to gather her things, Thomas stayed on the porch for a minute, watching the last rays of sunlight filter through the oak trees. The afternoon had shifted something between them, not dramatically, but perceptively. The careful professional distance they'd maintained had softened a bit into something more genuine. A tentative friendship built on the appreciation for the island and the commitment to the inn.

It wasn't the passionate connection they once shared as young adults, but Thomas didn't expect it to be again. Too much life had happened in between, too many choices made and paths taken. There was value in this careful partnership they were building - professional respect seasoned with shared history, collaboration that honored what they'd once meant to each other without demanding more than either was ready to give.

But as Thomas walked to his truck, he couldn't shake the feeling that 'enough' was becoming a harder boundary to hold with each passing day. Isabella's laughter echoing across the hidden cove, her hand brushing his when he'd helped her from the kayak, the way she'd looked at him when he'd almost said too much about their shared vision...

Perhaps some foundations, once disturbed, refused to return to their original positions. Maybe some stories demanded to be finished, regardless of how carefully you tried to leave them buried.

The question was whether he was brave enough - or foolish enough - to find out which kind of story theirs really was.

CHAPTER 10

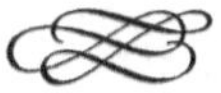

The Architectural Review Board meeting was scheduled for seven o'clock in the Wexley Island Municipal Building, a stately brick structure that housed the island's very limited government functions. Isabella arrived thirty minutes early, which was her customary time. She wanted time to set up the presentation materials and get herself centered a little bit before the proceedings started.

She'd spent the past week carefully preparing for the meeting, knowing it was a key challenge for the inn's renovation. The initial plans had received conditional approval months earlier, but this more detailed review would assess modernization aspects that needed special consideration for a historic property.

The meeting room was formal but not intimidating. It featured wood paneling, with comfortable chairs arranged around a large conference table. Pictures of the island's historic buildings decorated the walls, silent reminders of the architectural heritage the board was responsible for protecting. She positioned her presentation boards on easels at the front of the room, ensuring each was perfectly level and properly lit.

She had dressed very carefully for the occasion in a tailored navy suit that displayed her professionalism without being showy. Every detail mattered when presenting to a board known for its focus on minutiae.

As she reviewed her notes one more time, the door opened and Thomas entered, carrying additional materials. He looked polished in a blazer and dress shirt, his typical work attire upgraded for the formal meeting.

"Everything ready?" he asked, setting down his portfolio.

"I think so," Isabella said, gesturing toward the display. "I've arranged the boards to flow from historical context through necessary modernizations and then to the final aesthetic vision."

He nodded approvingly as he examined the

presentation. "That's a great idea, Isabella. Clear, comprehensive, and respectful to the historical elements, while making a strong case for the updates needed."

His confidence bolstered her own. They had worked closely over the past week to refine their approach, anticipating all potential objections and preparing thorough responses. His intimate knowledge of the board's concerns had been very valuable in the preparation.

"Grayson Williams arrived early," he said, glancing toward the hallway. "He's talking to the board chairman now."

Isabella wasn't surprised. "Trying to set the stage before the formal meeting begins, I guess."

"It's standard procedure for Grayson," Thomas said, "but we've done our homework. The modernizations we're proposing are all supported by historical preservation guidelines, and they are necessary if the inn wants any commercial viability."

Board members started arriving shortly after, filling the room with conversation. Isabella recognized several faces from Maggie's garden party and greeted them, noting with satisfaction that most of them responded with genuine friendliness. Vivian Pierce arrived last—of course, impeccably dressed, and wearing an expression that mixed neutrality with disapproval.

The chairman called the meeting to order promptly at seven, outlining the procedures for those in attendance. Isabella and Thomas would present their plans and then take questions from the board and comments from any other interested parties. The board would then deliberate and vote on approval, conditional approval, or outright rejection.

When invited to begin their presentation, Isabella stepped forward. She'd given countless presentations during her corporate career, often to skeptical executives with far more intimidating demeanors than the Architecural Review Board.

"Good evening," she said. "Thank you for the opportunity to present our renovation plans for The Wexley Inn. As you know, this historic property has stood at the core of the island for over a century and a half, serving as both a community gathering spot and a link to shared heritage."

She outlined the historical significance of the inn, using pictures from different eras. Then she transitioned into current renovation challenges, explaining how the building systems needed to be updated to meet modern safety codes and guest expectations.

"Our approach balances preservation with necessary modernization," she said, pointing toward detailed floor plans. "Every single decision has been guided by the simple question: how can we honor the inn's history while ensuring its viability for the next one hundred years?"

Thomas joined her to present the technical aspects of the renovation. He explained the methods they would use to update plumbing and electrical systems, and how they would preserve original architectural elements. His expertise was evident as he addressed specific structural challenges and proposed solutions. He talked about relevant preservation guidelines and successful precedents from similar historical properties.

The presentation concluded with Isabella's vision for the completed inn. This vibrant community landmark would once again host celebrations, provide accommodations for visitors, and serve as a living connection to the island's heritage.

"The Wexley Inn has always been more than just a building," she said in closing. "It's a place full of memories, a gathering place for generations of islanders, and a physical embodiment of the community's values. This renovation will honor that legacy, while ensuring that the inn can continue to serve these functions for generations to come."

When they finished, the room stayed silent for a moment, a response Isabella interpreted as positive in her experience. Whenever there were immediate questions, they often indicated confusion or resistance; however, silence suggested that the presentation had been compelling enough to warrant reflection.

The board chairman finally broke the silence. "Thank you for the presentation. The board will now ask questions for clarification before opening the floor to public comments."

The initial questions were straightforward and technical in nature. There were clarifications about materials, timelines, and specific preservation techniques. Isabella and Thomas answered each with confidence, their thorough preparation evident in the detailed responses they provided.

Then Grayson Williams leaned forward, his expression concerned. "Ms. Montgomery, your plans for updating the kitchen to commercial standards would require removing a significant part of the original layout. How do you reconcile that with preservation principles?"

Isabella anticipated this question. "The kitchen presents a unique challenge," she said. "Its current configuration not only fails to meet health department requirements for commercial food service, but it also poses a significant safety hazard because of outdated electrical and gas systems." She pointed the board's attention to a detailed diagram. "Our solution preserves the kitchen's original footprint and several key historical elements, including the brick hearth and the built-in cabinetry. However, it also reconfigures work areas to meet these modern health codes. We've talked to preservation specialists who have successfully modernized similar kitchens, including the Dillon House in Charleston and the Hambrie House in Savannah."

Before Grayson could follow up, Thomas added, "I want to make sure it's noted that the kitchen has already undergone at least three major renovations throughout the inn's history, most recently in the 1960s. So what is there now is not the original kitchen, but a mid-century interpretation that itself modified historical elements."

The context seemed to satisfy most of the board members, though Grayson's expression remained skeptical.

The questions continued, with Vivian Pierce focusing particularly on the bathroom renovations planned for each guest room.

"Adding private bathrooms to each room is a significant departure from the inn's original design," she said. "Historically, guests would have had shared facilities at the end of each hallway."

"That's correct," Isabella said, "and we've preserved one of those original shared bathrooms as a historical feature on the third floor. But modern guests expect private bathrooms, and we want to provide them with what they need to ensure the inn's commercial viability. I highly doubt anyone here would prefer to share a bathroom with strangers rather than have their own private facilities when staying at the inn."

She directed attention to the architectural plans. "We've designed each bathroom addition to be minimally invasive to the original room layouts. We will utilize existing closet spaces where possible and ensure that all new features complement the historical aesthetic. The plumbing will be concealed within existing walls wherever feasible, so that we can minimize any structural changes."

After nearly forty-five minutes of detailed questioning, the chairman opened the floor to public comments. Isabella braced herself, unsure of what to expect from the island residents.

To her surprise, the first speaker was Charlotte Stewart, who rose to offer enthusiastic support for the project.

"My family has lived on this island for four generations," she said. "Some of my fondest childhood memories involve celebrating at The Wexley Inn. What Ms. Montgomery and Mr. Langley have presented tonight shows a deep respect for our island's heritage, and I want to wholeheartedly support their plans."

Several other residents followed with similar endorsements, many referencing historical details from the presentation that resonated with their memories of the inn. Isabella felt a growing sense of optimism.

Then Vivian Pierce's closest ally on the island, Amelia Ashford, approached the podium with a different perspective.

"While I appreciate the efforts to preserve certain elements at the inn," she said in a very measured tone, "I remain concerned about the cumulative impact of these modernizations on the building's historical integrity. When we begin compromising on preservation standards for commercial reasons, we risk losing what makes our island unique."

Isabella tensed slightly, recognizing the potential impact of this argument on board members who valued preservation above all else.

Before she could even think of a response, an unexpected voice joined the discussion.

"If I may," Luella Washington said, rising from her seat at the back of the room.

The board chairman nodded, clearly recognizing her significance at the proceedings.

"I have lived and worked at The Wexley Inn for over forty years," she said. "I've seen renovations come and go, some that were respectful of the building's character, and others that were less so. And what Ms. Montgomery proposes is the most thoughtful approach I've ever witnessed. Preserving what matters while also acknowledging that the buildings have to change to remain useful."

She looked around the room, her expression challenging anybody to dispute her unique perspective.

"A building preserved exactly as it was, but sitting empty, serves absolutely nobody in this community. The inn always was meant to be lived in, worked in, celebrated in, and her plans will make that possible."

The simple eloquence of Luella's statement seemed to resonate with many of the people in the room. Isabella felt so grateful toward the older woman whose endorsement carried more weight than dozens of technical arguments could have.

After a few more comments, the chairman closed the public portion of the meeting and announced the board would deliberate in private.

Isabella and Thomas gathered their materials as the room cleared, neither of them speaking until they were alone in the hallway.

"Well, I think that went better than I expected," Isabella said.

"Luella's intervention was very effective," Thomas agreed. "There's no arguing with somebody who's literally lived in that building's history for nearly half a century."

"So should we wait for the decision?" she asked, glancing toward the closed meeting room door.

He checked his watch. "Their deliberations take at least thirty minutes, sometimes longer. You know, there's a small café across the street that stays open late on meeting nights just for this purpose. Coffee is decent, and it's better than just standing in this hallway."

The Island Bake Shop was warm and inviting, with comforting aromas of fresh pastries still lingering in the air, even though it was late at night. A few other attendees for the meeting had also sought refuge there, quietly talking at tables scattered around the room. Isabella and Thomas found a corner spot by the window where they could see the entrance to the municipal building.

"Well, regardless of the outcome, your presentation was great," Thomas said, as they settled in with their coffees. "You addressed every concern thought-fully and respectfully."

"We addressed them," she corrected, "and your technical explanations were crucial, especially talking about the structural modifications."

He smiled slightly. "I guess we make a good team."

Isabella's pulse quickened at the observation. They did work well together - too well. It reminded her of late nights in the architecture studio, how their ideas had flowed seamlessly, and how right it felt to create something together. That same dangerous ease was creeping back, and she didn't know whether to embrace it or run from it.

The simple observation hung between them, carrying way more weight than its casual delivery suggested. Their different perspectives and comple-mentary skills created a more effective whole than either of them could achieve individually.

"Charlotte's support was unexpected," Isabella said, trying to steer the conversation back to safer ground. "I knew she was friendly at Maggie's party, but such a public endorsement probably carried a lot of weight."

"Oh, Charlotte rarely speaks at these meetings," Thomas said, "and when she does, people listen. Her family's been on the island for a long time, which gives her opinions a certain weight in the community."

They continued discussing the meeting while waiting, dissecting questions and responses, and trying to identify areas where they might need additional documentation if the board requested more information. The professional discussion helped calm Isabella's nerves about the pending decision.

After about forty minutes, they saw board members starting to exit the building.

"They finished deliberating," Thomas said. "We should head back."

The chairman was waiting for them in the meeting room, along with two other board members, including, notably, Grayson Williams. His presence during the delivery of the decision suggested that the outcome could be complicated.

"Ms. Montgomery, Mr. Langley," the chairman began very formally. "The board has reviewed your plans carefully, and we've considered both the technical requirements and public input."

Isabella tried to maintain her professional composure, but her heart rate accelerated to the point that she was afraid everybody could hear it banging against her chest wall.

"We've decided to grant conditional approval for your renovation plans," he continued. "The majority of the proposed work does meet our guidelines for historical preservation while also taking into consideration necessary modernization."

Relief washed through Isabella, although the word "conditional" kept her from celebrating prematurely.

"The conditions are as follows," he proceeded. "First, the kitchen renovation must incorporate more of the original cabinetry than currently planned. Our historical consultant will work with you to identify specific elements that should be preserved."

Thomas nodded and made notes. That was a reasonable request that wouldn't significantly impact their plans.

"Second, the bathroom additions must use historically appropriate fixtures and finishes, with samples to be approved by the board before installation."

Again, it was manageable. They'd already planned to use period-appropriate fixtures anyway.

"Finally," the chairman concluded, "the exterior color scheme has to adhere strictly to the original palette and be based on paint analysis of the earliest accessible layers. Mr. Williams has specifically requested this condition."

Grayson offered a thin smile that didn't reach his

eyes. The last condition, although seemingly minor, could potentially restrict their design options for the inn's exterior appearance. Paint analysis was notoriously subjective, and Isabella suspected Grayson would advocate for the most restrictive interpretation possible.

We accept these conditions," Isabella responded. "Thank you for your thorough consideration."

As they gathered their materials to leave, Grayson approached them directly.

"Congratulations on your conditional approval," he said, his smile as sharp as broken glass. "Those conditions may seem minor now, but I've found that historical paint analysis can be… surprisingly complex. And time-consuming. I do hope you've built adequate contingency into your timeline. Historical accuracy is so important to maintaining our island's unique character."

The threat was clear from the start. Grayson planned to manipulate every requirement, turning reasonable demands into bureaucratic quicksand. Paint analysis could take weeks, involving multiple rounds of testing and board review. He was betting she'd run out of time, money, or patience - and then he'd be there with his buyout offer, more aggressive this time.

"We are committed to historical accuracy in all

aspects," Isabella replied evenly, "and I'm sure the analysis will confirm appropriate choices for the inn's exterior."

Once outside the building, Thomas let out a low whistle. "Conditional approval with minimal modifications? That's actually a pretty significant win, despite all of Grayson's maneuvering."

"That paint analysis requirement seems designed to create obstacles," Isabella said as they walked to their cars.

"It is, but I've dealt with similar tactics from others. We'll hire an independent historical paint analyst with impeccable credentials to conduct the study. Grayson can argue, but he sure can't dispute scientific evidence from a recognized expert."

Isabella smiled. "You've navigated these waters many times before, haven't you?"

"More than I care to remember," Thomas admitted. "I've watched these same battles play out for years - different faces, same arguments about change versus tradition, progress versus preservation. You learn to read the patterns, understand what's really being fought over beneath the surface disagreements."

They reached Isabella's car first, pausing beside it. The stress of the meeting gradually dissipated, replaced by the satisfaction of having cleared another hurdle.

"We should celebrate this victory," Thomas suggested. "Small as it may seem, getting a conditional approval with such minor modifications is pretty big."

"Oh? What did you have in mind?" Isabella asked, surprised by the suggestion, but not opposed to it.

"Well, the Island Bake Shop is known for more than just the coffee we had. Their peach cobbler is legendary, and they're still open for another hour."

The invitation was casual, framed as a professional celebration, but Isabella sensed a shift beneath the surface. They had maintained strict boundaries - every interaction centered on the renovation, every moment careful and controlled. However, tonight felt different, like standing on the verge of something she couldn't quite identify. Part of her wanted to keep those walls up; another part was exhausted from hiding behind them. Their conversations always focused solely on the renovation. Even their kayaking trip had been presented as project research. But tonight felt different. It felt like a moment of connection that didn't need to be weighed down by their complicated past.

"Peach cobbler sounds perfect," she said with a smile. "Lead the way."

They returned to the cafe, which had grown quieter. The owner greeted Thomas by name, clearly a regular customer, and recommended the cobbler fresh from the oven with vanilla bean ice cream.

They settled at a corner table with their desserts and coffee, the formality of the board meeting giving way to a more relaxed conversation. The small table meant they sat closer than they usually did during work discussions. Isabella noticed details she'd been trying not to see - the way laugh lines deepened around his eyes when he smiled, how his hands moved expressively when he talked about the inn, the silver at his temples that somehow made him more attractive rather than less.

"I still can't believe Luella showed up to speak," Isabella said, savoring a bite of the exceptional cobbler. "She never even mentioned she was going to attend."

"Well, that's Luella," he said, chuckling. "She appears exactly when needed, says precisely what needs saying, and then returns to her domain as if nothing unusual happened."

"Well, she's become important to the project, not just for her historical knowledge, but for her practical insights about how the inn actually functions day to day," Isabella said. "She sees this renovation as her legacy, too. The inn has been her life for so long."

"And she wants to see it restored properly before she retires," Thomas said, taking a bite.

"Has she mentioned retirement?" Isabella asked, surprised. "She's never even indicated to me that she's considering it."

"Not directly," Thomas admitted, "but she's mentioned several times that she wants to see the inn 'settled right', before she's done. I think she's just waiting to make sure it's in good hands before she steps back."

Isabella thought about it. "I hope she'll stay involved even after the renovation's complete. Her knowledge of traditional Lowcountry cuisine is epic, and I've been taking notes during our cooking lessons."

"Cooking lessons?" Thomas raised an eyebrow, clearly amused. "Oh, I didn't realize Luella had taken on an apprentice."

Isabella chuckled softly. "Yeah, well, I'm very much a beginner. She's teaching me classic dishes that we might put on the menu, such as shrimp and grits, she-crab soup, and Frogmore stew. She's remarkably patient, considering my limited experience with cooking at all, specifically Southern cooking."

"You're full of surprises, Isabella Montgomery," he said, his expression warm. "Corporate hotel executive turned innkeeper and now Lowcountry chef in training."

"Hardly a chef," she said, "but I want to understand every aspect of what makes this place work. In corporate hotels, I managed operations remotely - tracking reports, metrics, and budget lines. But here? I'm learning to make she-crab soup from scratch, gaining an understanding of why certain dishes hold significance for this community. The food isn't just fuel - it's memory, tradition, connection."

Their conversation flowed easily as they finished dessert, talking about the renovation, but also occasionally venturing into more personal territory, like Thomas's recent fishing trip with the crew after completing a difficult phase of the electrical work, and Isabella's discovery of a beautiful walking path on the eastern shore of the island.

Other people left in the cafe occasionally looked their way with some curiosity. Isabella was starting to become accustomed to the constant observation that came with island life.

"We're providing excellent fodder for the island gossip mill," she said, amused.

"Oh, sharing peach cobbler after a board meeting? Scandalous," Thomas replied dryly. "Although I suppose in a community this size, any interaction beyond professional meetings may raise eyebrows."

"You know, Maggie mentioned that our history hasn't exactly remained a secret," Isabella said, broaching the subject directly for the first time. "Apparently, it's common knowledge around here that we knew each other in college."

He nodded, his expression turning more thoughtful. "Island memories are long, and connections are traced meticulously. When you arrived and hired me for renovations, it didn't take long for someone to make the connection."

What Isabella didn't reveal was that she'd heard whispers of more than just college romance - vague mentions of 'circumstances' and 'obligations' that had brought Thomas back to the island. She'd tried to dismiss the speculation, but curiosity ate at her. What truly happened thirty years ago?

"Does it bother you?" she asked. "The speculation?"

Thomas thought about the question for a moment. "Not for my sake. I've lived here long enough to develop a little bit of immunity to the gossip, but I wouldn't want it to affect your renovation or your standing in the community."

"Oh, I've navigated corporate politics for decades," Isabella assured him. "Island gossip is actually refreshingly straightforward by comparison. At least people here speculate openly rather than behind closed boardroom doors."

That drew a laugh from Thomas. "I guess that's one way to look at it, though I'm not sure refreshingly straightforward is how people would describe Wexley's social dynamics."

As the cafe prepared to close, they gathered their things and walked outside. The night had grown cooler, stars brilliantly visible in the sky above the island. They paused beside Isabella's car.

"Thank you for your work on the presentation," she said. "We wouldn't have received approval without your expertise and knowledge of the island."

"Well, it was a team effort," he said. "Your vision for the inn is what convinced the board, despite Grayson's objections."

She nodded and then hesitantly added, "And thanks for suggesting we celebrate. It was nice to enjoy an accomplishment rather than immediately focusing on the next challenge."

"Something I've learned over the years," Thomas said, "taking time to acknowledge progress makes the remaining work feel less daunting."

They said their good nights and drove their separate ways. Isabella returned to her cottage with a sense of satisfaction. The evening had shifted something in their carefully maintained professional relationship. Not dramatically, but she perceived it. Sharing dessert and conversation outside of a renovation had humanized their interaction, giving glimpses of the people they had become.

As she got ready for bed, she found herself thinking about Thomas's comment about island gossip. The rumors about their past relationship didn't really bother her. She had come to Wexley Island to start fresh and build her own legacy. She didn't expect that the process would require confronting old wounds, or that the man who once broke her heart would become vital to her plans' success. And she definitely didn't expect how difficult it would become to remember why she built those careful walls in the first place.

Whether the transformation would lead to anything beyond their current professional relationship remained to be seen, but for now, she was content that progress had been made in both.

The board's conditional approval was another victory, despite Grayson's attempts at sabotage. But as Isabella turned off the light, she realized that the real challenge wasn't the architectural review boards or the paint analysis requirements.

The real challenge was figuring out whether she could trust her growing feelings for Thomas - or if she was risking the same heartbreak that had nearly destroyed her thirty years ago. Because every shared laugh, every moment of perfect teamwork, every time their eyes met across a room, she felt the walls crumbling a little more.

Tomorrow would bring new challenges. Tonight, she simply acknowledged that the careful professional distance she'd maintained was becoming harder to defend with each passing day.

CHAPTER 11

Thomas stood at his kitchen counter, chopping vegetables for dinner. Emma would be arriving from Atlanta within the hour for her weekend visit, and he wanted to ensure they shared a proper meal. These visits had become more frequent since she'd met Isabella and shown interest in the renovation, which pleased him but also made him a bit uneasy.

The sound of his phone ringing interrupted his methodical food preparation. He wiped his hands on a kitchen towel and looked at the caller ID. It was Emma.

"Hey, sweetheart," he answered. "Are you on your way?"

"Just crossed the causeway," she said, her tone a bit too casual. "Be there in fifteen."

"Well, perfect timing. Dinner's almost ready."

"Sounds great. Oh, and Dad, I was thinking maybe we could invite Isabella to join us tomorrow night. I brought some design magazines with ideas for the inn's marketing materials I wanted to show her."

He paused, his knife hovering over a red bell pepper. This was the third time Emma had suggested including her in their plans during her visits. While he appreciated his daughter's acceptance of Isabella, he couldn't help but wonder about her motivations.

"I'm sure Isabella has her own plans for the weekend," he said carefully. "I thought we were going fishing tomorrow."

"We can do both," Emma chirped. "Fishing in the morning, dinner with Isabella in the evening. Besides, I already texted her to see if she's free."

Thomas sighed. "Emma, you shouldn't put Isabella on the spot like that."

"Oh, relax, Dad. I just asked if she had plans. She hasn't even responded yet." Her tone turned more serious. "Unless you don't want her to join us for some reason. Is something wrong between you two? I thought the board meeting went well."

"Everything is fine," he said. "The meeting was a success. We got conditional approval with minimal modifications. But I don't want you playing matchmaker, Emma. Isabella and I have a professional relationship, and it's working well. I don't want to complicate that unnecessarily."

"Who said anything about matchmaking?" Emma replied with an exaggerated innocence that didn't fool Thomas for a minute. "I just want to discuss those marketing ideas. That's all. Very professional."

He shook his head, though his daughter couldn't see it. "We'll talk about this when you get here."

After hanging up, Thomas returned to his dinner preparations. Emma's interest in connecting with Isabella had shifted from initial wariness to active encouragement of a closer relationship. While he appreciated that his daughter had formed her own positive opinion of Isabella, her transparent attempts at pairing them as a couple created a very awkward dynamic that he wasn't sure how to navigate.

The truth was, his feelings for Isabella had grown increasingly complicated as they worked together. Their professional collaboration had turned into genuine respect and a tentative friendship. Moments like their kayaking trip to the hidden cove or their celebratory dessert after the board meeting had created a comfortable connection that might have suggested something deeper. However, significant barriers remained, including the unresolved truth about why he had ended their relationship thirty years earlier.

Emma knew that story now, but Isabella didn't, and until she did, any deeper connection between them would be built on an incomplete foundation.

The sound of Emma's car in the driveway pulled Thomas from the thoughts he was having. He pushed aside his concerns and focused on welcoming his daughter, happy to see her regardless of her matchmaking schemes.

She burst through the door with her typical energy, dropping her weekend bag in the entryway, and hugged him. An adult herself, she was a successful professional with her own life. Still, something about her returning to the island always seemed to reconnect her with a more carefree version of herself.

"Something smells great," she said, looking over his shoulder at the kitchen counter. "Please tell me that's your famous paella."

"With extra shrimp just for you," he said. "So how was the drive?"

"Not bad. I left early enough to beat the worst of the Atlanta traffic."

She moved around the kitchen with familiar ease,

grabbing plates and glasses while Thomas finished making the meal.

"The island looks stunning right now with all the summer flowers blooming, and the evening light is breathtaking."

"Best time of the year here," Thomas agreed, "before the worst of the summer heat sets in, but warm enough for the beach."

They settled into comfortable conversation as they finished dinner together, Emma sharing updates about her work projects and friends in Atlanta, while Thomas discussed recent developments at the inn.

It wasn't until they were seated at the table, paella served and wine poured, that Emma returned to the subject of Isabella.

"So she texted back while we were eating," she said casually, taking a sip of her wine. "She's free tomorrow night and would be happy to join us for dinner. I said we could cook here rather than going out."

Thomas gave his daughter a look. "You're just determined to make this happen, aren't you?"

Emma looked at him. "I like her, Dad. She's smart, accomplished, and genuinely passionate about the inn. And yes, I've noticed how you talk about her. There's something there, whether you want to admit it or not."

"It's complicated, Emma."

"Life is complicated," she countered. "It doesn't mean you should avoid connections that could be meaningful."

She put down her fork and turned more serious. "Mom has been gone for fifteen years. You've dedicated yourself to your work and to me, but what about your own happiness?"

He sighed, recognizing the genuine concern behind his daughter's persistence. "I appreciate that you want me to be happy, Emma, but my history with Isabella isn't something that can just be easily set aside. There are many things she doesn't know, things that might change how she sees me."

"You mean the real reason you left her?" Emma said quietly.

Thomas nodded, tracing the rim of his wine glass with his finger. "I made that decision without giving her any choice in the matter. I thought I was doing the right thing at the time."

"Then tell her the truth now, Dad," Emma suggested. "Allow her to decide how she feels about everything. Maybe she'll be angry, but maybe she'll understand. At least it's the honest way to go about it."

"And what if knowing hurts her all over again? Or makes working together impossible?"

"Dad, you taught me that sometimes you have to take risks even if you aren't sure what the outcome will be. You'll never know if you don't try."

Thomas thought about his daughter's words, struck by her wisdom. When had his little girl grown up into such an intelligent, well-spoken woman?

"When did you get so smart about relationships?" he asked with a slight smile.

Emma chuckled. "I observe and learn. Just because I'm still single doesn't mean I don't understand how people work." Her expression softened. "I just want to see you happy, Dad. And I think Isabella might be part of that happiness, if you give it a chance to build without being on shifting sand."

"One dinner," Thomas finally conceded. "But no obvious matchmaking, Emma. Promise me."

"Scout's honor," she replied, holding her hand in a mock pledge. "Though I was never actually a scout, so take that as you will."

He shook his head and smiled. "You're impossible."

The next morning dawned clear and perfect for fishing. The temperature was mild, there was a light breeze, and visibility on the water was excellent. Thomas and Emma set out early in his small boat, going to her favorite spot in the tidal creek where redfish could be found this time of year pretty reliably. Fishing had always been their special activity since Emma was old enough to hold a rod, a tradition that continued into her adulthood. Some of their best conversations had happened on these little excursions, quiet, peaceful mornings surrounded by beauty, creating space for meaningful connections.

"Do you remember when I caught that huge redfish when I was ten?" Emma asked as they anchored in a little cove. "The one that was almost as big as I was?"

"Oh, how could I forget?" Thomas laughed, preparing their rods. "And then you refused to let me help you land it and insisted on bringing it in yourself, even though it nearly pulled you overboard."

"Well, stubbornness is a family trait," Emma said with a grin. "Mama always said I got a double dose, one from each of you."

"Well, she was right about that," he agreed. "She used to say watching us argue was like seeing the same person disagree with themselves."

Emma cast her line with practiced skill, the lure landing exactly where she intended. "I miss her," Emma said quietly. "But it's different now. The missing doesn't swallow me whole anymore. Sometimes I feel guilty about that, like if I'm not actively hurting, I'm somehow forgetting her. Is that weird?"

"No, not weird at all," Thomas said, casting his own line. "Grief changes over time. The love remains, but the sharp edges of loss start to soften."

They fished in silence for a while, the casting and reeling creating a meditative quality. Birds called overhead, and occasionally a fish jumped nearby, creating ripples across the otherwise calm water.

"You know, I've been thinking about making a change," Emma said eventually, her tone casual. "I mean professionally."

"What kind of change?" he asked, giving her his full attention.

"Well, I think I might leave the agency and start my own marketing consultancy. You know, focus on specifically helping traditional businesses develop authentic digital presences without losing their core identity."

"Well, that sounds perfectly aligned with your skills and interests. What's holding you back?"

She reeled in her line slowly. "Honestly, fear of disappointing you. You've always been so proud of my corporate success, you know, my steady climb up the ladder."

"Emma," Thomas said, surprised. "I'm proud of you, no matter where you work or what title you hold. I'm proud of you for your intelligence, your integrity, and your creativity. Those qualities will serve you well, whether you're in a corporate setting or running your own business."

"Really?" She looked at him directly. "You wouldn't think I was being impulsive or taking an unnecessary risk?"

"Taking thoughtful risks is how we grow," he said. "I took a risk coming back to this island to start my own restoration business when everybody thought I was going to establish an architectural firm. It wasn't the conventional path, but it was right for me and for our family."

She nodded, relaxing. "That's part of what inspired me, actually. Watching Isabella take a similar risk with the inn, you know, leaving her corporate success. It made me realize I want to have that same sense of ownership and purpose to my work."

"Well, then you should pursue it," he said. "You have the skills, the connections, and the vision to make it successful, and I'll always support you however I can."

"Thanks, Dad," she said. "That means more than you know."

Thomas felt a pull on his line, which interrupted the moment.

"Hey, I think I've got something," he said, starting to reel in what proved to be a pretty respectable redfish.

They spent the next few hours catching fish, releasing most of them but keeping two for dinner, and discussing Emma's business plans in more detail. They enjoyed the pristine beauty of the tidal ecosystem, and by the time they were headed back to the dock, Thomas felt the day had already been a success, no matter what the evening would bring.

As they cleaned their catch at the dock's fish cleaning station, Emma returned to the subject of dinner with Isabella.

"You know, I was thinking we could grill the fish with some of those herbs from your garden. Simple but impressive. Oh, and maybe that rice pilaf that you make that everybody loves."

"Sounds good," Thomas said, focusing on filleting the fish. "What time did you tell her to come?"

"Seven. That gives us lots of time to clean up and prepare everything." Emma studied her father's face. "So are you nervous about tonight?"

He considered denying it but opted for honesty.

"I guess a little bit. Our interactions have been mostly professional, you know, with clear boundaries, but this feels different."

"Oh, it's just dinner, Dad," Emma said. "And I'll be there to buffer. You know, no pressure, just good food and conversation."

He nodded but wasn't totally convinced he was willing to trust his daughter's judgment. "Just remember your promise. No obvious matchmaking."

"Yes, subtle matchmaking only. Got it," Emma said with a mischievous smile.

Thomas rolled his eyes.

By six-thirty, his cottage had been transformed from its usual bachelor state to something that looked more welcoming. Emma had insisted on fresh flowers for the table, proper cloth napkins instead of paper ones, and softly playing background music.

"It's not a formal dinner party. You act like we're at Maggie's house," Thomas protested as Emma adjusted the table setting for the third time. "Isabella won't care if the napkins are perfectly straight."

"Details matter," Emma said. "And it's not just about impressing her. It's about creating a welcoming atmosphere for conversation."

He raised an eyebrow at his daughter's enthusiasm but didn't argue anymore. The fish was marinating, the rice pilaf was prepared, and a simple salad was waiting in the refrigerator. Everything was ready except maybe Thomas himself. He had changed his clothes twice before settling on a blue button-down shirt that Emma once told him brought out his eyes, paired with his best jeans. Nothing fancy, but a step up from his usual work attire. He had even trimmed his beard, a maintenance task he often neglected when he was busy.

At precisely seven o'clock, the doorbell rang. Thomas took a deep breath, suddenly feeling absurdly nervous for what was, as Emma pointed out, just dinner with a colleague.

Isabella stood on the porch, looking casually elegant in white jeans and a soft teal blouse, her honey-blonde hair loose around her shoulders instead of up in its usual professional style. Thomas found himself momentarily speechless. He'd grown used to professional Isabella - hair pulled back, work clothes, focused intensity. This relaxed version reminded him painfully of the girl he knew in college, and the decades between them seemed to collapse for a heartbeat. She held a bottle of wine in one hand and a small gift bag in the other.

"Right on time," he said, stepping back to welcome her inside. "Please come in."

"Thank you for inviting me," she said, handing

him the wine. "I hope white is okay. I thought it might pair well with fish."

"Perfect choice," he said. "Emma mentioned you were bringing marketing materials to talk about."

"Oh, just some ideas," she said, following him into the main living room where Emma was arranging a cheese plate. "But nothing that can't wait until after dinner."

"Isabella," Emma greeted her warmly. "I'm so glad you could join us. Dad caught redfish this morning, so you're in for a treat."

"Well, that sounds wonderful," Isabella said, offering the gift bag. "Just a small hostess gift. When you mentioned your interest in marketing materials for the inn, I thought you might find this useful."

Emma opened the bag to reveal a beautifully bound book of historical Lowcountry hotel advertisements and brochures.

"Oh my gosh, this is amazing. Where did you find it?"

"At an antique bookshop in Charleston," Isabella said. "The owner specializes in ephemera from historical Southern hotels and resorts. I just thought it might give you some inspiration for the inn's marketing aesthetic."

"Oh, it's perfect," Emma said. "Thank you so much."

Thomas observed the exchange with interest, noting the rapport that had developed between his daughter and Isabella. There was no awkwardness or forced politeness; instead, there was a natural connection.

"Can I offer you a glass of wine?" he asked Isabella. "Or maybe some sweet tea if you'd prefer that."

"Wine would be lovely, thank you."

Thomas opened the bottle, and Isabella glanced around his home with undisguised curiosity. His cottage was modest but well-designed, with an open floor plan that maximized his water view and showcased his craftsmanship through custom-built-ins and carefully restored original features.

"Your home's beautiful," she said. "The woodwork is extraordinary."

"Dad did most of that himself," Emma said proudly. "The house was practically falling down when he bought it fifteen years ago."

"It was a good project during a difficult time," Thomas explained, handing her a glass of wine. "You know, focusing on restoration gave me some purpose after Sarah passed."

Her expression softened. "Creating something beautiful from something broken can be healing."

"That's exactly right," he said quietly.

The moment of connection passed between them. Then Emma smoothly shifted the conversation to something lighter, talking about their fishing adventure that morning with lively detail. Isabella soon found herself laughing at the exaggerated story of Thomas nearly falling overboard while landing a particularly energetic fish.

The evening progressed with surprising ease. Thomas grilled the fish on the back deck while Emma and Isabella prepared the sides, chatting the whole time about the inn renovation. Emma's marketing ideas and island stories were also hot topics. By the time they sat down to eat dinner, any initial awkwardness had dissipated.

"This is delicious," Isabella said when she took her first bite of the fish. "There's nothing quite like fish served the day it's caught."

"Dad's the real chef in the family," Emma said. "I could manage the basics, but he's the one with the culinary skills."

"I wouldn't go that far," Thomas said. "I took some cooking classes after Sarah died, you know, just to make sure Emma would have some decent, healthy meals, but also to give me something new to learn."

"Oh, he's being modest," Emma told Isabella. "He

became quite accomplished. His dinner parties are legendary."

"Dinner parties?" Isabella said with surprise. "I didn't picture you as an entertainer."

"Very small gatherings," Thomas clarified. "Just close friends, and only occasionally. Hardly legendary."

"Still, it's impressive," Isabella said. "Cooking is a skill I've only just started to appreciate thanks to Luella's patient instruction."

The conversation turned to Luella's cooking lessons and the traditional Lowcountry recipes Isabella was learning for the inn's future menu. Thomas found himself increasingly relaxed as the meal continued, enjoying the interaction between the three of them. Emma was keeping her promise to avoid obvious matchmaking, although he noticed she was creating opportunities for him and Isabella to connect directly and stepping back from the conversation.

After dinner, they moved to the back deck, where they enjoyed coffee and a simple dessert of fresh berries and cream. The evening air had cooled, and the view of the tidal creek, illuminated by the moonlight, created a peaceful backdrop.

"You know, I've been meaning to ask," Isabella said, turning to Emma. "How did you become interested in marketing? Thomas said you studied business in college, but marketing specifically seems to suit your creative instincts."

She smiled. "I actually started in architecture, you know, following in Dad's footsteps, but I discovered I was more interested in how people perceive and interact within the spaces than designing them."

"Oh, that's so fascinating," Isabella said, with genuine interest. "So the marketing became a way for you to explore that interest from a different angle."

"Yes, exactly. I still love architecture and design. They inform my approach to marketing, especially with businesses that have physical locations like the inn, but understanding how space influences experiences is critical to creating authentic marketing materials."

As Emma explained her philosophy further, Thomas watched as Isabella engaged with her - the way she asked thoughtful questions and offered relevant insights from her own career in hotel management. The two women clearly connected on both professional and personal levels, finding common ground despite their different backgrounds and generations.

Eventually, Emma looked at her watch and stood up. "You know, I just remembered I promised to video chat with a friend at ten. Can't believe I almost forgot." Her tone implied she hadn't truly forgotten, and the timing of this sudden obligation seemed oddly convenient.

Thomas gave his daughter a knowing look. This was clearly a part of her subtle matchmaking strategy. "Of course. I can clean up."

"I should probably be going anyway," Isabella said, rising as well. "It's getting late, and I have an early meeting with a plumbing contractor tomorrow."

"Oh, at least stay and finish your coffee," Emma suggested. "The night is too beautiful to just rush off." She gave Isabella a warm hug. "Thanks again for the book. It's absolutely perfect for what I had in mind."

After Emma disappeared inside, Thomas and Isabella found themselves alone on the deck, the soft sounds of the marsh creating a gentle soundtrack to their moment. Rather than awkwardness, Thomas felt comfortable in the quiet between them.

"Emma is really great," Isabella said after a moment. "You must be so very proud of her."

"Oh, I am," he said. "She's the best thing in my life. Smart, kind, determined. Even during her rebellious teenage years, I never doubted she would find her way."

"Well, she seems to have inherited your eye for detail and your appreciation of craftsmanship. I noticed how precisely she arranged the table setting earlier."

He laughed softly. "Oh, that's her mother's influence. Sarah was meticulous about presentation. She said the experience of a meal begins before the first bite is taken."

"A philosophy that applies to hospitality as well," Isabella said. "The guest experience starts the moment they see the property, long before they check in."

"Exactly why the exterior restoration of the inn is as important as the interior," he said. "First impressions really matter."

They fell into an easy conversation about the renovation's progress, the upcoming challenges, and their shared vision for the completed project.

"I really should be going," Isabella said again, although she made no immediate move to leave. "Thank you for the lovely evening. Dinner was wonderful."

"Well, thank you for coming," Thomas replied, "and for being so generous with Emma about her marketing ideas. She respects your opinion a great deal."

"The feeling is mutual. Her insights about positioning the inn digitally while honoring the historical character are exactly what I've been looking for."

Isabella smiled. "You've raised an exceptional young woman, Thomas."

"I had help," he said. "Sarah was a fantastic mother."

Isabella nodded. "May I ask, if it's not too personal, how you managed after she passed away? Raising Emma alone while running your business must have been incredibly challenging."

The question was asked with such genuine care that he found himself answering honestly. "It was the hardest thing I've ever done. Emma was in elementary school when Sarah was diagnosed the first time. The years of Sarah's illness were a balancing act, being there for both of them while trying to keep the business afloat. After she died..." He paused, surprised by how the memory could still tighten his chest after all these years. "After she died, Emma and I became each other's lifeline. We grieved differently - she needed to talk, I needed to work - but we held each other up through the worst of it. I don't know if I would've survived those first years without her."

"Well, that kind of bond is precious," Isabella said.

"It sure is. Emma wanted to move back to the island after graduation to help me, but I insisted she pursue her career in Atlanta. Sarah would have wanted that for her, to build her own life, not sacrifice her opportunities out of concern for me."

Isabella looked at him for a moment before speaking. "You've always put others first, haven't you? Emma, Sarah, your clients, the island community. Who takes care of you, Thomas?"

The unexpected question hit him like a physical blow. No one had asked him that in years, maybe ever. Isabella had always seen through his defenses, even in college, always known when he was carrying more than he let on. Thirty years later, she still possessed that uncanny ability to cut through his carefully maintained self-sufficiency to the vulnerable truth beneath. He had indeed structured his life around caring for others rather than himself.

"I manage," he finally said, not quite answering the question.

She seemed to recognize his discomfort and gracefully changed the subject. "I should really head home. Early morning tomorrow."

He walked her to the car, the night air cool against their skin. At her vehicle, she turned to face him. "Thanks again for dinner. It was lovely to spend time with you and Emma outside of work."

"We enjoyed having you," he said. "Perhaps we could do it again sometime."

The invitation slipped out before he'd fully thought through what he was offering - not just dinner, but a possibility, a hint that their relationship might grow beyond the inn's completion. Her eyes widened slightly, and he knew she'd heard the unspoken question beneath his words.

"I'd like that," she said. The words escaped before she could question them, before the cautious voice in her head could remind her that getting closer to Thomas Langley was risky. That she still didn't understand why he'd left her or that trusting him again meant risking her heart a second time. But watching him with Emma tonight, seeing the man he'd become - devoted father, skilled craftsman, thoughtful host - made those old defenses feel increasingly pointless.

The taillights of her car vanished around the bend, but Thomas couldn't shake the feeling that something important had changed tonight. The professional distance they'd carefully maintained had broken, maybe beyond repair. And he wasn't sure if that scared him or gave him relief. When he went back inside, he saw Emma waiting in the living room, her video call noticeably missing.

"So," she said, "how'd it go?"

"It was a pleasant evening," he said neutrally. "Isabella is good company. She always has been."

She studied him with knowing eyes. "You like her, and not just professionally, Dad. You genuinely like who she is."

He sighed. "Yes, I do. She's thoughtful, intelligent, passionate about her work, easy to talk to—"

"And beautiful," Emma added.

"And beautiful," Thomas conceded with a smile, "though that's hardly the most important quality, especially at my age."

"Well, it doesn't hurt," she said, grinning. "So, what happens now?"

He started gathering dishes from the deck. "Nothing happens now, Emma. We continue working together on the inn. We maintain a friendly, professional relationship."

"And you continue to avoid telling her the truth about why you left thirty years ago?"

Thomas set the dishes in the sink, turning to face his daughter. "It's not that simple."

"Actually, it really is that simple," she said. "Difficult? Yes. Potentially painful? Absolutely. But simple in concept. You tell her the truth, and let her decide what to do with it."

"And what if it damages the renovation project? If it makes working together absolutely impossible?"

"Then you deal with that consequence," Emma said firmly. "But hiding from the truth isn't fair to either of you. And Dad, I saw how you look at her. This isn't just about clearing your conscience. There's something real developing between you two. Something that probably never died. Whether you're ready to admit that or not."

He couldn't argue because Emma was right. Tonight had proven what he'd been trying to ignore - his feelings for Isabella went far beyond professional respect or nostalgic affection. When she'd asked who took care of him, when she'd looked at him across the table with those knowing hazel eyes, he'd felt seen in a way he hadn't in decades. Maybe hadn't felt since the last time he'd held her, thirty years ago, before everything fell apart.

"I'll think about it," he said, not committing.

Emma seemed to recognize this was about as much as she was going to get tonight. She kissed his cheek and headed upstairs to her room, leaving Thomas alone with his thoughts.

Alone in his quiet kitchen, Thomas washed the dinner dishes and reflected on the evening. Isabella burst into laughter when Emma shared fishing stories. The way she'd touched his arm when thanking him for dinner. How she'd looked standing on his porch with her hair down, like stepping out of a memory he'd locked away years ago.

Emma was right about one thing - something

real was growing between them, something that seemed inevitable despite his best efforts to stop it. The real question wasn't whether he had feelings for Isabella, but whether he was brave enough to tell her the truth that had kept them apart for thirty years, knowing it could ruin whatever fragile bond they were rebuilding.

Some foundations, once cracked, couldn't bear weight again without being rebuilt from the ground up. The question was whether they dared to do the work, or whether the safer choice was to leave some things buried.

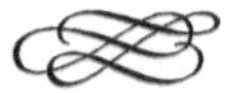

Isabella straightened her linen dress as she entered the Victorian-style headquarters of the Lowcountry Ladies Club. The monthly luncheon was in full swing - elegant women in their summer linens, perfectly styled hair catching the afternoon light, the melodic sound of Southern drawls blending with the gentle percussion of crystal against fine china. Money and tradition permeated every corner of the room. Although she had attended a few of these gatherings since arriving on Wexley, she still felt the subtle scrutiny that always followed her entrance. The brief lull in conversations was quickly replaced by glances masked with polite, closed-lip smiles.

"Isabella, darling," Maggie Beaumont waved from

a table near the window. It overlooked the carefully manicured gardens. "I've saved you a seat."

Grateful for her friend's reliable support, Isabella made her way across the room, exchanging greetings with several women who had warmed to her since the Architectural Review Board meeting. Their acceptance, while tentative, represented significant progress in her integration into island society.

"You look lovely," Maggie said as Isabella sat beside her. "That color brings out your eyes beautifully."

"Thank you," Isabella said with a smile. "Although I think I could arrive in a potato sack and you would always find something complimentary to say."

Maggie laughed, a warm, sincere sound that drew attention from nearby tables. "Oh, nonsense. You know I'm ruthlessly honest. Just ask Vivian."

"Speaking of whom?" She nodded discreetly toward the entrance where Vivian Pierce had just arrived. Impeccably dressed in her pale pink suit that managed to look classic and yet intimidating.

"She doesn't look at all pleased to see us together," Isabella said quietly.

"Oh, Vivian hasn't looked pleased about anything since 1992," she said dryly. "Pay her no mind. Tell me instead about your dinner with Thomas and Emma. I heard it was quite enjoyable."

Isabella almost choked on her water. "Wow, news really travels fast on this island."

"Honey, faster than lightning through a wire fence," Maggie said, laughing. "Betty at the market probably knew what y'all ate for dessert before you'd finished washing the dishes. Charlotte Stewart's niece is dating one of the boys who works at the island market. He delivered groceries to Thomas yesterday morning and saw Emma setting a lovely table. Now, one doesn't arrange flowers and use good china for a casual family dinner."

Isabella shook her head, amused and disconcerted by the island's efficient gossip network. "It was just dinner with colleagues. Emma wanted to discuss marketing ideas for the inn."

Maggie hummed skeptically. "And did you discuss marketing the entire evening?"

"Among other things," Isabella said. "Emma is very insightful about positioning the inn's historical character for the contemporary audience."

"Oh yes, she's a clever girl," Maggie agreed. "Takes after her father in that regard. Seeing beyond the surface of what truly matters to what truly matters." She looked at Isabella with shrewd eyes. "And how was spending time with Thomas outside of work?"

Isabella tried to think of ways to deflect the question, but realized it was futile. "It was nice," she said finally. "It's different seeing him in his home environment with his daughter. He's clearly an excellent father."

"Oh, one of the best," Maggie nodded. "Those two have been through a lot together. Sarah's illness was devastating for them both, but they sure supported each other beautifully through it."

Isabella felt a pang of sympathy, imagining Thomas and a younger version of Emma trying to navigate such profound loss together, alone. "He mentioned taking cooking classes after she passed, said he wanted to make sure Emma had good meals when she visited."

"Well, that's our Thomas," Maggie said softly, "always thinking of others before himself. You know, it's his greatest strength and his greatest weakness." She paused as servers approached with the first course, waiting until they had walked away before continuing. "He cares for everyone else but rarely allows anyone to care for him."

The observation resonated with Isabella and echoed her own question to Thomas the previous evening about who took care of him.

Before she could respond, Charlotte Stewart

joined their table, followed by two other women Isabella only recognized from the garden party.

"Isabella, we were just discussing the inn renovation," Charlotte said as she settled into her seat. "Eliza Wright mentioned the original woodwork in the main staircase has been completely restored. She says it's magnificent."

"Thomas's team has done remarkable work," Isabella confirmed. "The craftsmanship is really extraordinary."

"Oh, Thomas has always had a gift for restoration," one of the women commented. "Remember what he did with the Beaumont Library, Maggie? Those floors were beyond saving, according to every other contractor on the island."

"And now they're the envy of every home in The Palms," Maggie said with pride. "Which reminds me, Isabella, have you given any more thought to our discussion about the inn's opening celebration? December will be here before we know it."

The conversation flowed easily to plans for the inn's reopening, and several women offered suggestions about local organizations, caterers, and cross-promotion with some of the island businesses. Isabella appreciated the genuine interest and the valuable insights from community members.

It wasn't until dessert was being served that she

finally noticed Vivian Pierce making her way determinedly toward the table with a thin smile fixed on her perfectly made-up face.

"Isabella," she said, greeting her with a very practiced cordiality. "I've been meaning to ask you how the paint analysis is progressing. Grayson mentioned that you've engaged a specialist from Charleston."

"Yes, Dr. Eleanor Simmons from the Historical Preservation Institute," Isabella said. "She's the leading expert in historical paint analysis in the Southeast, and her preliminary findings should be available next week."

"Oh, how thorough," Vivian replied, her tone suggesting that maybe that was a little excessive. "But I understand you've been spending quite a bit of time with Thomas Langley, you know, discussing the renovation, of course."

The deliberate emphasis and pointed look that accompanied the statement made her implication unmistakable. Isabella maintained her composure, aware that conversations around her had quieted as the women strained to hear her response.

"Well, Thomas is the restoration contractor for the project. Naturally, we do spend a lot of time discussing the work. We want to make sure everything goes well."

"Of course," Vivian nodded, her smile never reaching her eyes. "Although I understand these professional discussions have become quite... personal. Dinner at his cottage with his daughter present—how lovely. One does hope the renovation's timeline isn't being compromised by... other considerations."

The direct reference to her private evening with Thomas and Emma confirmed Isabella's suspicion that this encounter was staged to create discomfort and public speculation about her and Thomas. Before she could even think of a response that wouldn't feed the attempt at gossip-mongering, Maggie thankfully intervened.

"Vivian, darling, how's your nephew's contracting business these days?" she said with a deceptive sweetness. "Is he still struggling to secure projects on the island? Maybe if he developed an expertise in historical restoration, instead of focusing on those dreadful modern monstrosities, he might be a little more successful. Not everyone can match Thomas's skill, of course, but surely he could improve if he had proper training."

The strategic counter-strike, reminding everybody that Vivian's nepotistic attempt to secure the Beaumont restoration for her unqualified nephew, hit its mark perfectly. A faint flush appeared on

Vivian's cheeks, and several of the women at nearby tables looked at each other with knowing glances.

"Actually, my nephew is doing quite well with projects on the mainland, thank you," Vivian replied stiffly. "Not everybody appreciates the constraints of historical preservation. Some clients prefer contemporary design."

"How fortunate the mainland offers such opportunities for someone like your nephew," Maggie said, smiling. "Oh, if you'll excuse us, Isabella and I were just talking about the holiday decoration plans for the inn's opening. We'd love your input at the committee meeting next week, if you're available, of course."

Effectively dismissed, Vivian had little choice but to retreat with as much of her dignity intact as she could when she departed. Conversations around the room gradually resumed their normal volume and flow.

"Thank you," Isabella said quietly to Maggie. "That was a master class."

"Well, island politics is a contact sport," she replied with a shrug. "Vivian forgets I've been playing it much longer than she has." She patted Isabella's hand. "Don't let her bother you. Her influence here isn't what it used to be, especially since the review board approved your plans despite her relentless objections."

Isabella nodded, but she couldn't completely dismiss the discomfort of having her personal life become fodder for island gossip. She knew there was going to be some curiosity about her past connection to Thomas, but she didn't enjoy the public scrutiny of their current relationship, whatever it might be. It felt invasively personal.

The luncheon concluded shortly after, with Isabella saying goodbye to several women who had become friendly over the past months. As she got ready to leave, Charlotte Stewart approached her privately.

"I wanted to mention," she said in a low voice, "that most of us remember how Thomas was after Sarah passed away. He withdrew from everything except for work and taking care of Emma. It's been fifteen years, and this is the first time any of us has seen him show interest in somebody. So whatever may or may not be developing between you two, it's a good thing. Don't let Vivian's pettiness suggest otherwise."

Touched by the unexpected support, Isabella thanked her. As she drove from the club toward the inn, she found herself thinking about the complex social dynamics of Wexley Island. What initially seemed like a unified wall of resistance had gradually revealed itself to be a tapestry of individuals with nuance, each holding varying perspectives, allegiances, and values.

At the inn, Isabella found Daphne Chen reviewing fabric samples with a local upholsterer in what would eventually become the main sitting room. The space was looking more beautiful by the day, with the original moldings restored and hardwood floors refinished to a warm glow that complemented the beautiful afternoon light streaming through the tall windows.

"Oh, Isabella, perfect timing," Daphne called, waving her over. "We're trying to finalize these upholstery selections for the custom pieces. I've narrowed it down to these three options for the main seating grouping."

Grateful for the distraction from her luncheon, Isabella looked at the design decisions for the next hour. The work was progressing very well, with many of the upstairs guest rooms nearing completion and the main public spaces starting to reveal their restored grandeur.

As the afternoon progressed, Isabella found herself constantly aware of Thomas's absence. He'd mentioned that he would be sourcing reclaimed heart pine for the dining room floor today, a quest that took him to a salvage yard in Savannah. She found herself missing his steady presence, his thoughtful insights, a realization that both pleased and unsettled her at the same time.

Around four o'clock, she was surprised to see Emma enter the inn, looking professional in her tailored slacks and silk blouse, with a portfolio tucked under her arm.

"Emma, I didn't know you were still on the island," Isabella said.

"I extended my stay through tomorrow," she said. "I wanted to follow up on our marketing discussion, if you have some time. I wrote some preliminary concepts for the inn's brand identity, and I even sketched some things."

"Oh, I'd love to see them," Isabella said. "Let's go to the library. It's the quietest space right now."

They settled in a partially restored library, where built-in bookshelves lined the walls and comfortable reading chairs had been positioned near the windows. Emma spread her sketches across the table, showing the visual identity she'd developed for the inn that honored its historical character.

"Wow, these are remarkable," Isabella said, genuinely impressed with her ideas. "You've really captured the balance I've been trying to articulate -

respecting the tradition without feeling stuffy or outdated."

"That's exactly what I was aiming for," Emma nodded. "The inn has such a rich history, but it needs to feel welcoming to guests of today, not like a museum where they can't touch anything."

They talked about concepts in detail, with Isabella offering insights while Emma explained her design choices from a marketing perspective.

"You have an extraordinary talent for this," Isabella said. "Have you considered focusing your career more specifically on historical properties and their branding needs?"

A flicker of something - maybe surprise or recognition - crossed Emma's face. "It's funny you should ask that. I've actually been considering a career shift in that direction. There's something particularly satisfying about helping historical places find their voice in the modern world."

"Well, you would excel at it," Isabella said. "Your understanding of how to honor history is exactly what these properties need."

"Thank you. That means a lot, especially coming from someone with your experience." She hesitated for a moment and then added, "I mentioned the idea to Dad this weekend. He was supportive of me potentially leaving the agency to start my own consultancy."

"Why is that a surprise?" Isabella asked.

"I don't know. I've always thought he took pride in my corporate success, you know, my steady climb up the ladder and being in the security of an established firm." She shrugged her shoulders. "But he said he's proud of me regardless of where I work or what title I hold - that what matters are my skills and character, not my employment status."

"That certainly sounds like Thomas," Isabella said, nodding. "He's never been impressed by titles or status, only integrity and craftsmanship."

"He hasn't changed in that way, has he?" Emma said. "Even after all these years."

They both understood the fundamental character traits that defined Thomas Langley, regardless of the decades that had passed or the circumstances that had shaped his life.

Before Isabella could say anything, her phone chimed with a text message.

"Speaking of your father," she said, "he's on his way back from Savannah with the reclaimed flooring. Apparently, it's even better quality than he had hoped to find."

"Oh, I'm sure that made his day," Emma said, smiling. "He gets so excited about materials in a way most people would reserve for sports victories or lottery wins."

Isabella laughed. "I've noticed. The day he found those original doorknobs in the attic, you would have thought he'd discovered buried treasure."

"Oh, in his mind, he had," Emma said. "That's what makes him so good at what he does. He sees the value in things that others might discard or overlook."

They shifted their conversation back to marketing materials, but Isabella kept thinking about Emma's words. Thomas had a gift for recognizing the value beneath surface imperfections. It was one of the qualities she had always admired about him.

As they wrapped up their meeting, Emma picked up her sketches. "Well, I should head back to Dad's place. I promised I would make dinner tonight since he cooked yesterday."

"It was wonderful seeing your ideas," Isabella said. "I'd be delighted to work with you on the inn's marketing strategy, whether through your current agency or other arrangements."

Emma's eyes lit up. "I would love that. The inn is exactly the kind of project I want to focus on. Something with authentic history and soul, not just commercial appeal."

They walked together to the inn's entrance, where they found Luella seated on the porch, watching the late afternoon light filter through the oak trees.

"Emma Langley," Luella greeted her with obvious affection. "Twice in one weekend. Your daddy must be pleased to have you home so often these days."

"Hey, Miss Luella," Emma said, leaning down to kiss her cheek. "Dad's always happy to have me visit, although I think he appreciates his peace and quiet when I leave, too."

"Mmm-hmm," Luella hummed. "That man's had enough peace and quiet to last three lifetimes. He needs a little commotion now and then to keep his blood flowing."

She looked at Emma and Isabella. "You two been plotting something? Got that look about you."

"Just discussing marketing for the inn," Isabella said, amused.

"Marketing, is it?" Luella raised an eyebrow. "Fancy word for telling stories about a place so folks want to visit. This inn's got stories enough for three hundred marketing campaigns if you know where to look for them."

"That's exactly what makes it so special," Emma said, "and why I'm so excited to help develop its brand identity."

Luella nodded. "Well, good to see young people appreciating history instead of just tearing it down to build something shiny and new. Your daddy raised you right."

After Emma left, Isabella settled into the rocking chair beside Luella, content to share a few moments of quiet observation as the day transitioned into evening. Deer had emerged from behind the inn, grazing peacefully on the overgrown lawn that would eventually become a formal garden.

"Heard you had quite a time at the ladies' club luncheon today," Luella said after a while. "Vivian Pierce making trouble as usual."

Isabella sighed. "News gets around really quickly here."

"Like a wildfire in August," Luella said. "But don't let it bother you. Island gossip is like the tide. Comes in, goes out, regular as clockwork. What seems important today will be forgotten by next week when somebody else does something worth talking about."

"Well, I hope you're right," Isabella said. "I didn't come here looking for personal complications or drama. I want to restore the inn and create something meaningful. I want to enjoy my life."

Luella studied her thoughtfully. "Life's funny that way, sugar. You come lookin' for one thing, and it hands you somethin' else entirely. Question is whether you're smart enough to recognize what you need when it shows up, even if it ain't what you were expectin'."

The cryptic observation hung in the air between them as the deer continued grazing, untroubled by any human concerns.

"Luella," Isabella began hesitantly. "Can I ask you something personal?"

"You can ask," the older woman said. "Might even answer, depending on what it is."

"Are you sure you don't know why Thomas ended our relationship in college? I'm talking about the real reason, not the one he told me at the time. I've spent thirty years telling myself it doesn't matter anymore, that I've moved on. But being here with him, working together, feeling..." She stopped, unsure how to finish. "I need to know if what he told me was the truth, or if there's something more."

Luella's expression, as always, remained impassive, but something flickered in her eyes.

"What did he tell you back then?"

"Well, not much, really. Just left a note that he had to go home. I tried calling him for weeks, but he never responded. I took that as an answer." Isabella found the words still had a little bit of their original sting, even though decades had passed. "It came out of nowhere, you know, just as I was returning from my summer internship. We had plans, like a future we had mapped out together, and suddenly it was over."

Luella was quiet for a long moment, watching the deer with seemingly absorbed interest. When she finally spoke, her voice carried the wisdom of someone who chose her words deliberately.

"Honey, some stories aren't mine to tell," she said. "But I will say this. Thomas Langley is a man who's always done what he thought was right, even when it cost him everything. Sometimes what seems like abandonment from one perspective is actually a sacrifice from another. There are people on this island who know pieces of what happened back then. Not the whole story. Thomas kept that close, but people know enough to have opinions. You start askin' around, you might hear things that'll confuse you more than clarify. Better to get it straight from the source."

She considered the response, sensing there was more meaning beyond the surface than Luella was willing to explicitly state.

"That doesn't really answer my question."

"No," Luella said. "It doesn't. But some answers you need to get from the source when the time is right." She turned her penetrating gaze directly to

Isabella. "The question is, are you asking because you need to know for your own peace of mind, or because it matters for what might be developing between the two of you now?"

The directness of the question caught Isabella off guard. She'd been so careful to maintain professional boundaries with Thomas, yet Luella had seen right through it.

"I'm not sure," Isabella admitted finally. "Maybe both."

Luella nodded, seemingly pleased with the honest uncertainty. "Then maybe it's time to have that talk with Thomas. Ask him straight out why he left. Because whatever's growin' between you two now, it's growin' on shaky ground if you don't know the truth. And honey, secrets have a way of comin' out at the worst possible time, usually when they can do the most damage."

Before Isabella could respond, the sound of a truck approaching drew their attention. Thomas pulled into the driveway with his vehicle loaded with reclaimed flooring.

"Speak of the devil," Luella murmured, a hint of amusement. "Timing was always that man's specialty, sometimes good, sometimes not so good."

Thomas parked near the side entrance and

approached the porch, his expression brightening when he saw them. Despite the long drive to and from Savannah, he looked energized rather than tired.

"Ladies," he greeted them with a warm smile. "Enjoying the evening?"

"Oh, just watching deer and solving the world's problems," Luella said dryly. "Found your flooring, I see."

"Better than I hoped," Thomas confirmed. "Heart pine from an 1860s warehouse in Savannah, same vintage as the inn's original floors, and the patina is perfect. We won't even need to artificially age it to match the existing sections."

His genuine excitement over the discovery was charming. Isabella found herself watching how his face changed when he talked about materials and craftsmanship, the boyish enthusiasm that made him seem younger, the passion that initially drew her to him decades ago. It was risky how easily he could still make her forget why she had built those walls around her heart.

"That's wonderful news," Isabella said. "You want to show me?"

"Absolutely," Thomas nodded.

As they walked toward his truck, Luella called after them. "Don't forget what I said, Isabella. Some conversations need to happen face-to-face and not through the island grapevine."

Thomas glanced back with a questioning expression, but Isabella merely shook her head, indicating they would talk about it later.

At his truck, he lowered the tailgate and showed the flooring planks, their rich amber color glowing.

"It's beautiful," Isabella said, running her hand along one of the exposed edges. "This color variation is extraordinary."

"That's what makes reclaimed heart pine so special," he said. "Every board has its own story to tell through its unique grain pattern and color variations. This wood right here has witnessed over 150 years of history."

As he continued explaining the technical aspects of installing and finishing the flooring, Isabella watched his face. His genuine reverence for craftsmanship was compelling.

They were interrupted by the arrival of another vehicle, a sleek silver Mercedes that Isabella recognized immediately as belonging to Grayson Williams.

Thomas's expression shifted. "Unexpected visitor," he said, as Grayson emerged from his car impeccably dressed. "Want me to stay?"

"Please," Isabella nodded, grateful that he was there to support her.

Grayson approached with his practiced smile. "Isabella, Thomas, working late, I see."

"Just reviewing some materials for the dining room," Isabella said. "What brings you by, Grayson? I don't believe we had a meeting scheduled."

"No appointment necessary among friends, surely," he replied. "I was just driving past and saw your car. Thought I'd stop to discuss the paint analysis requirement. I understand Dr. Simmons has begun her work."

"She has," Isabella said, "and as I mentioned to Vivian at lunch today, we should have the preliminary results next week."

"Excellent," Grayson said. "I hope Dr. Simmons understands the importance of historical accuracy to our community. Some experts from Charleston tend to apply, let's say, flexible standards that might not meet Wexley's expectations."

"Well, Dr. Simmons has an impeccable reputation," Thomas interjected. "Her analysis methods are considered the gold standard in historical preservation circles across the Southeast, so we're confident her findings will satisfy even the most stringent interpretation of the requirements."

The subtle emphasis on *most stringent* made it

clear Thomas recognized Grayson's attempt to create additional obstacles.

Grayson's smile tightened. "Well, we all want what's best for the inn, don't we?" he said, his tone sharp. "It's such an important part of our island's heritage. Speaking of which, Isabella, have you given any more thought to my offer? The market for luxury properties continues to strengthen, and my investment group has recently increased our acquisition budget."

"My position hasn't changed, Grayson," Isabella said firmly. "The inn isn't for sale. I told you I came to Wexley to restore it as a hospitality business, not to flip it for development."

Grayson's expression hardened briefly before he regained his smooth facade. "Admirable commitment. Though I do hope you've considered all the ongoing challenges of managing a historic property - renovation delays, cost overruns, staffing issues in a seasonal economy." He paused thoughtfully. "And of course, financing can become… complicated if lenders start questioning a project's viability based on community feedback. Banks do tend to listen when influential board members voice concerns."

"Yes, I'm well aware of business realities," Isabella said, painting on a fake smile. "My financial projections account for these factors, and I'm very confident in the viability of the inn as an ongoing operation."

"Well, of course." Grayson nodded. "Should circumstances change - and they often do with projects of this scope - my offer remains open. For now." The slight emphasis on the final words carried an unmistakable edge. "In the meantime, I do look forward to reviewing Dr. Simmons' analysis with the board. Historical accuracy is so important, wouldn't you agree, Thomas?"

"Absolutely," Thomas said evenly. "Which is why we've engaged the most qualified expert available."

Grayson departed quickly after that, and Thomas and Isabella stood in silence for a moment, watching his Mercedes disappear down the driveway.

"Boy, he's not giving up, is he?" Isabella said.

"Not likely," Thomas confirmed. "This inn property represents the last big parcel of the historic district that hasn't been developed or permanently preserved. And Grayson's not the type to just sit back and wait for you to succeed. If he can't buy you out, he'll find other ways to apply pressure. I've seen him do it before - financial pressure, regulatory complications, social isolation. He's patient and he's ruthless. For someone with Grayson's ambitions, it's the ultimate prize."

"Well, he won't be getting it," Isabella said firmly.

"This inn is going to be restored, reopened, and operated exactly as I've planned."

Thomas smiled. "I don't doubt that for a moment. You're at least as stubborn as Grayson, with the advantage of actually owning the property."

"What was Luella talking about earlier?" he suddenly said. "Something about having a conversation face-to-face?"

Isabella hesitated, Luella's advice echoing in her mind. Was now the right time to ask Thomas directly about their past, while they stood in the inn's driveway with the workday ending and other pressing matters on their minds?

"Just Luella being Luella," she said, laughing, "dispensing wisdom whether requested or not."

Thomas chuckled. "Well, she's been doing that for as long as I've known her. The remarkable thing is how often her unsolicited advice turns out to be exactly what you needed to hear."

"Yeah, beginning to notice that pattern," Isabella agreed.

As Thomas got ready to leave, he paused for a moment. "I meant what I said at dinner last night, about doing it again sometime. Maybe with Emma's not-so-subtle matchmaking efforts."

The directness of his acknowledgment of both

the dinner's success and Emma's transparent intentions surprised Isabella.

"I would like that," she said honestly.

A pleased smile crossed his face, warming his blue eyes in the fading light. "Good. I'll call you."

Isabella watched him drive away and found herself reflecting on the day's events - Vivian's pointed comments, Luella's cryptic advice, and now Thomas's unexpected invitation. The careful boundaries she had tried to establish when she found him on the island were becoming more permeable.

She wasn't sure if reopening her heart to Thomas Langley was wise. The man had shattered her once without explanation, and now here she stood, contemplating dinner alone with him, feeling the same dangerous pull she'd felt at twenty-two. But watching the deer graze in the golden light, standing in front of the inn she was bringing back to life, Isabella recognized that some risks might be worth taking, even if they terrified her.

The inn itself seemed to stand witness to the possibility. Perhaps their relationship could undergo a similar restoration.

With this thought, she turned back toward the inn, ready to finish the day's work before going home. Whatever conversations needed to happen would have to wait for the right moment. But as she returned to the inn, Isabella couldn't shake Luella's warning about secrets coming out at the worst possible time. She'd built her entire project on this island, poured her life savings and dreams into this restoration.

If there were truths about Thomas's past she didn't know - truths that might complicate everything - she needed to hear them before her feelings made her too vulnerable to devastation.

The question was whether she had the courage to ask.

CHAPTER 13

Thomas knelt on the dining room floor of the inn, carefully aligning a piece of reclaimed heart pine with the existing floorboards. The morning light streamed through the tall windows and brought out the amber tones in the wood. Around him, his crew worked with focused precision, each one contributing to the restoration with their own practiced skills.

"That's fitting beautifully," Wade said, pausing beside Thomas. "Can't hardly tell where the old floor ends and the new one begins."

"Well, that's the idea," Thomas replied. "Once we apply the finish, this color variation will blend even more naturally."

He stood, brushing sawdust from his knees, and looked around the room. The dining room was nearing completion, with the original crown molding restored, the walls replastered, and the floor now being carefully repaired. The space was gradually reclaiming its former elegance.

The sound of voices in the hallway drew his attention. Isabella entered, accompanied by a middle-aged woman Thomas recognized as Dr. Eleanor Simmons, the historical paint analyst.

"Thomas," Isabella greeted him with a warm smile. "Dr. Simmons has completed her preliminary analysis, and I thought you might want to join us for her report."

"Absolutely," Thomas said, wiping his hands on a cloth before extending one. "Dr. Simmons, good to see you again. I do hope your investigation has been productive."

"Fascinating, actually," she said. "This building has quite a story to tell through its paint layers. Shall we find somewhere to review my findings?"

They settled in the library where Isabella had established her temporary office during the renovation. Dr. Simmons spread her documentation across the table, including detailed photographs, microscopic analysis of paint samples, and a comprehensive report outlining her conclusions.

"The exterior of the inn has been painted at least fourteen times since its construction," she said.

"What's particularly interesting is the color palette has remained remarkably consistent throughout history, just minor variations in the shade."

She produced a fan of color samples, each one meticulously labeled with dates and locations. "The original color scheme, which dated to the 1870s, featured this warm white for the clapboard and these specific green tones for the shutter and trim. The porch ceiling was painted this particular shade of light blue, which, as you know, is a tradition in Lowcountry architecture that's believed to deter insects and evil spirits."

Thomas looked at the color samples with interest, noting their alignment with his own research. "These match the tones that were visible in the earliest photographs we found," he said. "They're consistent with the other buildings of the same period that I've restored on the island."

"Exactly," Dr. Simmons said, nodding. "There's a clear historical precedent for this color scheme, not just on the building, but throughout the region. My report documents this thoroughly, of course, with references to other historically significant structures."

Isabella reviewed the findings with evident satisfaction.

"This is exactly what we needed."

"The colors are beautiful and historically accurate - and thoroughly documented to satisfy even the most demanding interpretation of the review board's requirements," Thomas said, thinking of Grayson's transparent attempt to create obstacles.

After reviewing the interior color findings, which also revealed equally interesting historical patterns, they thanked Dr. Simmons for her thorough work. The specialist left with promises to provide her final report within the week.

"Well, this is excellent news," Isabella said once they were alone. "With Dr. Simmons' analysis so thoroughly documented, even Grayson can't object to our color selections."

"He'll try," Thomas said, "but her credentials are impeccable and her methodology is beyond reproach. I know that we've satisfied this condition exactly as required."

Isabella smiled, clearly pleased. "One more hurdle cleared. The renovation's really coming together now, isn't it?"

He nodded. "The structural work is almost complete. The system updates are progressing on schedule, and now we have documentation about the paint. Barring any major surprises, we're on track for your holiday opening."

"I can hardly believe it," Isabella said. "After so

many years with corporate hotels, where projects drag on beyond projected timelines, this efficiency is refreshing."

"Hey, don't jinx us," Thomas said with a smile. "We still have plenty of work ahead, and old buildings have a way of revealing unexpected challenges just when you think you're in the clear."

As if the cautionary words summoned him, Wade appeared in the doorway, a concerned expression on his face.

"Hey, Thomas, we've got a situation in the kitchen. A plumbing contractor just found something you should see."

Thomas exchanged a glance with Isabella. "Duty calls," he said. "Let's see what surprise the inn has in store for us today."

The "situation" proved to be significant: a previously undiscovered cast-iron waste pipe embedded in a structural wall, which had severely deteriorated and required immediate attention.

Thomas spent the next several hours working with the plumbing contractor to develop a solution that would fix the problem without jeopardizing the timeline for the kitchen renovation. By late afternoon, they had come up with a workable plan, although it would require additional costs, materials, and labor.

Thomas found Isabella in the front parlor, looking at fabric samples with Daphne for the custom furniture that would furnish the space.

"I hate to interrupt," he said, "but we do need to discuss the kitchen plumbing issue."

Daphne tactfully excused herself, leaving Thomas to explain the problem and the proposed solution to Isabella. He outlined the technical details, the necessary modifications for the renovation, and the budget implications.

"Bottom line," he said, "we're looking at approximately eight thousand dollars in additional costs and maybe a week's delay in the kitchen completion."

Isabella absorbed the information calmly. Where many clients would have expressed frustration, she simply asked insightful questions about the technical aspects.

"So if we address it properly now, then we'll prevent future problems that could be a lot more costly and disruptive once the inn is operational, correct?"

"Exactly."

"Well, then the additional expense is unfortunate, but necessary," she said. "Cutting corners on plumbing is never wise."

"Especially in a commercial kitchen where health code compliance is essential," Thomas responded.

"Well, then, let's proceed with your recommended solution," Isabella said decisively. "I'd rather spend the money now than deal with a catastrophic failure later."

Their conversation was interrupted by the arrival of the building inspector, who was scheduled to review the electrical work completed the previous week. Thomas excused himself to accompany the official through the property, leaving Isabella to return to her design discussion with Daphne.

The inspection went smoothly, with the inspector noting the high quality of the electrical upgrades. As they completed the final portion of the review, Thomas looked out the window and saw dark clouds gathering on the horizon. The previously clear sky was giving way to the ominous gray that signaled an approaching summer storm.

After the inspector departed with clean approval, Thomas sought out Wade to let the crew know to secure the site before the weather deteriorated.

"Make sure all the materials are covered and the equipment is stored inside," he said. "The storm looks like it could be significant."

Wade nodded and organized the team to batten down the work site.

"Weather alert just came through on my phone.

Severe thunderstorm warning for the next six hours. They're predicting high winds and heavy rain."

Thomas grimaced, knowing it was going to slow progress. "Get everyone home safely before it hits. We can assess any impacts tomorrow."

The crew hurried to secure the site and then departed as Thomas found Isabella in the library, looking at the inspection report.

"Clean approval on all electrical work," she said, smiling. "Excellent news."

"It is," Thomas agreed, "though this approaching storm is going to dampen the celebration, I'm afraid. There's a severe weather warning in effect for the next several hours."

Isabella glanced toward the windows where the darkening sky confirmed his warning. "I guess I should head home before it hits. I have paperwork to finish that doesn't require me to be on-site."

"That's probably wise," Thomas said. "You don't want to get stranded here if you can be at home."

They walked together to the front entrance, where the wind was already intensifying, bending the branches of oak trees and sending early fallen leaves skittering across the driveway.

"Drive carefully," Thomas said. "These summer storms can develop quickly."

"It's not that far," she said, chuckling. "But what about you? Are you heading home?"

"Soon," he nodded. "I want to double-check that everything's properly secured first. That dining room floor installation is at a vulnerable stage. I'd sure hate for water damage to compromise the work we've done."

Isabella hesitated for a moment, glancing again at the sky. "Would you like help before you go? It might be faster with two people."

The offer touched Thomas. "I appreciate that, but I've got it covered. No sense in both of us getting caught in a downpour."

With a final farewell, Isabella left, her car disappearing down the oak-lined driveway just as the first large raindrops started to fall.

Thomas went back inside to complete his inspection of the property, checking all the windows, covering sensitive materials, and ensuring the temporary roof patches were secure.

The storm intensified rapidly, rain falling in sheets driven by gusting wind. Thunder crashed overhead, and lightning illuminated the sky. He was completing his final checks when he heard an unexpected sound in front of the building - a car engine and a door slamming.

Moments later, Isabella appeared in the doorway,

drenched despite the brief distance from her car to the entrance.

"A tree blew down on my street. Deputy had it barricaded before I even got close - said it won't be passable for hours yet."

"Are you all right?" he asked.

"Fine, just wet," she said, smiling. "I thought I might beat the worst of it, but the storm moved in faster than I expected."

A particularly violent gust of wind rattled the windows, followed by a crash from upstairs. They exchanged glances before hurrying toward the sound.

The source became immediately apparent when they reached the third floor. A section of the temporary roof covering had torn away, allowing wind-driven rain to pour onto the partially renovated guest rooms. Water already pooled on the hardwood floor, threatening to seep between the boards and damage the ceiling below.

"This is like deja vu, isn't it?" Isabella said, laughing.

"We've got to contain this quickly," Thomas said. "There are tarps in the storage room downstairs. We can create a barrier to direct the water away from the floor."

Isabella nodded. "I'll get towels to soak up what has already spilled."

They separated, gathered supplies, and came back together minutes later to work in the dim light. Since the power had predictably failed shortly after the storm's intensity increased, they secured a heavy tarp across the exposed section of the roof, creating a channel that directed the water into buckets.

The work was challenging, requiring them to balance on ladders in near darkness, only occasionally illuminated by lightning flashes. Rain continued to pour through the opening until they managed to secure the tarp, soaking them both despite their efforts to stay dry.

"Hold this corner," Thomas said, passing Isabella one end of the tarp while he secured the opposite side to an exposed beam. Their hands brushed briefly during the exchange, which heightened the tension of the moment. The contact sent a jolt through Thomas, unrelated to the storm. Even soaked and exhausted in near darkness, he was hyperaware of her - the determined set of her jaw, how skillfully she moved, how perfectly they worked together. This partnership felt inevitable, like something that had been waiting thirty years to reconnect.

When the immediate crisis was contained, they

turned their attention to soaking up water with towels and moving furniture away from the affected area.

"I think it's the best we can do until the storm passes," Thomas said finally, looking around. "The tarp should hold unless the wind gets a lot worse."

Isabella nodded and pushed her damp hair back from her forehead. "What about the rest of the roof? Should we check any other areas?"

"Good thinking," Thomas agreed. "Let's do a complete inspection while we're already soaked."

They checked the remaining rooms on the third floor and found two minor leaks, which they addressed with temporary measures. By the time they completed their inspection, they were thoroughly drenched, but the inn was as secure as they could make it.

"We should get out of these wet clothes," Thomas said as they walked to the main floor. "I keep some spare work shirts in my truck. They'll be big on you, but at least they're dry."

"Oh, that would be wonderful," Isabella said, shivering. "I hadn't planned on an impromptu shower today."

Thomas retrieved the shirts from his vehicle and then dashed through the downpour, returning even wetter than before. The shirts were in plastic bags, thankfully. He handed Isabella a clean button-up shirt and then gestured toward the small bathroom.

"You can change in there. I'll use the staff bathroom near the kitchen."

When they reconvened in the library several minutes later, the incongruity of their appearance - Isabella in a men's shirt that nearly reached her knees and Thomas with his hair still dripping onto the shoulders of his dry shirt - created a moment of shared amusement that broke the tension.

"This is quite a look," Isabella said with a self-conscious laugh, tugging at the oversized shirt. Her damp hair curled around her makeup-free face, and without her usual professional polish, she looked younger, more vulnerable.

Thomas thought she'd never been more beautiful. "A man's shirt suits you," he said, his voice coming out rougher than intended.

Their eyes met, and the air between them shifted - charged with something beyond camaraderie or shared crisis.

The dim light of the battery-powered lantern Thomas had taken from the emergency supplies made the library feel intimate and separate from the outside world.

"I can't believe we're dealing with another storm

again. This is becoming a pattern," Isabella said as she settled into one of the library's reading chairs.

"Summer thunderstorms are usually pretty fast-moving, although we're almost into fall at this point, so I'm not really sure what this one's doing." He sat down across from her. "When they stall over the island, they can last for hours, though, and based on the radar I checked before the power went out, we might be in for a longer one."

"At least we're dry, sort of, and the inn is as secure as we can make it," she said.

"Yeah, it usually takes a few hours even after the rain stops," Thomas said. "The tide can play a factor, too. If the storm coincides with a high tide, the flooding will take longer to subside. Where's Luella?"

"Honestly, I'm not sure. She had talked about maybe going to visit her niece in Charleston, so maybe she got stuck over there."

They fell into comfortable conversation as the storm raged outside, talking about the renovation, all the upcoming tasks, and some of the island residents.

"You know, I've been meaning to thank you," Isabella said during a lull in the conversation, "for dinner the other night with Emma. It was great to spend time together outside of work. I haven't really done a lot of social things since I moved here, other than the Ladies Club, of course."

"We enjoyed having you," Thomas said sincerely, "and Emma was particularly pleased to share her marketing ideas with you. She's so grateful that you're supportive of her potential career change."

"She really has a remarkable talent."

"Well, that's a nice thing to say," Thomas said with a smile.

A comfortable silence fell between them, with just the drumming of the rain on the roof and occasional rumbles of thunder. Now more distant, as the storm started moving past the island.

"Can I ask you something?" Isabella said, "About the past?"

Thomas felt apprehension, sensing they were approaching territory they had so far avoided in their professional interactions. But maybe it was the isolation of the storm or the natural intimacy that had developed by sharing the emergency response - he felt like the question was going to be more inevitable than intrusive.

"Of course," he said, as his heart rate accelerated.

Isabella sucked in a deep breath and then slowly blew it out before asking her question. "Why did you really end things between us?" Her gaze was steady despite the vulnerability in the question. "It's been thirty years, and I've made peace with what happened, but I've never understood why one day we were planning our future together and the next you were gone. Did you think our relationship was a mistake or something?"

The question hung in the air between them. Thomas had known the moment might come and even tried to initiate the conversation himself - with Emma's encouragement, of course - but now it had arrived, and he found himself struggling to find the right words.

"It wasn't a mistake," he said finally, his voice quiet. "What we had was real and important. I loved you, Isabella. That was never the issue."

"Then what was?"

Thomas took a deep breath. "Shortly after you left for your internship, my father's business collapsed completely. Bad investments, mounting debts - he was facing bankruptcy and potentially jail time." He paused, the shame still fresh after so many years. "I was desperate. I called Sarah's family because they had money and had once been fond of me."

He met Isabella's eyes. "They agreed to help, but only if I married Sarah immediately after graduation. It wasn't a loan, it was a transaction. My father's freedom in exchange for giving Sarah what she'd always wanted."

Understanding dawned in Isabella's expression. "They blackmailed you."

"I told myself I was being honorable, doing the right thing. But the truth is, I had no choice. It was marry Sarah or watch my father lose everything, and possibly his freedom. Sarah never even knew what her parents did." His voice dropped. "Emma came a year later, and she's the only part of that choice I've never regretted."

"So you sacrificed everything - your dreams, our future - to save your father." Isabella's voice was steady, but her eyes welled. "That wasn't abandonment, Thomas. That was impossible circumstances and people who manipulated your honor against you." She was quiet for a long moment. "I spent thirty years thinking I hadn't been enough, that you'd realized you'd made a mistake with me. Knowing the truth doesn't erase those years, but it... It helps me understand we were victims of circumstances, not failures of the heart."

"I should have told you then," Thomas said. "Should have given you the choice to wait or to walk away knowing the truth. Instead, I chose for you."

"You were twenty-two and terrified," Isabella said

gently. "I understand why you did what you did. I just wish..." She trailed off.

"Wish what?"

"That you'd trusted me enough to let me stand beside you through it. Even if the outcome had been the same. Thank you for trusting me with this now," Isabella said. Then, more quietly: "I need you to know I'm not that twenty-two-year-old girl anymore who needed protecting from hard truths. I've built my career on handling crises and making difficult decisions."

Thomas nodded, though something in her tone suggested a specific concern. "Of course. I see how capable you are every day with the inn."

But even as he said it, part of him wanted to shield her from the challenges ahead - Grayson's escalating pressure, the financial complexities, the island politics. Old protective instincts died hard.

"Does Emma know all of this?" Isabella asked, surprised.

"Yes. We discussed it during your first visit after you arrived on the island. She was curious about our history. She's been not-so-subtly encouraging me to clear the air with you ever since."

"Well, that explains a few things about her interest in our dinner together," Isabella said, amusement passing across her face.

"She's not exactly subtle in her matchmaking efforts," Thomas agreed.

"You know, I appreciate your honesty now, even if it was long delayed," Isabella said. "I understand why you made the choice you did. Emma is clearly the center of your world, and you've been an extraordinary father to her. I can't imagine you being anything less."

The generosity of her response, free from recrimination or bitterness, touched Thomas. "Thank you for that. It means more than I can express."

Isabella nodded. "So with Sarah, your marriage to her was it…"

"It was a good partnership," Thomas replied honestly. "We shared a lot of respect for each other and commitment to Emma, and had common values. Sarah was truly a remarkable woman - intelligent, practical, principled - and we built a solid life together, even if it wasn't the grand passion of youthful romance." He paused for a moment, wanting to be truthful. "She knew about you - not the full circumstances of our breakup - but that you had been important to me, and she was okay with that. Well, she was secure in who she was," Thomas explained. "She once said that, 'her loss was my gain, wasn't it?' That was

Sarah. Direct, no nonsense, but with a generous heart."

Isabella smiled. "She sounds like someone I might have liked under different circumstances."

"Oh, you would have," Thomas agreed. "You're similar in some ways - that core of strength, that practical approach to challenges. Emma sees that in you, too. She mentioned it to me after meeting you."

The comparison seemed to please Isabella, although she didn't comment directly on it. Instead, she stared out the window where the rain had finally subsided to a gentle drizzle. "The storm's passing," she said. "The road should reopen soon."

Thomas recognized that subtle shift in conversation as a signal that she needed some time to process. Thirty years of wondering had been answered in a single conversation. It was natural that she would want space to consider things.

"Probably within the hour," he said, respecting her unspoken request to return to more neutral territory. "You know, we should check the temporary repairs once more before we leave. Make sure everything's holding up. This seems to be becoming a common thing, us getting stuck here in the house during a storm."

She laughed and nodded her head as they rose

from their chairs. They made their final inspection, and the interaction remained comfortable, but slightly more reserved.

The road reopened as predicted, allowing them to depart as darkness settled over the island. Standing beside their respective vehicles in the driveway, they found themselves in a moment of uncertain farewell.

"Thanks again for your help with the roof," Thomas said.

"We make a great emergency response team."

She smiled. "We do. And thank you for the shirt. I'll wash it and return it tomorrow."

"Oh, no rush," Thomas said, waving his hand. "Thanks for listening, and for understanding."

She met his gaze directly, her expression thoughtful. "You know, thirty years is a long time to wonder about something. I'm glad to finally know the truth." She paused for a moment. "I do need some time to process it all, but I'm grateful for your honesty."

"Of course," Thomas said. "Take all the time you need."

As Thomas drove through the rain-washed evening, he felt both lighter and more settled than he'd been in years. He'd finally told Isabella the truth, and she'd responded with grace and understanding he hadn't deserved.

Some lessons, it seemed, took more than thirty years to learn.

CHAPTER 14

Isabella stood at the center of what would become the inn's grand lobby and watched as the workers carefully restored the original crown molding. It highlighted the intricate details of the plasterwork - acanthus leaves and delicate rope patterns - that Thomas's craftspeople had meticulously repaired.

Two weeks had passed since the storm that trapped them together at the inn and led to Thomas's revelation about their past. Two weeks of professional collaboration continued, even though personal undercurrents were clearly present. Isabella had requested time to process his explanation, and Thomas had given her the space. They had gone back to the comfortable professional rapport they had built during the months of renovation. But something had unquestionably shifted between them.

The truth, finally spoken after three decades, had lifted an invisible barrier. Of course, their talk remained focused on the renovation, but the tension from their unacknowledged history was gone, replaced by a more genuine connection.

"The molding looks perfect," Daphne said as she joined Isabella. "You can't even tell which sections are original and which have been recreated."

"Oh, Thomas's craftsmen are the best of the best," Isabella said. "Their attention to detail makes all the difference."

"Speaking of details," Daphne continued, opening her portfolio, "I've finally finalized the fabric selections for all the guest rooms. Each one will have its own subtle color scheme but maintain an overall cohesion for the house."

Isabella examined the selections. Over the past months, Daphne had proven herself not only talented but also intuitively aligned with Isabella's vision for the inn.

"These are perfect," she said. "When can we expect delivery?"

"Six weeks for custom pieces, and everything should arrive in plenty of time for the holiday opening. Which reminds me, have you finalized the date for the grand opening celebration?"

"December fifteenth," Isabella said with a nod. "It gives us a comfortable buffer after construction completion for staff training and a soft opening, but we'll still be able to capture some of the holiday season."

They were interrupted by Luella, who entered with her signature mix of authority and casual familiarity. "Kitchen cabinets are being delivered," she announced. "Thought you'd want to know."

"Thanks, Luella," Isabella said. "I should be there to oversee the installation."

As they walked toward the kitchen, Luella watched Isabella with a shrewd look on her face. "You seem different lately. More settled somehow."

Isabella smiled slightly. "Oh, do I?"

"Mmm-hmm," Luella hummed, as she commonly did. "Like someone who's finally got an answer to a long-standing question, maybe?"

Her knowing look made it clear she suspected as much. Rather than responding directly, Isabella changed the subject. "Wow, this kitchen is really coming together. Once the cabinets are installed, we can schedule the equipment delivery."

"Avoiding the subject, I see," Luella said, unperturbed. "That's fine. Some conversations need to happen in their own time."

She stood in the kitchen entrance for a moment, where workers were unloading the custom cabinetry designed to complement the room's historical character. "Just remember that understanding the past doesn't necessarily dictate the future. All that part's still up to you."

With her cryptic advice delivered, Luella walked into the kitchen to inspect the cabinets, leaving Isabella to stand there, reflecting on what she had just said.

It was true that learning the real reason behind Thomas's abrupt ending of their relationship had given her long-sought clarity. The knowledge that his decision had been driven by responsibility and honor, rather than a change of heart, had healed an old wound she had carried for decades.

But understanding it created its own complexity. What did it mean for their relationship now? The circumstances that had separated them no longer existed. Emma was grown, Thomas had been widowed for fifteen years, and they both had built successful careers, which ultimately led them back to each other through the inn's renovation.

Did this convergence of their separate paths

suggest the possibility of a relationship, or was it merely a coincidence?

These questions had occupied Isabella's thoughts over the last couple of weeks as she tried to focus on the inn's restoration. The project, of course, was her primary focus, but she couldn't deny that her feelings for Thomas had evolved beyond professional, maybe even into friendship territory, or beyond.

The kitchen delivery took up the rest of the morning, and Isabella worked with the installation team to ensure the cabinets were placed according to the plans. The commercial kitchen was one of the most significant updates in the renovation, blending historical aesthetics with practical needs for running a hospitality business.

By early afternoon, the cabinet installation was well underway and progressing smoothly enough that Isabella felt comfortable leaving it to the skilled workers without her direct supervision. She headed to the library, where she had a scheduled meeting with potential staff members for the inn's eventual operation.

The hiring process had begun in earnest, and Isabella was looking for people who understood both hospitality and the unique character of the inn they would be representing. Today's interviews were for key positions: assistant manager, head of housekeeping, and front desk supervisor. These were all roles that would be important in establishing standards from the outset.

As she reviewed the résumés one last time before the interviews started, she thought about how much her life had changed since buying The Wexley Inn. What began as just a work project had become something more complicated and personal. The inn was not only a business, but also a part of the community, a form of creative outlet she hadn't realized she needed, and unexpectedly, a way to reconnect with her past.

The afternoon interviews proved promising, with several candidates seeming both technically qualified and possessing the personal qualities Isabella sought. By the time the final applicant departed, she had made preliminary selections for every position, pending reference checks and, of course, second interviews.

As she organized her notes from the meetings, Isabella heard a familiar voice in the hallway - Thomas, speaking with one of his crew members about the dining room floor installation. There was just something about his voice that comforted her in a way she hadn't expected. It brought an involuntary smile to her face.

Moments later, he appeared in the library

doorway with a blueprint rolled under his arm. He always had the best arms. That was something she had never forgotten about him.

"Sorry to interrupt. Do you have a minute to talk about the veranda railing design?"

"Of course," Isabella said, clearing space on the table for the blueprint. "How's the dining room coming along?"

"Beautifully," Thomas replied. "The floor is going to be ready for finishing by the end of the week. We're a little bit ahead of schedule there."

He unrolled the blueprint and showed drawings of a proposed restoration for the inn's wraparound veranda. The original railing had been replaced several times over the decades, with the current version dating to the 1960s renovation. At the time, they had prioritized maintenance over historical accuracy.

"I found photographs of the original 1870s railing design," Thomas explained, showing some historical images pinned to the corner of the blueprint. "It was more ornate than the current version, with these distinctive spindle patterns and decorative corner posts."

"It's beautiful," Isabella said as she studied the detailed craftsmanship, while trying not to look at Thomas's dimple. "Can it be accurately reproduced?"

"Absolutely," Thomas confirmed. "I have a wood-worker on my team who specializes in these kinds of historical reproductions. He can create this pattern exactly using the same kind of wood as the original."

"And it will meet current safety codes?" Isabella asked, again trying not to make eye contact. She could smell his cologne. This was getting difficult.

"With minor modifications to the height and spacing," he nodded. "The changes won't be visually apparent, but they'll satisfy code requirements."

As they discussed the technical aspects of the railing restoration, she became acutely aware of his presence as they bent over the blueprint. Their shoulders occasionally brushed as he pointed out different elements of the design, creating brief moments of contact that seemed charged with electricity.

"I think this is exactly right," Isabella said, approving the design. "It restores the important architectural feature while making sure guests are safe. When can the work begin?"

We can start the fabrication immediately," Thomas said. "Installation would follow the exterior painting, probably in about three weeks."

When they finished their business, a brief silence settled between them. It wasn't uncomfortable, but it was filled with the feeling of unspoken words.

Thomas appeared about to say something beyond their professional discussion when Daphne arrived, accompanied by a delivery person carrying fabric samples.

"Perfect timing," Daphne said, unaware of the moment she had just interrupted. "The mill sent these advance samples for the custom upholstery fabrics. I wanted to see the actual colors before they began production."

Thomas excused himself and went back to the dining room, leaving Isabella to examine the fabric samples with Daphne. As he left, his gaze briefly met Isabella's, conveying something—perhaps regret over the interrupted moment, or maybe he was just glad to get out of there. She had no idea if he was developing feelings like she was. Right now, all she felt was an uneasy sensation in her stomach.

The remainder of the day passed in a blur of activity, including fabric approvals and staff reference checks. By late afternoon, Isabella found herself mentally exhausted but satisfied with the day's progress.

As the workday ended and the construction crew began to leave, Isabella took a final walk through the property, noted the day's accomplishments, and set her priorities for the next morning. The inn was shifting from a construction site into a coherent building, with finished spaces starting to outnumber those still under renovation.

She found Thomas in his makeshift workshop set up in what would become the storage room, carefully restoring an original newel post from the main staircase. His focus was complete, and his hands moved with the practiced precision of someone who had spent decades mastering his craft. Isabella paused in the doorway, watched him work for a moment, and then announced her presence. There was something compelling about observing how absorbed he was in the task, the reverence with which he handled the historic wood, restoring it to its original beauty with patient, skilled effort.

"That's coming along beautifully," she finally said, stepping into the room.

He looked up and smiled. "It's responding well to restoration. The wood is sound underneath years of paint and neglect."

"Rather like the inn itself," she said, walking over to look at his work more closely.

"Exactly like that," Thomas said. "Good bones, just needing the right care to reveal its true character again."

Isabella ran her finger lightly over the partially restored newel post, feeling the smooth sections he had already refinished. "I've been thinking about what you told me," she said quietly, and a little more spontaneously than she had intended. "About why you ended things between us all those years ago."

Thomas set down his tools to give his full attention.

"And, well, I understand why you made the choice you did," she continued, meeting his gaze. "Accepting responsibility for your child, being present for Emma - those were all honorable decisions, and I would have expected nothing less from you even back then."

"Well, thank you for saying that," he said, looking both relieved and still regretful. "Though I wish I'd been honest with you at the time."

She nodded. "The truth would have been painful but less confusing than believing that what we had meant nothing to you."

"It meant everything," Thomas said softly. "Leaving you was the hardest decision I ever made in my life."

The simple honesty of the statement hung in the air between them.

"So where does that leave us now?" Isabella asked, the directness of her question surprising both of them.

Thomas thought for a moment before responding. "Well, that depends on what you want, Isabella.

We've both lived full lives in the years since. We're different people than we were then, but I've come to care for you again - or maybe still - in ways that definitely go beyond this professional collaboration."

The admission touched Isabella. It reflected the same consideration he always had when he approached his restorations.

"I've developed feelings for you, too," she said. "But I'm cautious. We're in the midst of an important project, one that matters a lot to both of us, and complications could certainly jeopardize that."

"I understand," Thomas nodded. "The inn deserves our best work, no matter what's going on in our personal lives."

"And yet," Isabella continued, "I definitely don't want to ignore what's happening here either. Maybe we could take our time, be mindful of our professional responsibilities, but remain open to the possibility of something more."

A smile spread across his face, warming his blue eyes. "I'd like that very much."

There were no dramatic declarations or impulsive actions, just two mature adults trying to acknowledge their past and present at the same time.

"I should go," Isabella said finally. "Early meeting tomorrow with the landscape designer."

"Of course," Thomas said. "Though before you

go, would you like to have dinner with me Friday night? Not to discuss work - just dinner."

"I'd like that," she said with a smile. "Where should we meet?"

"Let me surprise you," he said. "I know a place I think you'll enjoy."

As Isabella drove home, she felt a sense of lightness that had been absent in recent years. The conversation had been brief but significant. She wondered what would come of this second chance at a relationship with Thomas. It was a little terrifying, but worth the risk.

Friday evening arrived with the most perfect early autumn weather. Clear skies, a gentle breeze, and temperatures mild enough in the Lowcountry to be comfortable for outdoor dining. Isabella carefully dressed for her dinner with Thomas, selecting a simple blue linen dress that complemented her coloring without looking overly formal.

When he arrived precisely at seven, he looked handsome in his khakis and sport coat, his salt-and-pepper hair slightly tamed from his usual workday style. It reminded her of their much younger days, when he would pick her up for a date.

"You look beautiful," he said.

"Thank you," she replied, accepting the compliment. "You clean up pretty well yourself, Thomas Langley."

He drove them not to one of the island's restaurants she had expected, but to a small marina on the western shore. A modest sailboat awaited them.

"Dinner on the water?" she asked, pleasantly surprised.

"If that's okay." He nodded. "It's the perfect evening for sailing, and there's a cove I thought you might enjoy. Nothing fancy, just simple food in a beautiful setting. If that's—"

"Well, it sounds wonderful," Isabella assured him.

The sailboat proved to be Thomas's own, a well-maintained vessel, as any of his personal belongings would be. He handled it with practiced ease, navigating out of the marina and into the open water beyond, raising the sails to catch the gentle breeze.

"I didn't know you sailed," Isabella said, as they glided smoothly across the water, the island's shoreline receding behind them.

"Oh, it's been a passion since just after college, though I didn't have much time for it when Emma was young. But these past few years, I've rediscovered the pleasure of being on the water."

Isabella found herself enjoying the peaceful movement of the boat and the opportunity to see Thomas in a different context - relaxed, engaged with something he clearly loved. They talked easily as they sailed, their conversation flowing naturally between observations about the beauty of the coastline and personal topics, like books they'd enjoyed recently, places they'd traveled since college, and experiences that had shaped them over the years.

After about forty minutes of sailing, he guided the boat into a sheltered cove surrounded by marsh grass and ancient oaks.

"This is breathtaking," Isabella said.

"One of my favorite spots," he agreed as he dropped anchor. "Feels removed from everything, but it's only a short sail from the marina."

From a small cabin below deck, he carried up an insulated basket with their dinner - local specialties like shrimp caught that morning, fresh bread from the island bakery, and seasonal vegetables from the farmer's market that he'd cooked himself at home. A bottle of white wine completed the simple yet thoughtful meal.

They dined as the sun set, watching the spectacular colors across the sky reflect off the water around them. They continued talking, and the conversation flowed easily, as if the thirty years hadn't passed since their college relationship ended.

"So, when did you know you definitely wanted to focus on historical restoration? You were studying architectural design in college with plans for building new construction."

Thomas wiped his mouth. "It evolved gradually after I came back to the island. I started with small renovation projects while Emma was young, you know, work that I could schedule around her needs. And then I realized I had a certain sensitivity to the character of these old buildings." He smiled slightly. "Of course, my father's influence. He treated these historic properties with such respect."

"Well, it suits you," she said. "The patience, the attention to detail, the respect for history."

"What about you? Corporate hotel management is definitely different from restoring a historic inn. What made you decide to make that change?"

Isabella looked out over the darkening water, gathering her thoughts.

"I had achieved everything I set out to accomplish professionally. I had all the titles, the responsibilities, and the respect of my peers, but I always felt like something was missing. I was maintaining other people's visions, but never creating my own." She looked back at Thomas. "When the opportunity to purchase the inn appeared, it felt like the right moment to just build something that truly reflected my values and not some corporate list of priorities."

"And has it met your expectations?" he asked. "The inn project, I mean."

"Oh, it exceeded them," she said. "Not just the renovation, although that's been very satisfying so far, but the connections that I've made here with the community and the building's history and the people who share my vision." She looked at him directly. "And with you."

There was a quiet moment of intimacy between them. Thomas reached across the small table between them and took her hand.

"I never expected to find you again," he said softly. "Certainly not here, not like this. It feels like a second chance I don't deserve, but I'm very grateful for."

"Well, maybe we both needed the years between," she said, "to become the people who could appreciate this opportunity."

The feeling of his hand in hers felt so familiar, yet so new.

He nodded, his thumb tracing gentle patterns across her knuckles. "Wise as always, Isabella Montgomery."

As darkness settled around them completely, stars emerged from the sky. They moved to sit side by side on the boat's cushioned bench. The evening had cooled a bit, and Thomas draped a light blanket around Isabella's shoulders, his arm remaining comfortably behind her.

They sat in silence for a bit, watching the moon rise over the marsh, its silver light creating a magical quality. The moment felt both new and familiar—echoes of their younger selves, yet deepened by life experiences that had shaped them in the intervening years.

"I guess we should head back soon," Thomas said eventually, although he made no immediate move to raise the anchor. "The tide will be turning."

Isabella hummed, equally reluctant to end their evening. "This has been lovely. Thank you for sharing it with me."

He turned slightly to face her, his expression visible in the moonlight. "Thank you for being willing to explore whatever this is becoming between us. I know it's complicated - our history and the renovation and all the island community watching our every move."

She smiled. "Life is complicated, but that doesn't mean we should avoid all connections that might be meaningful."

"You sound like my daughter," Thomas said. "She said almost the same thing to me recently."

"Smart woman, your daughter. Must take after her father."

"And her mother," Thomas added honestly. "Sarah was very insightful about people and relationships."

As they prepared to return to the marina, raising anchor and readying the sails, Isabella found herself thinking about the evening's significance. It hadn't been dramatic or flashy, but rather just an exploration of what could happen between the two of them. Thomas had struck a careful balance— romantic without being overwhelming.

Back at the marina, he secured the boat and walked her to her car.

"Thank you again for a wonderful evening," Isabella said. "It was perfect."

"I'm glad. Perhaps we could do it again sometime. There are other beautiful spots around the island I'd love to show you."

"I'd like that very much."

They stood close together in the quiet marina, the moment holding potential for further connection. Gently, Thomas leaned forward, his hand lightly touching her cheek as he kissed her. The contact was soft and brief, but held so many memories at the same time.

When they parted, she felt a sense of rightness that had been absent in her life for longer than she cared to think about. This was not the breathless excitement of youthful romance, but something more profound—a connection grounded in respect and shared values.

"Good night, Isabella," Thomas said softly.

"Good night, Thomas."

CHAPTER 15

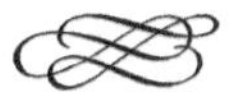

The weekend passed in a golden haze. Saturday morning texts that made her smile over her coffee. A quiet dinner Sunday evening at the Waterfront Restaurant on the mainland, where they had talked until the staff started stacking chairs around them. Thomas had kissed her good night in her cottage doorway, his hand cradling her face with such tenderness that she leaned into it like a flower turning toward the sun.

Now, Monday morning found Isabella alone in the inn's library, the early light streaming through the windows that Thomas's crew had painstakingly restored. She sat at the antique desk she'd claimed as her temporary workspace, her laptop open to a spreadsheet of vendor invoices, trying to focus on details that would transform the inn into a beautiful business.

Her email chimed, a slight sound that would later feel like the first rumble of an earthquake. The sender's name made her pause, coffee cup halfway to her lips. Claire Rousseau, CEO, Rousseau International Hotels.

It wasn't the first time she'd seen an email with those words, but she had carefully avoided it. Now, as she sat in front of her computer, she had nowhere to go. She set down her coffee cup, her heart suddenly hammering in her chest.

She knew the name. Anyone who'd ever spent any time in luxury hospitality knew the name. Rousseau International wasn't just another hotel chain. It was the benchmark for historic property restoration throughout Europe. The company that had pioneered the concept of preserving architectural heritage while creating world-class guest experiences. She'd studied their properties in business school, used their case studies and presentations, and dreamed of working for them back when she still believed that corporate hospitality could be a meaningful occupation.

She clicked the email open, her hands unsteady.
Dear Ms. Montgomery,

Your work in luxury historic hospitality has gained recognition, especially your exceptional and innovative methods for balancing preservation with operational excellence. Your experience at Belmont Hotel Group showed a rare understanding of how historic properties can retain their soul while meeting modern standards, and this philosophy closely aligns with Rousseau International's mission.

We're expanding our European operations significantly over the next five years, acquiring and restoring landmark properties across France, Switzerland, Italy, and Spain. This expansion requires exceptional leadership - somebody who understands not just hotel management but the deeper responsibility of stewardship that comes with these historical properties.

We want to offer you the position of Vice President of European Operations, based in our Paris headquarters. This role would provide executive oversight of our entire European portfolio, which currently consists of twelve properties and is expected to expand to twenty within three years. You'd work directly with our board of directors, architectural consultants, and government preservation agencies to shape our expansion strategy and operational standards.

More importantly, you'd have the autonomy to implement your vision across multiple premier properties with resources and institutional support that few positions in our industry can offer. This isn't merely a management role—it's an opportunity to influence how an entire generation of historic European hotels approach the balance between preservation and hospitality.

I've attached the initial details of the compensation package, which I believe you'll find reflect both the importance of the role and our sincere desire to welcome you into the Rousseau family.

I understand you've recently started a personal project, which shows your dedication to hands-on restoration work. That entrepreneurial drive is exactly what we appreciate. However, I encourage you to consider whether your vision might have a bigger impact if applied to multiple landmark properties, each with its own story to tell.

Given the scope of the role and our expansion timeline, we need your decision within two weeks. I recognize this is a tight schedule, but securing the right leadership is essential for our plans, and we want someone in the position shortly after the first of the year. We are willing to be flexible about your transition if you accept.

I hope to hear from you very soon.

Warmest regards,

Claire Rousseau

Isabella stared at the screen, her breath shallow. She opened the attachment with trembling fingers.

The compensation package was absolutely staggering - more than double what she'd earned at her peak in corporate hospitality. Executive housing was located in the most exclusive part of Paris. Equity participation would make her a genuine stakeholder in the company's growth. A professional development budget that exceeded what most hotels spend on their entire management team. Four weeks' vacation and travel expenses for property visits across Europe.

Vice President of European Operations for Rousseau International.

It was the position she had fantasized about during those soul-crushing corporate meetings where bean counters dismissed her preservation proposals as too expensive. The role she had envisioned holding someday when she was stuck reviewing budget spreadsheets instead of walking through buildings that held centuries of stories.

The validation that everything she had learned, every compromise she made, and every political battle fought in corporate hospitality had been building toward something truly meaningful. She could do for a dozen historic European properties what she is doing for The Wexley Inn. She could establish standards, create templates, and demonstrate that preservation and profitability are not mutually exclusive. She could train a generation of hoteliers who understand that these buildings are not just assets, but responsibilities.

The vision struck her with such unexpected force. The Wexley Inn would open, succeed, and become exactly what she'd envisioned, but it would be one inn, one restored property on a small island off the South Carolina coast. A beautiful project, indeed, a meaningful accomplishment, but ultimately small.

What if she could do this ten times? Twenty? What if, instead of creating just one haven for travelers seeking a connection to history, she could build a network of them across Europe's most beautiful cities?

The thought felt simultaneously thrilling and treasonous.

She closed the laptop abruptly as if the email would contaminate her if she looked at it too long. Her hands were shaking. She pressed them against the desk's cool surface, trying to ground herself.

But this was her dream: The Wexley Inn - building something entirely her own, making decisions without corporate oversight, and creating a business that reflected her values without compromise. She'd walked away from security and status specifically to have this freedom. She'd poured her entire life savings into these walls, spent months learning about the Lowcountry history and island politics, and earned the trust of people like Maggie and Luella, who didn't give it easily.

And Thomas. Oh gosh, Thomas. She was falling in love with him, had maybe never stopped loving him, the feelings just buried under thirty years of other lives lived. The way he looked at her across the room made her feel seen in ways no one ever had. The careful way he restored the inn's architectural details mirrored the cautious way he seemed to be restoring the broken pieces of her heart.

She stood up quickly and walked to the window, looking out at the grounds where the workers were arriving for the day. The inn was almost done, the bones restored, the systems updated, the finishing touches underway. In just a few weeks, they would open the doors. Guests would sleep in these rooms and dine in that kitchen. They'd walk through the gardens she'd meticulously planned right down to the colors of the flowers. The building would live again, serve its purpose, and become a part of the island's fabric.

But the treacherous thought wouldn't leave her alone. One inn. Just one.

Someone would have that job. Why not her? Didn't she deserve it?

She pressed her forehead against the cool glass, watching Thomas's truck pull into the driveway. He got out, grabbed his tool belt from the cab, and said something to Wade that made the other man laugh. He moved with such easy confidence here, so entirely at home. This was his island, after all, his community, his territory, in ways that it might never be hers, no matter how many ladies' club luncheons she attended or how graciously Maggie championed her.

What if something happened to the inn? What if Grayson found some way to sabotage it, despite the review board approval? What if she couldn't make the business successful in a seasonal market with a limited local population?

What if - and this fear felt almost too disloyal to acknowledge - what if she'd made a terrible mistake putting all of her eggs in this one beautiful, fragile basket?

The European job was about security, not just financial security, although that mattered a lot. It was also about professional security and the validation that she belonged in the industry at the highest level. If she failed at The Wexley Inn, she'd become a cautionary tale, the corporate executive who couldn't quite succeed as an entrepreneur. But if she accepted the Rousseau position, she'd be seen as a visionary who learned from hands-on restoration work to lead strategic expansion. She could frame it that way. The inn was just a learning experience, a proof of concept, a stepping stone to something bigger. It was not a failure but a successful experiment that taught her what she needed to operate at true scale.

The rationalization tasted bitter even as she formed it. Isabella pulled out her phone and looked at Thomas's contact information. She should tell him. They had just agreed to explore this relationship carefully, honestly. Keeping something this important a secret was exactly the kind of dishonesty that would destroy trust.

But what would she even say? *I got offered my dream job, and I'm considering leaving even though we just decided to try dating again.* It sounded absurd, it sounded cruel, and it sounded exactly like she was already looking for an exit before they even started.

Besides, she hadn't even decided anything. This was just an email, an offer to consider. She was keeping her options open. That didn't mean she was planning to leave. Smart business people always explore opportunities. They always stayed aware of their market value and always maintained flexibility. She would think about it, research the company, review the package again, and consider any implications. This wasn't dishonesty; it was just due diligence.

The guilt that twisted through her chest suggested otherwise, but Isabella pushed it down. She closed the email app on her phone, sat up straight, and prepared to greet Thomas with a smile that would reveal nothing about the turmoil churning beneath her carefully maintained surface.

Two weeks. She had two whole weeks to decide whether to choose the dream she'd built with her own hands or the dream that someone else was offering her on a silver platter. She told herself she hadn't already begun to lean toward the latter, and she almost believed it.

Thomas took his entire crew to Charleston that afternoon. A specialty lumber supplier had finally found the period-appropriate trim molding for the veranda restoration, and he wanted to personally inspect it before committing to the purchase. He had kissed Isabella goodbye that morning in the inn's driveway, a brief touch of the lips that sent warmth through her that lingered hours later.

Should be back by four, he had said, his hand

lingering on her waist. *Then we'll go for those final paint selections.*

Perfect, she'd replied and watched the truck disappear down the oak-lined driveway.

Now it was just past two, and she was alone at the inn except for the kitchen appliance installation crew working in the back. She'd been reviewing the staff training schedule she'd developed, which included orientation, safety procedures, guest service standards, and the careful balance of professionalism and warmth she wanted to define the inn's culture.

Then she heard the front door open.

"Hello, Isabella."

She recognized Grayson Williams' voice immediately, the smooth Carolina drawl that reminded her of poison honey. Her jaw tightened as she set her pen down and walked to the entrance hall.

He stood in the center of the restored space, expensive shoes gleaming on the finished floor, looking around with an appraising eye that made her skin crawl. He wore perfectly tailored khakis and a crisp white button-down with his silver hair styled in a casual perfection that had required significant effort to achieve. Every inch of him screamed old money and older entitlement.

"Grayson," she said, keeping her voice neutral. "I don't recall us having an appointment scheduled."

"No appointment necessary among neighbors, surely." His smile was all practiced charm and no warmth. "I was in the area, had a meeting with the Historical Society board, and I thought I'd stop by to see the progress firsthand. The transformation is quite remarkable. Thomas and his crew have done exceptional work."

The compliment felt like a trap. Isabella didn't move from her position in the doorway and didn't invite him further inside.

"Thanks. As you can see, though, we're in the final phases, and if there's something specific you need to discuss…"

"Actually, there is," Grayson said, interrupting her as he walked deeper into the hall, trailing his fingers along the restored wainscoting.

The building was hers, and his presumption of touching anything felt very violating.

"I wanted to discuss a matter that's come to my attention. As a member of the Architectural Review Board, I felt it was only fair to give you advance warning before it becomes *official*."

The pause before the final word was deliberate, ominous. Isabella's stomach tightened.

"What are you talking about?"

"Well, the county has received several community concerns about the inn's permits," he said casually while examining the crown molding restoration, as if they were just talking about the weather. "Nothing terribly specific, you understand, but questions about the historical accuracy of certain modifications, safety compliance in the kitchen renovation, environmental impact of the updated septic system - the usual sorts of concerns that pop up when outsiders…" He paused, letting the word settle. "… undertake major renovations without a full understanding of local standards and expectations."

Outsiders. There it was. The reminder that, despite months of work, despite her friendship with Maggie and attending Ladies Club meetings, despite everything, she would always be someone who didn't truly belong here.

"Our permits were approved months ago," Isabella said, maintaining a steady voice even though rage was brewing in her chest. "Everything we've done has adhered to the approved plans exactly. Thomas has documented every modification, material choice, structural decision, and the Review Board approved all of it."

"Oh, I'm certain you followed the letter of the law," Grayson said, turning to face her directly. His eyes were cold despite the pleasant tone. "But when community members raise concerns, especially long-time residents with deep ties to this island, the county is obligated to conduct a formal review hearing. And these processes can be quite time-consuming, usually at least three to four months for resolution, sometimes longer if the concerns prove substantial or appeals are filed."

Three to four months?

The words hit like a physical blow, pushing them way past Christmas, past the holiday season when low country tourism peaked, past the carefully planned grand opening in December. Her loan had a milestone-based funding tied to the opening timeline. Delays would trigger penalty rates or even allow the bank to call the loan entirely. Her staff hiring was contingent on specific start dates. Vendor contracts had delivery windows and cancellation fees. The marketing campaign Emma had designed was built around the December 15th opening. Everything - the entire careful house of cards that she'd constructed - could collapse if the timeline were disrupted.

"And who filed these concerns?" Isabella managed to keep her voice steady, but her hands clenched at her sides.

"Complaints are always anonymous, as is permitted under the county procedure." Grayson's expression was maddeningly neutral, almost fake sympathetic, but she knew he was loving every bit of this. "The regulations are designed to protect community members who might fear retaliation for raising legitimate concerns. I'm sure you understand the principle, even if the application is inconvenient."

Anonymous, of course. No one to confront, no way to address the concerns directly, just vague allegations that would require months of bureaucratic red tape to resolve. It was brilliant, really—weaponizing the community protection regulations to destroy a person who had no community protection of her own.

"I wouldn't worry too much," Grayson said, pulling his wallet from his pocket and taking out his business card, placing it on the refinished hall table. "These things often resolve themselves quite naturally once the right people on the island feel reassured about the property's future direction. So one's concerns about, shall we say, compatibility with island values are adequately addressed."

There it was. The threat was barely veiled, the extortion dressed up in concerned community language.

Isabella felt her pulse pounding in her ears. This man - this entitled, manipulative man who saw historic buildings as nothing more than demolition opportunities and profit margins - was going to destroy months of hard work, hundreds of thousands of dollars, and her entire dream because she refused to sell to him.

"And how," she said quietly, carefully controlling each word, "would those community concerns be *'adequately addressed,'* Grayson?"

His smile widened slightly, satisfied that she'd asked the question.

"Well, that really depends on which direction you decide to take the property. My investment group's offer still stands, of course. In fact, considering how much you've already accomplished and the value you've added through your restoration efforts, we're willing to significantly increase our original offer. You could walk away from this project with a substantial profit and avoid the headaches that come with managing a property like this in a small, insular community. As you know, they don't always welcome outsiders with open arms."

The emphasis on *outsiders*. Again. The reminder that she would always be exactly that, no matter how hard she worked or how carefully she navigated island politics.

"I'm not selling." The words came out flat, final.

"Well, then, I wish you the very best navigating

the review process." His tone turned cooler, the pretense of neighborly concern dropping away. "Though I should mention - purely as a courtesy, you understand - these hearings can become quite expensive. Legal representation doesn't come cheap in these specialized areas like historic preservation law. Expert witnesses to refute community concerns can run tens of thousands of dollars, and the appeals procedures, should the initial review not go in your favor, add additional costs. Not to mention the opportunity costs of a delayed opening."

He moved toward the door and then paused as if an afterthought had just occurred to him.

"And of course, there's also the matter of your lender. Banks become really nervous when the community substantially opposes a project. They might even have questions about the property's ultimate viability or whether the local market will support an operation facing such significant resistance. Your loan terms likely have provisions addressing such contingencies, I would think. You know, performance clauses, timeline requirements, that sort of thing. You might want to review those carefully."

He was threatening her financing directly now, not even bothering to pretend otherwise, threatening to drag her through bureaucratic hell and financial ruin until she was forced to sell at whatever price he deigned to offer.

Isabella opened the front door, her hand gripping the knob so tightly that her knuckles turned white. "Thanks for the warning, Grayson. I'll be sure to have my attorney review any official complaints the county receives, and I will ensure Thomas documents every single decision we've made with such thoroughness that any review process will be very straightforward. Professional representation is so important in these matters."

He walked to the door, pausing directly in front of her. Up close, she could smell his cologne. Expensive. Offensive.

"You know, Isabella, I've been developing property on this island for many years. I've seen people like you before - the idealists who think passion and good intentions could overcome economic reality and political complexity - but some battles aren't worth fighting. Pride is an expensive luxury. Sometimes the smart choice, the actual mature choice, is to recognize when you're outmatched and accept the generous offer that allows you to move on to projects with fewer, shall we say, complications."

He walked down the porch steps and then turned back.

"Oh, one more thing, just as friendly advice, of

course. You might want to carefully consider how much Thomas's support is genuinely worth in a situation like this. He's well-respected, for sure, but his influence has limitations, especially with county-level bureaucracy. His own business reputation could suffer if he's closely tied to a project that ultimately fails. Loyalty is a admirable trait, but I'd really hate to see him caught in the fallout of your overreach."

Now, a threat to Thomas. The suggestion that standing by her could damage him. It made something cold settle in Isabella's chest.

She didn't respond and just stood there watching as Grayson got into his sleek Mercedes and drove away, leaving her trembling with rage and fear on the porch that she'd given everything to restore.

After he left, she stood there in the entrance hall, her hands shaking. She'd been monumentally, childishly naive to think Grayson would accept defeat. After the review board approved her plans, men like him didn't give up. They just changed tactics, probed for weaknesses, and waited for opportunities to strike.

She was vulnerable. Dear God, she was so vulnerable. She'd put every penny of her savings into this project. She'd staked her whole professional reputation on making it succeed. She'd allowed herself to put down roots and to make friends, to fall in love with a man and a place and a vision of a future that suddenly felt as fragile as the old window glass Thomas's crew had carefully preserved.

Her phone felt so heavy in her hand as she pulled it out to call Thomas. She needed to tell him about the threat because she would need his help navigating the island's politics. She didn't fully understand them, even now, but Grayson's parting words echoed in her mind. The suggestion that Thomas's reputation could be damaged just by being associated with her and the inn?

What if standing by her cost him? What if helping her fight these complaints made him look unprofessional or too personally involved? His business depended on his relationships with property owners across the island. He had a reputation as an honest person who played by the rules and maintained good standing with county officials and review boards.

She couldn't be the reason his reputation was damaged. She couldn't drag him into her mess.

But she also couldn't handle this alone. That admission made it feel like defeat, but it was true. She'd spent her career navigating corporate politics, managing all kinds of bureaucratic hierarchies, and leveraging institutional power to get things done, but this was different. This was a small island where thirty years of accumulated relationships mattered more than any corporate organizational chart.

This was Thomas's territory, not hers. She needed him.

She hit his contact, her hands still trembling.

"Anonymous complaints."

Thomas's voice came through the phone, but she could hear anger simmering underneath his calm exterior.

"Tell me exactly what he said, Isabella. Every word you can remember."

She was back at her cottage now, unable to stay at the inn after Grayson left. The space had felt violated, contaminated by his presence and his threats. She'd sent the kitchen crew home early, locked up, and driven to her rental with hands that wouldn't stop shaking on the steering wheel.

Now she paced the small living room, too upset to sit, and recounted the conversation in detail.

Thomas listened without interrupting. She imagined him taking notes in that methodical way he approached every problem.

"Three to four months," she finished, her voice breaking slightly. "That pushes us past the holidays, past the opening date, past everything. The loan terms, Thomas. There are milestone requirements tied to that timeline. Performance clauses. If we can't open by December 31st, the bank can call the entire loan or increase the rates to the point where the project becomes unviable financially. I would lose everything."

Silence on the other end. She could hear him breathing, could imagine his jaw tight.

"Son of a—" he started, and then stopped himself. There was such venom that it almost made her smile despite everything. "He's done this before. Tried to create bureaucratic nightmares until developers gave up and sold. But he's never been this blatant, never this targeted."

"So what do I do?" The question came out smaller than she intended. She hated that pleading note in her voice, hated feeling so helpless. "I can hire attorneys and fight the complaints formally, but it all takes time we don't have. And money I can't afford to spend on legal battles when I need every penny for operations."

"All right." Thomas's voice shifted, adopting that

calm, problem-solving tone she recognized from when he faced technical or complex challenges. "Here's what we're going to do. First, we don't respond to any official communications from the county until we've looked at them together. Don't acknowledge the complaints. Don't try to address them directly. We need to see exactly what's been filed before we can craft our response."

"Okay."

"Second, I'm going to look into this. I have relationships with people at the county office. Bill Patterson handles permits, and he's an honest guy. I need to understand what's actually been filed, who's behind it, and what the real exposure is."

"But if you ask questions, won't that—" She hesitated, Grayson's words about damaging Thomas's reputation echoing in her mind. "Won't that make you look too personally involved? I don't want to drag you into…"

"Isabella." He cut her off gently. "I'm involved. This is my project, too, and I've been navigating these island politics my whole life. I know how to have a quiet conversation that doesn't create exposure for either of us."

"And you're sure?"

"Yes, I'm sure. Grayson uses intimidation, making problems seem so overwhelming that people break down under the perceived pressure, but his actual power is limited. These anonymous complaints might sound threatening, but there are ways to handle them that won't require months of hearings or costly legal fights. I need to understand what we're really up against first."

Some of the tension in Isabella's chest eased slightly. He knew this world in ways she didn't. He understood the unspoken rules, the pressure points, and the ways to navigate bureaucracy that weren't in any manual.

"So what should I do in the meantime?"

"Get some rest. Don't let this consume you tonight. Tomorrow, I'll start making the calls, having the conversations. By the end of the day, I'll have a clear picture of what we're actually dealing with."

"Thomas." She paused, not sure what she wanted to say. *Thank you* felt inadequate. *I'm scared* felt too raw. *What if we can't fix this* felt too defeatist. "I'm happy you're here."

She heard him exhale softly.

"I'm not going anywhere, Isabella. We're going to figure this out together."

After they hung up, she felt somewhat steadier, a little less like she was drowning. Thomas would help. He would navigate the politics, use his relationships, and find solutions that she couldn't see from her position.

But what she didn't know and what she couldn't see was exactly what he meant by *"having conversations"* and *"addressing the complaints."*

Thomas Langley's instinct to protect the people he loved from burdens was as natural as breathing and just as unconscious, and she didn't know exactly what he meant by those words.

Thomas hung up the phone and immediately started looking through his contacts, his jaw set in determination. Bill Patterson at the county office, Gerald Stewart at the bank, Robert Henderson, who chaired the Architectural Review Board. He would fix this. He'd use every relationship, every favor owed, every ounce of political capital he'd built over three decades. He'd protect Isabella's dream and her investment and future, whatever it took.

The small voice in his head whispered that he was repeating the exact pattern that had destroyed them thirty years ago - making decisions for her rather than with her, prioritizing protection over partnership.

He pushed all of that firmly aside. This was

different. She had asked for help. He was providing it. He wasn't controlling anything. He was being a good partner. Wasn't he?

Thomas arrived at the county planning office before most of the staff, parking in the nearly empty lot. He'd been awake since four, lying in bed, staring at the ceiling, mentally rehearsing conversations he needed to have. By the time dawn broke, he had showered, made coffee that went cold while he looked at his notes, and then driven to the mainland with a sense of grim purpose.

Bill Patterson was just unlocking his office door when Thomas appeared in the hallway. Bill was mid-fifties, soft around the middle in the way that men who spent their days behind desks were, and had thin, sandy hair and reading glasses that were perpetually perched on the top of his head. They'd known each other for twenty-five years, served on the Historical Preservation Committee together, coached opposing Little League teams when their kids were young, and shared countless Thursday morning breakfasts at the diner where local contractors and county officials conducted the real business of building permits over eggs and grits.

"Thomas." Bill's expression held a mixture of warmth and discomfort as he stepped into his office. "I wondered when you'd be coming by."

"So there are complaints filed about The Wexley Inn permits." It wasn't a question.

Bill sighed and set his coffee and briefcase down on his desk. "Three anonymous complaints filed Monday afternoon, right before the close of business. There are historical accuracy concerns, questions about safety compliance in the kitchen modernization, and environmental impact issues with the septic system upgrades. You know, all vague enough that they technically require review, but all specific enough that we can't dismiss them out of hand."

"Let me see them."

Bill hesitated and then pulled up a file on his computer screen. "Thomas, you know I shouldn't—"

"Bill?" He interrupted. "We've known each other for two and a half decades. You were at Sarah's funeral. You sent Emma a graduation gift when she finished college. We've done business together long enough to know that I'm not asking you casually." Thomas leaned against the doorframe, his voice quiet but firm. "Let me see the complaints."

After a long pause, Bill printed three pages and handed them over. Thomas read through them slowly, his jaw tightening with each paragraph. The complaints were skillfully written, clearly authored by someone who knew exactly which buttons to press.

They expressed concerns about "deviation from approved historical preservation standards" without specifying the nature of those deviations. They questioned whether "modern commercial kitchen equipment complies with historical character requirements" without identifying the specific requirements. They also raised the issue of "potential environmental impact from increased wastewater volume" without providing any supporting data regarding the actual impact.

Vague enough that they would be very hard to disprove, but specific enough to trigger mandatory review processes - and anonymous enough that there was no one to confront and no way to address concerns directly.

"This has Grayson Williams written all over it," Thomas said flatly.

"I can't comment on who filed anonymous complaints." Bill's tone was neutral, but his expression said everything.

"Bill, we both know who benefits from delaying The Wexley Inn opening, and we both know who's been trying to get that property for years. The complaints are anonymous, but the motivation isn't."

Bill ran his hand through his thinning hair, a gesture Thomas easily recognized from countless committee meetings where Bill was caught between regulations and common sense. "What do you want me to tell you, Thomas? The complaints meet the technical requirements for review. They raise legitimate questions. Even if we both suspect the motivation is less than pure, I can't just ignore them because we think we know who filed them."

"I'm not asking you to ignore them," Thomas said, sitting down across from Bill's desk. "I'm asking what it would take to expedite the review process, to address them quickly without months of hearings that serve no purpose except harassment."

Bill was quiet for a moment, staring at his computer screen. When he spoke, his voice was lower and more careful. "Independent expert verification would help. Updated safety certifications, environmental impact assessment from a licensed engineer, all of which take time and money. And you know as well as I do that even without documentation, the formal hearing process has minimum time frames built in. We're looking at six weeks minimum, more than likely two to three months."

"Or?" Thomas heard the agitation in Bill's voice.

"Or," Bill looked up, meeting Thomas's eyes directly, "a letter of assurance from a recognized island historical expert—someone whose professional reputation the review board trusts implicitly, someone who could personally vouch for the project's adherence to preservation standards and safety requirements. It would carry significant weight with the board and could potentially allow us to expedite the review considerably."

Understanding settled in Thomas's stomach. "You're talking about me."

"If you were willing to formally vouch for the historical accuracy and the safety of the renovation - stake your professional reputation on it - that would address most of the concerns. It wouldn't eliminate a hearing entirely, but it could shorten the process to just a few weeks instead of months."

"And what if something goes wrong? If there are problems down the line that the complaints were supposedly warning about?"

Bill's expression was sympathetic, but firm. "Well, then your reputation is on the line, along with the property owner's. You'd be personally vouching for the work, Thomas. It's not a decision to make lightly. If legitimate issues do come up later - like structural problems, environmental damage - well, you'd be implicated as the expert who told everyone it was fine. You could be looking at legal problems if it got bad enough."

Thomas thought about the inn, about the months of work, about every decision documented and every modification approved. He thought about Isabella's voice when she had called him yesterday, the fear beneath her composed exterior. He thought about Grayson Williams and his smug certainty that he could destroy this project using bureaucratic harassment.

"Draft the letter," Thomas said. "I'll sign it. But draft it today. I'll come back this afternoon to sign it."

Bill looked at him for a long moment. "You sure are putting a lot on the line for a client."

"She's not just a client." The words came out more revealing than Thomas meant, but he didn't take them back.

Something changed in Bill's expression, an understanding. "All right. I'll have it ready by two o'clock."

Gerald Stewart looked uncomfortable when Thomas asked for a private meeting. They had known each other even longer than Thomas had known Bill. Gerald's father and Thomas's father had been friends. They fished together and sat on the church board before the Old Island Church was destroyed by the hurricane of '89. Thomas and Gerald grew up swimming in the same creeks, dating girls from the same high school, and building their businesses in parallel as they both settled into adult lives on the island they loved.

But now Gerald sat behind his polished desk in the corner office with its view of the marina, his ruddy face creased with concern, his banker's caution warring with decades of friendship.

"Thomas, I cannot discuss a client's financial details. You know that. There are privacy regulations and fiduciary responsibility."

"Gerald, we both know Grayson Williams is trying to sabotage Isabella's project. All those anonymous complaints to the county are designed to trigger concerns about loan viability, and I need to know what her actual exposure is so I can help her get through this without destroying her financially."

Gerald was quiet for a long moment, his fingers drumming on the desk.

"The renovation loan has milestone-based funding with strict timeline requirements," Gerald finally said, keeping his voice low. "If the inn doesn't open by December 31st, doesn't start generating actual revenue as projected, then technically the bank has the right to call the loan entirely or significantly change the terms. I mean, we're talking about interest rate hikes that could make the project completely unviable. Isabella's personal guarantee covers any shortfall between the property value and the outstanding loan amount."

Thomas felt like ice was coursing through his veins. "Which means if Grayson succeeds in delaying the opening past the deadline, she doesn't just lose her business, she loses everything. Her retirement savings, her investment, and maybe her personal assets."

"Well, that's the worst-case scenario, but yes," Gerald said, looking pained. "Thomas, I like Isabella a lot. She's smart, though. She's doing everything right. But the bank has obligations to our investors, our regulatory oversight, and if a property faces community opposition, if there are questions about permit compliance or anything else, if the timeline slips significantly…well, we have to protect our position."

"What would it take to waive those timeline requirements, to give her more flexibility if the delays happen through no fault of her own?"

Gerald's expression shifted. "A co-signer with sufficient assets and established local ties. Somebody that the bank trusts to ensure the project will be completed, even with setbacks. Somebody whose own reputation and financial stability would also be at stake."

The implication was clear. Thomas felt the trap closing. Saw exactly where this was headed, but Isabella's terrified voice on the phone—*I'd lose every-thing*—echoed in his mind.

"What are we talking about in terms of exposure?"

"Roughly $350,000 if the loan were called at the current balance. Less if the property sells quickly, more if it doesn't, or if delays cause more deteriora-tion. But Thomas, you'd be personally liable for—"

"I understand what I'd be liable for." His voice was steady, even though his gut was churning.

$350,000. It was more than he had in liquid assets, but his business was solid. His properties were paid off. His reputation would support additional credit if needed. He could cover it. It would hurt. He might require selling assets he'd planned to leave to Emma, but he could do it.

"Draft the paperwork, Gerald. I'll co-sign her loan."

"Thomas…" Gerald leaned forward, his expres-sion pleading. "Think about this carefully. You're betting everything - your business, your savings, your financial security, Emma's future - on a project you don't even control, on an uncertain timeline, in support of somebody you've known for what, a few months? Look, I understand you're…whatever… involved with Isabella, but mixing personal feelings with finances this significant—"

"I'm not mixing anything. This is good business. The inn is sound, the renovation is top quality, and the only risk is this bureaucratic harassment from a developer with a grudge. Once we get past Grayson's complaints, the project will succeed."

"But if it doesn't—"

"It will." Thomas stood, the decision made. "Draft the paperwork. I'll come by tomorrow morning to sign it."

Gerald watched him with an expression that looked like a mixture of admiration and concern. "And you're sure about this?"

"Totally." Thomas met his old friend's eyes. "Need anything else from me?"

"Just your sanity," Gerald muttered, "but apparently you've already lost that."

CHAPTER 17

Thomas met Robert Henderson in the club's nearly empty dining room, where the Thursday morning breakfast crowd had thinned to just a few retired members lingering over coffee and newspapers. Robert, a seventy-two-year-old with silver hair, was a retired architect who had chaired the Architectural Review Board for fifteen years, showing a mix of expertise and stubborn integrity. Thomas respected Robert. He had also known Thomas's father and encouraged him to pursue architecture in college. He even hired Thomas for his first major restoration project when Thomas was just twenty-five and trying to build his business. So their relationship went beyond professional courtesy. Robert was as close to a mentor as Thomas had found after his father died.

"Morning, Thomas." Robert's voice remained just as strong despite his age, carrying the crisp diction of someone who'd grown up in Charleston. "You sounded urgent on the phone. Problems with Wexley Inn?"

Thomas slid into the booth across from him, waving off the server who approached with coffee. "I'm just going to get to the point. Grayson Williams is filing anonymous complaints about the inn's permits. All kinds of crap. Historical accuracy concerns, safety questions, environmental stuff - all conveniently vague enough but technically requiring formal review."

Robert's expression darkened. "That son of a gun… That man has done more to damage this island's architectural character than any developer in fifty years, building all these commercial monstrosities. Every historic property he gets his hands on is demolished for some horrible building."

"Well, the complaints are designed to delay opening past the holiday, trigger loan performance clauses, and force Isabella to sell at whatever price he offers. It's pure harassment. We both know it."

"You're probably right." Robert took a sip of his coffee. "But complaints are legally filed, Thomas. The board has to review them. I can't just dismiss them because we know Grayson's motivations."

"I'm not asking you to dismiss them." Thomas leaned forward, his voice low. "I'm asking that the review be conducted fairly and quickly. Isabella Montgomery has done everything right. She's hired the best experts. She's followed every guideline and exceeded all the preservation standards at every turn. This project deserves a fair shake, not to be destroyed by somebody who sees historic buildings as nothing more than obstacles to profit."

Robert studied him for a long moment, his sharp blue eyes missing nothing. "You're vouching for the project personally?"

"Yep. Completely. I've documented every decision and every modification, even every material choice. I'll stake my whole reputation on the quality and accuracy of this restoration."

"You're already staking your reputation." Robert's tone was gentle. "Bill Patterson called me yesterday, said you're signing a letter of assurance. That puts you in a vulnerable position if anything goes wrong."

"Nothing will go wrong. The work is solid."

"Well, the work may be solid, but you're putting a lot on the line for a client, Thomas. Or is she more than a client at this point?"

Thomas met his eyes. "She's not just a client."

Understanding crossed over Robert's weathered face. He looked concerned. "I see. Does she know you're doing this? Making all these guarantees, putting your reputation and finances at risk to protect her project?"

"She knows I'm helping navigate the complaints."

"That's not what I asked."

Thomas didn't answer.

Robert sighed, shaking his head slowly. "Thomas, I've known you since you were a kid. I watched you build this magnificent business from nothing, raise your daughter by yourself after Sarah died, and establish yourself as the finest restoration specialist in this whole area. You're one of the most honorable men I know, but you tend to try to protect people by making decisions for them rather than with them."

"This is different."

"Oh, is it? Or are you doing it again? What did you do thirty years ago? Deciding what's best for someone you love without giving them a say in the matter?"

His reference to Thomas's past with Isabella - which Robert knew something about, although not the whole story - made Thomas flinch.

"I'm fixing a problem," Thomas said quietly. "Using all the resources I have to address an unjust situation. That's not me just making decisions for her. That's me being supportive."

"Well, supporting her would be telling her about

the guarantees you're making and letting her decide whether she wants you taking on this level of risk on her behalf." Robert leaned back. "But you're not going to tell her, are you?"

Again, Thomas didn't answer.

"I'll expedite the review," Robert said after a long silence. "I'll make sure the process is fair and thorough, and I'll push for a reasonable timeline. But that's the best I can do within the board's regulations."

"That's all I'm asking. Thank you."

"Oh, don't thank me yet." Robert's tone turned grave. "Because if this goes sideways - if this project fails, and your relationship with Isabella implodes when she learns what you've done - you're going to have to live with the consequences of keeping her in the dark. And that's a burden I sure wouldn't want to carry."

Thomas sat alone in his workshop after his crew had left for the day, surrounded by his tools and half-finished projects. The familiar smell of wood shavings and linseed oil was usually comforting, but tonight it reminded him of all the careful work that could be undone by his good intentions gone wrong.

He had done it. He had signed Bill's letter of assurance, risking his professional reputation for the inn's compliance. He had signed Gerald's co-signer agreement, making himself personally liable for Isabella's loan if the bank called it in. And he had secured Robert's commitment to speed up the review process.

In two days, he had risked his reputation, his finances, and his political capital to protect Isabella's dream. He used every relationship, favor owed, and ounce of influence he'd built over thirty years on the island, yet he told her none of it. She knew he was "looking into" the complaints and having "conversations" with county officials. She didn't know he'd staked everything on protecting her, didn't realize that if this project failed, he would lose nearly as much as she would.

He convinced himself it was the right choice. She had asked for help, and he was providing it. She was already stressed about the complaints, without adding more worry about his financial risk. Why burden her with details that would only make her feel guilty or obligated? He was handling the problem before it could turn into her crisis. That was love, wasn't it? Protecting the people you cared about from burdens they didn't need to bear alone.

But Robert's words echoed in the quiet work-shop: *You tend to protect people by making decisions for them rather than with them.*

And Emma's voice from weeks ago: *You decided what was best for Isabella without asking. How is that different from what Sarah's parents did to you?*

Thomas pushed the thoughts away. This was different. He wasn't forcing Isabella to do anything. He was clearing obstacles for her, using his resources to solve a problem that threatened her dream. That was a partnership, not control. At least that was the rationalization he was giving himself.

He thought about calling her and telling her what he had done, explaining he'd co-signed her loan, that he'd put his reputation on paper vouching for the project. But what would he say? *I've risked everything to save your project without asking you if you wanted me to.* It would either sound patronizing or manip-ulative.

Besides, she'd probably get upset, would feel guilty about the risk he had taken, and feel under-mined, like he didn't trust her to handle her own challenges. Why had these things never occurred to him while he was signing papers all over town? Isabella had made it clear from the beginning that she wanted to build something on her own, make her own decisions without any oversight or interference.

No, it was better to just let her believe the complaints were being addressed through normal channels. It's better to let her focus on opening preparations without the stress of knowing how much he had put on the line. This wasn't about him.

Once the complaints were resolved, the review process completed, the inn opened successfully, and her loan was secure, maybe then he would tell her - when it was all settled and safe, when she could see it as a loving gesture instead of interference or control.

Yes, that was the right choice. The mature choice. The choice that protected both of them - both the project and their relationship.

He tried to convince himself of that as he locked up his workshop and drove home on the dark island roads, tried to ignore the still small voice whispering that secrets kept for someone's own good were still secrets, that decisions made to protect somebody without their knowledge were still decisions that usurped their agency, that the patterns we convinced ourselves we had outgrown had a way of coming back when fear made us forget the lessons we thought we had learned.

Isabella's phone rang at 9:15 in the morning, with the screen displaying an unfamiliar number that had a Paris country code. Thankfully, she was alone in the inn's library, supposedly reviewing finalization of staff training schedules but actually just staring at the same page for twenty minutes as her mind churned with worry about permit complaints, timeline delays, and whether she'd made a catastrophic mistake putting all of her money and time into this one project.

She almost didn't answer the phone. Her policy was always to let unknown international numbers go to voicemail, but when she saw it was Paris, she tapped her thumb to accept the call.

"Ms. Montgomery, this is Claire Rousseau. I hope I'm not calling at an inconvenient time."

The cultured French accent, warm and professional, sent a jolt through Isabella. She quickly stood up and stepped out onto the front porch, ensuring she could talk without the workers overhearing her. The morning was beautiful, calm, clear, and the kind of low country autumn day that made you understand why people had been living here on these islands for centuries.

"Not at all, Ms. Rousseau. Your email this week was very unexpected."

"Please call me Claire. I know it was unexpected, and we typically don't pursue executives who've left the industry, but Isabella, your work speaks for itself. I mean, twenty-five years of building programs that balanced profitability with preservation - you understand that luxury hospitality isn't just about all the amenities, but about creating meaningful connections between properties and guests. And that perspective is rare. It's exactly what Rousseau International needs."

They talked for twenty minutes, and Isabella found herself drawn in despite her better judgment. Claire wasn't like the corporate executives she'd worked with. She had a genuine passion beneath her polished professionalism, a fundamental understanding of what made historic property special.

Claire described Rousseau's portfolio with a level of knowledge that only comes from genuine care - the 18th-century palazzo in Venice they'd just acquired with its marble floors and frescoed ceilings, the château outside Lyon with its original medieval foundations and Renaissance additions, and the converted monastery in Switzerland where they preserved the cloisters and chapel while creating guest rooms that felt monastic but luxurious.

"We're not trying to create hotels that merely reference history," Claire said. "We're creating spaces where guests get to experience it. Not like they're museum visitors, but temporary residents. That's where your work at Belmont demonstrated you understand."

"Well, it sounds amazing," Isabella admitted, and she meant it. "But I'm curious why you're reaching out now. I've been out of corporate hospitality for nearly a year."

"Because of what you're doing now," Claire's voice sounded genuine and full of admiration. "We've been following your Wexley Inn project. It's a historic building in decline, requiring a huge restoration, with plans to operate it independently - it's exactly the kind of work we value. Someone who doesn't just manage historic properties but truly understands them from the ground up, who gets their hands dirty with the restoration itself rather than just reviewing plans and budgets."

Isabella felt a sense of pride but also discomfort. Someone at Rousseau had been tracking her project and following her progress.

"The inn is almost complete," Isabella said. "We're opening in December."

"And that's perfect timing. We wouldn't expect you to abandon a project midway. But Isabella, I need to be completely honest with you. We're making this offer now because we require exceptional leadership for our expansion, and we can't wait forever. Our board has approved substantial capital for these European acquisitions over the next five years, and the person who leads this expansion will influence how the entire generation of historic European hotels develops."

The vision was intoxicating. Not one inn, but at least a dozen. Not just Lowcountry, but Europe - Venice, Lyon, Zurich, and other cities. They'd acquired properties and would acquire more. Not proving she could restore one single building, but establishing standards that would influence the whole industry.

"Listen, I'm flying to Charleston next Thursday for meetings with potential investors," Claire continued. "Would you be available for lunch? Mossy Oaks Grill at one o'clock. Nothing formal. I'd love to meet you in person to share more about our vision and give you a chance to ask questions. No pressure, no commitment, just a conversation between two professionals who share a passion for historic properties."

Isabella's heart raced. If she agreed, it meant she was truly considering this offer. It meant leaving The Wexley Inn, the community she had been building, and Thomas, along with whatever was developing between them. But Grayson's threats had unsettled everything she believed in. She had invested all her savings, her professional reputation, and her emotional energy into that one property. A wealthy man with the right connections and no scruples could potentially destroy it through harassment.

The European position was security. Not just financial - although that mattered - but professional, and it gave her the validation that she belonged in the industry at the highest level. Although it felt disloyal, Thomas was maybe right to have protective instincts for her. Perhaps she had been so naïve, thinking she could succeed as an outsider on a small island.

"Thursday at one o'clock works," Isabella heard herself say. "See you there."

"Wonderful. I'll have my assistant send confirmation details and make the reservations. Isabella, I'm very much looking forward to meeting you. I have a feeling this conversation is going to be the start of something huge."

After they hung up, Isabella stood on the porch for a long time, gazing at the inn she had poured her heart into restoring. The building was nearly finished. In just a few weeks, they would open the doors. Guests would sleep in these rooms, eat in the kitchen, and stroll through the gardens. It was everything she'd imagined when she first saw the property. The dream she had built with her own hands.

But dreams could be fragile, and she had a responsibility to be smart. She couldn't let emotion override practicality. She wouldn't mention the meeting to anyone, not yet. There was no point in creating unnecessary concern. She was just gathering information, having a conversation, keeping her options open.

It wasn't dishonesty. It was due diligence. She forced herself to believe it.

She pulled out her phone and saw two texts from Thomas: one about the permit situation - *"Making progress, will update you this evening"* - and then one suggesting dinner tomorrow night at a restaurant on the mainland he thought she would love. She texted back, agreeing to dinner, adding a heart emoji that felt both genuine and fraudulent.

She loved Thomas - was falling in love with him, at least - had maybe never stopped loving him through all the intervening years. But love didn't pay for renovation loans if Grayson succeeded in delaying her opening, and love didn't protect her from losing everything if one wealthy developer decided to destroy her dream. Love didn't diversify risk, provide support, or validate that she'd made the right choices.

She looked at the Paris meeting confirmation on her calendar - one o'clock Thursday, Mossy Oaks Grill, Charleston - and felt guilt twist through her chest. She was just having a conversation, just listening to an offer, and being smart about her future.

She almost believed it.

CHAPTER 18

Isabella pulled into the bank's parking lot, her mind already thinking of a dozen tasks waiting at the inn that she needed to tackle. The grand opening was just three weeks away, on December 15th, perfectly timed to coincide with the holiday travel season. Every detail had to be perfect: staff training schedules, final inspections, and the Christmas décor she and Daphne had planned to celebrate the inn's Victorian heritage.

She'd barely slept, lying awake thinking about the Paris offer she still hadn't mentioned to Thomas, guilt gnawing at her every time she remembered Thursday's lunch meeting she had scheduled with Claire Rousseau. But she'd also been thinking about Thomas's hands on her face when he kissed her goodnight, the way he'd said *I love you* for the first time as they stood on her cottage porch under a sky full of stars.

The bank visit should have been a routine thing, just signing off on all the final loan disbursements now that the renovation was almost complete. Gerald Stewart's assistant had called on Friday afternoon, requesting that she come in Monday morning to finalize the paperwork. It was all just standard procedure.

She gathered her folder of documents and walked to the stately brick building, saying hello to the receptionist who had become familiar over the months of renovation financing. Gerald greeted her warmly, ushering her into his corner office with its view of the marina.

"Isabella, it's great to see you. The inn looks spectacular. I drove by yesterday and couldn't believe the transformation."

"Thank you, Gerald. We've been so fortunate to have a great team."

She sat in the leather chair across from his desk and pulled out her documentation. "I have the contractor completion certificates, the final inspection reports, and the updated project budget showing that we actually came in just under our estimate."

"Excellent, excellent," Gerald said, spreading the

papers across his desk, looking at them with careful attention. "Everything appears to be in order. The final disbursement should be processed by the end of the week, which gives you plenty of cushion before the opening."

Relief washed over her. The financial aspect had been her biggest stress - not the amount, which she budgeted carefully, but the timeline demands that turned each day into a possible crisis.

"That's wonderful news. The milestone requirements will all be met comfortably ahead of schedule."

"Well, we were concerned about those permit issues last month," Gerald said, making some notes on his documents. "But then we heard about the county complaints and potential review delays, and the loan committee had some serious discussions about risk exposure. But Thomas's personal guarantee really reassured us. Having someone of his stature and local standing co-sign gave us the confidence to keep the original terms rather than calling the loan or changing the rates."

The words seemed to come from far away, reaching Isabella through a strange ringing sound in her ears.

"I'm sorry, what personal guarantee?"

Gerald looked up, his expression changing to one

of concern. "Thomas's co-signature on your loan? He didn't tell you?"

Isabella felt the room tilt slightly, her hands gripping the arms of the leather chair. "Wait, Thomas co-signed my loan?"

"Well, yes. About two weeks ago, when those anonymous complaints were filed with the county, the uncertainty in the timeline created a risk exposure from the bank's perspective. If your opening were delayed past December 31st, as you know, we would have had to invoke the performance clauses. But Thomas offered to personally guarantee the loan, which essentially removed our risk. Gerald's discomfort was growing more apparent. "Isabella, you did know about this, didn't you?"

"No." The word came out flat. "I did *not* know."

"Oh." Gerald set his pen down carefully. "I assumed, given your relationship with Thomas, that this was something you had discussed by now."

"What exactly did he guarantee?" Her voice even sounded strange to her own ears, too calm, too controlled, while her hands were trembling.

Gerald pulled a file from his desk drawer, wishing he were anywhere else, if the look on his face was any indication. "He's personally liable for the loan balance if the bank has to call it. That's currently about $350,000, though it decreases as you make your payments, of course. He also vouched for the project's viability and your management capabilities, which carried significant weight with our loan committee."

$350,000. Thomas had put himself on the line for $350,000 - more money than some people saw in a lifetime - without even telling her. He had made decisions about her business, her loan, and her financial future without consulting her.

"And again, when did this happen?"

"Well, the paperwork was signed on November 3rd." Gerald looked genuinely distressed. "Now, Isabella, I'm very sorry. I truly thought you knew. This was presented as a mutual decision to protect the project during a difficult period."

November 3rd. The day after Grayson's threats. The day after she called Thomas panicking about the permit complaints. The day he'd said he would *look into it* and *make some calls*. This was what he had meant by handling it.

Isabella stood, her movements mechanical, like she was some kind of robot. "Thank you for the information, Gerald. I'll review the documents and get back to you about the disbursement."

"Isabella—"

"Thank you, Gerald."

She walked out of his office with her spine

straight and her hands clenched at her sides, just holding herself together through sheer force until she reached her car. Then she sat in the driver's seat, staring at the steering wheel, trying to process what she had just learned.

Thomas had guaranteed her loan, had put his own financial security at risk. He'd made decisions about her business without even consulting her. He'd gone behind her back to protect her from knowing how vulnerable her position was, and he had treated her like a child who couldn't handle adult problems.

The betrayal felt physical, a sharp, hot pain in her chest. Not because he had helped. She understood he'd been trying to solve a problem. But because he'd done it without telling her, without giving her a say, without respecting her enough to let her make her own decisions about her own business.

Flashbacks - just like all those years ago, when he decided what was best for both of them without giving her any choice in the matter. She had spent months believing they were building a genuine partnership, that this time it was different, that Thomas had grown, that she had grown, that they could be equals working together. And all along, he'd been making decisions for her, protecting her, managing her life without her knowledge or consent.

She started the car, her hands shaking with rage that she could barely contain. Isabella was usually a calm, cool, collected person, but right now she felt like she could wring his neck.

She drove toward the inn on autopilot, her mind replaying every conversation they'd had over the past couple of weeks. Every time he'd reassured her about the permit situation, every time he told her not to worry, that he was handling it.

This was not what handling it meant. Taking control, making guarantees she never would have agreed to given the choice, putting himself at risk without her knowledge, treating her like someone who needed rescuing instead of the capable professional who could solve her own problems.

By the time she pulled into the inn's driveway, the initial shock had turned into a cold fury. Thomas's truck was already there - of course it was - because he was always there, always working on her project, always helping her in ways she apparently couldn't understand or appreciate unless he hid them from her.

She found him in the dining room, kneeling beside the refinished floor with Wade, discussing the final coat of finish. He looked up when she entered, his face lighting up with that smile that usually made her heart skip a beat.

"Hey, I wasn't expecting you till this afternoon. How'd the bank meeting—" He stopped, clearly reading something in her expression. "Isabella, is something wrong?"

"I need to speak with you. Privately." Her voice was ice.

Wade looked between them and stood up quickly. "I'll just go check the veranda."

After Wade left, Thomas stood slowly. "What happened at the bank?"

"You tell me," she said, crossing her arms. "You tell me what happened at the bank, Thomas."

Understanding - and then guilt - flashed across his face. "Gerald told you about the loan guarantee."

"Gerald told me, because apparently everyone knew except me, that you co-signed on my loan. That you're personally liable for $350,000 if anything goes wrong. And that you did this two weeks ago without mentioning it to me once." Her voice was rising despite her efforts to stay calm. "Did I miss that conversation, Thomas? Did I somehow forget discussing that you put your entire financial future at risk for my project?"

"Isabella, don't—"

She held up a hand. "Don't you dare tell me you were protecting me. And don't you dare tell me how you were helping me. Was I supposed to find this romantic?"

"I was helping. Grayson's threats could have destroyed this whole project. The bank was panicking about timelines. My guarantee gave them confidence to maintain your original loan terms."

"Instead of what? Instead of telling me what was happening so I could make my own decisions? Instead of treating me like a partner who deserved to know about major financial commitments made on my behalf?"

"Well, you were already stressed about the complaints. I didn't want to add more burden."

"Burden?" Isabella's laugh was harsh. "You didn't want to burden me with decisions about *my own business*? About my name? About financial risks that could ruin both of us?"

Thomas's jaw tightened. "I had connections to solve the problem, and the bank trusts me. I've been doing business with them for years. My guarantee removed their objections. I did what needed to be done."

"You did what you thought needed to be done, without asking me." Isabella's control was fracturing. "You made decisions for me instead of with me. You treated me like I wasn't even capable of handling my own business."

"That's not what I was doing."

"Then what were you doing, Thomas? Because from where I'm standing, it looks like you went behind my back, used your connections to make guarantees that I never approved, and then hid it from me, because you assumed that I couldn't handle the truth. And that is not a partnership. That's not trust. That's control, dressed up as protection."

"Control? I was trying to help you." His voice rose to match hers. Thomas hardly ever yelled. She couldn't even remember a time she'd heard his voice raised this loud. "You called me terrified about Grayson's threats. You asked for my help navigating the crazy island politics. I used my resources to solve the problem before it became a full-on crisis. How is that control?"

"Because you didn't tell me what you were doing. You let me believe that you were making some phone calls and having some conversations. You never once mentioned you were going to put your own money on the line. You never gave me the option to say no. I don't want you taking that risk for me. You decided, all on your own, what was best for both of us."

"Because I love you." The words erupted from him with raw emotion. "Because I couldn't stand watching you struggle with something that I could easily fix. Because I have relationships and resources to protect what we've both built here, and I wasn't going to let Grayson Williams destroy your dreams through harassment."

"My dream. It's *my* dream, Thomas, not ours. Mine. You don't get to make decisions about it without my consent just because you love me. Love doesn't give you the right to control my business or my finances or even my life."

They stared at each other across the dining room. Thomas's phone rang and Emma's name flashed on the screen. He silenced it. It rang again immediately, Emma calling back.

"Answer it," Isabella said coldly. "Maybe she knows something else about my life that I don't."

Thomas hesitated and then picked up. "Emma, this isn't a good time…"

But Isabella could hear Emma's voice, urgent and worried, cutting through the attempt to defer the conversation. Thomas's expression shifted, looking at Isabella with something that seemed like dread.

"No, Emma, don't—" He stopped, listened, and then slowly lowered the phone.

"What does Emma know that I don't?" Isabella asked. "What does Emma know, Thomas?"

"She knows I co-signed your loan. I told her about it last week because—"

"Because what? Because you needed to tell some-one? Just not me? Not the person whose business you were making decisions about?" She felt hurt more than angry now. "You told your daughter, but not me. You told the bank, the county officials, you told everyone except the person most affected. Do you have any idea how that feels? To find out from my banker that my boyfriend secretly guaranteed my loan?"

"I was going to tell you."

"When? When were you going to tell me, Thomas? After the loan was paid off? After there was no more risk? Or were you going to keep it a secret forever and congratulate yourself on how well you protected me from knowing the truth?"

His phone rang again, and it was Emma calling back. This time he answered, voice tight. "Emma, I said I can't talk right now." But Isabella saw his expression change, saw guilt and conflict war across his features. "No, she doesn't know about that either."

The bottom fell out of Isabella's world. "I don't know about what. What else don't I know?"

He closed his eyes briefly, and when he opened them, he looked directly at her. "I also signed a letter to the county vouching for the inn's historical accuracy and safety compliance.

My professional reputation is tied to this project's success."

"You—" she couldn't even form words. "You put your reputation on the line, too?"

"To expedite the review process. Bill Patterson said a letter of assurance from a recognized expert—"

"I don't care what Bill Patterson said." Her voice cracked. "I care that you made a decision. You made decision after decision about my project without telling me. You've tied your finances and your professional reputation to this Inn and made yourself responsible for my success or failure, and you never even once thought that you should ask me if it was okay with me."

"You wouldn't have agreed to it," Thomas said. "You would have said no, insisted on handling it yourself, refused help even when you needed it."

"Exactly," Isabella shouted. "I would have said no, and that was my right to say no. This is my business, my risk, my decision to make, and you don't get to override it because you think you know better."

"I do know better. I've been navigating this island for over thirty years. I know how things work here. I know who to talk to and what commitments mean to people. You're brilliant at hospitality, at design, at restoration, but you don't understand the politics of this place. So I used my strengths to compensate for your weaknesses. That's what partners do."

And then there was silence.

"My weaknesses," Isabella repeated. "That's what you think this is? Me being too weak to handle the people of this island, so you need to step in and save me?"

"That's not what I meant."

"That's exactly what you meant. You think I'm not capable of navigating this world without you, and you think I need protecting and managing and rescuing just like you thought that thirty years ago when you decided for both of us that I was better off without you." Her voice broke again. "You haven't changed at all, have you, Thomas? You're still making my decisions for me, treating me like somebody who can't be trusted with the truth."

"Now that's not fair."

"Fair? You want to talk about fair?" Her laugh was bitter. "Let me tell you what's not fair. I left corporate hospitality to build something of my own, to make my decisions without oversight or interference, and I told you that. I wanted to prove that I could create something meaningful on my own terms, and you, the man I'm falling in love with, you've been undermining that the whole time, making decisions behind my back, treating it like it's your business to manage."

"I was trying to protect you."

"I don't need protecting. I need a partner, someone who respects me enough to tell me the truth and trusts me enough to handle my own problems."

They stared at each other, both breathing hard, a careful distance between them. Emma's name flashed on Thomas's phone again.

This time, Isabella reached over and answered it herself, putting it on speaker. "Emma."

"Oh gosh, Isabella, I'm so sorry." Emma's voice sounded distressed. "I didn't know he hadn't told you. I assumed that you would know about the loan guarantee. I never would have—"

"What else should I know?" Isabella's voice was eerily calm. "What else has your father done that he's kept from me?"

"Isabella, don't—" Thomas reached for the phone, but she pulled it away.

"Emma, what else?"

Emma was quiet for a long moment. "He's been having conversations with the Architectural Review Board. He made assurances to them about the project, too, but he's just trying to use favors he built up over the decades. I know he's just trying to help you. He has good intentions. He loves you so much."

"Thank you for being honest with me." Isabella ended the call and handed it back to Thomas.

"Isabella—"

"I interviewed for a job in Paris," she said abruptly.

The words seemed to land like a physical blow because Thomas's face went white. "What?"

"Vice President of European Operations for Rousseau International Hotels. They made me an offer two weeks ago. I have a meeting with the CEO on Thursday in Charleston to discuss details." She watched his expression shatter. "I haven't mentioned it to you, haven't told you I'm considering leaving, haven't even given you any say in decisions that would affect both our lives."

Thomas seemed unable to process what she was saying. "Wait, you're planning to leave to take a job in Paris? I don't understand."

"I don't know what I'm planning, but I've been keeping it a secret and making decisions about my future without consulting you, protecting you from information that you might find upsetting. Does that sound familiar?"

The parallel hit him visibly. "That's different."

"Oh, is it? How is it different, Thomas? Because

you think your secrets are justified, but mine aren't? Because you were protecting me, but I'm just planning to abandon you?"

"Yes." The word exploded from him. "Because you weren't trying to save me. I was trying to save what you were building here, and you're planning to destroy it anyway. I kept secrets to protect you, and you kept secrets to plan your exit."

"I kept secrets because I'm scared." Her voice broke completely. "Grayson's threats showed me just how vulnerable I am here because I've put everything into this project, and one wealthy man with the right connections could destroy it. Because I'm falling in love with you, but you hurt me once before, and I don't know if I can survive you doing it again. So yes, I've been keeping my options open, creating an escape plan, protecting myself because clearly I can't trust you to be honest with me."

"You're gonna leave." He said it flatly, as if the realization had just landed. "You were interviewing for jobs in Paris while kissing me, while telling me you loved me, while planning our future together."

"And you were guaranteeing my loan while claiming partnership. You were making decisions about my business while pretending to respect me." Her tears were falling now, hot and angry. "At least I was protecting myself. You were controlling me."

"I was protecting you," he corrected.

"Stop saying that. Stop pretending this was about protecting me when it was really about controlling the outcome because you can't stand feeling helpless. You did this with your father. You made his decision for him. You did this with me. Made my decision for me. And you probably did it with Sarah. Made decisions for her without asking. It's who you are, Thomas. You manage and control and decide for everyone else because you're so scared of being helpless again that you'd rather destroy the trust than risk not being in control."

Thomas flinched as if she'd slapped him. "You're right." His voice was hollow. "You're absolutely right. I made your decision for you thirty years ago, and I've been making decisions for you the last couple of weeks. I thought I was being helpful, being protective, and being a good partner, but really, I was just too afraid to face the challenges. Too afraid to let you face challenges without me trying to fix the outcome."

The admission should have felt like a victory, but instead it felt like devastation.

"But let's be honest about what you do, Isabella. You're devising an exit plan because commitment scares you. You're planning to leave before I get the chance to leave you first. It's what you do when things get tough. You jumped between corporate jobs instead of staying long enough to build roots, but now you're running from me, from us, because you - who's actually willing to commit - would have to risk vulnerability."

"That's not—"

"Isn't it?" His eyes met hers. The pain there was almost unbearable. "Be honest. You don't really want that Paris job. It's more corporate hospitality, the thing that you left to escape, but it's safe and familiar. It's an escape route from having to trust me, from having to stay in one place long enough to build something real."

She opened her mouth to deny it, but the words wouldn't come because he was right. She didn't want the Paris job, not really. She wanted The Wexley Inn. She wanted the community she was building. She wanted Thomas and the life they could create together, but the thought of wanting it terrified her.

"Maybe we're both too broken for this," Isabella finally said, exhausted. "Maybe thirty years wasn't enough time. Maybe we're just going to keep hurting each other because we can't seem to break these patterns that destroyed everything the first time."

"Maybe you're right." Thomas's voice was hoarse. "Maybe some things are just too broken to fix. You know, some foundations are too cracked to ever bear weight again."

They stood in the beautiful dining room that they restored together. The space that should have represented their collaboration felt like a monument to their failure.

"I should go," Isabella said.

"Yeah." Thomas didn't move to stop her.

She walked to the door and then turned around. "For what it's worth, I really do love you. I really thought this time could be different."

"So did I." His smile was heartbreaking. "I guess we were both wrong."

Isabella left before her tears could completely blind her. She got in her car and drove without knowing where she was heading, eventually reaching the beach access across the road where she and Thomas had first gone kayaking to the hidden cove. She sat in her parked car as the afternoon light faded, her phone displaying missed calls from everyone - Maggie, Daphne, Emma. She couldn't answer any of them. She couldn't even explain what had just happened or process the devastation of losing Thomas all over again.

This time in a fight where they had both been right and both been wrong.

Her phone buzzed with a text from Thomas. *I'm sorry for all of it. You deserved better than I gave you.*

She stared at the message for a long time before she finally responded with *So did you. I'm sorry.*

Then she turned off her phone and sat in the darkening car, watching as the sun set over the marsh. She wondered how something that had felt so right could have gone so catastrophically wrong. And then she wondered if there was any possible way they could come back from this, or if they had destroyed whatever chance they had at a second beginning.

CHAPTER 19

Isabella woke up in her bed with swollen eyes and a headache that felt like her skull was splitting open. For a brief moment, she didn't remember why, but then it all came rushing back - the bank, the fight, Thomas's face when she told him about Paris, and how they'd torn each other apart in that beautiful dining room.

Her phone had seventeen missed calls and twenty-three text messages, but she ignored all of them. She just couldn't go to the inn today, couldn't face Thomas, couldn't even pretend to be professional. Everything had shattered so completely, and for once in her professional life, she couldn't fake it.

She sent a single email to Daphne: *Not feeling well. Please handle any decisions that can't wait. Will check in tomorrow.* Then she turned off her phone and pulled the covers over her head.

Thomas stood in the entrance hall to the inn, staring at the grand staircase they had restored together, and remembered how Isabella's face had lit up when they revealed the refinished banister, how she had run her hand along the carved wood with such reverence, and how he had fallen more in love with her in that moment.

"Boss?" Wade's voice cut through his paralysis. "You want us to keep working on the veranda trim, or…?"

Thomas looked at his friend. "Oh yeah, yes, the trim, that's right. Make sure the miters are tight. We don't want any gaps showing when the paint goes on."

Wade nodded slowly, looking concerned. "You okay, man? You look like you haven't slept."

"I'm fine. Just keep… keep working."

After Wade left, Thomas pulled out his phone and stared at Isabella's last text. *So did you. I'm sorry.* He typed and deleted a dozen responses. *Can we talk?* No, it was too soon. *I love you.* Too little, too late. *Please don't leave.* Too selfish. Finally, he just put his phone away and forced himself to focus on his work. The inn opening was nineteen days away - nineteen days to finish a project that felt poisoned now, nineteen days to figure out if there was any way to fix what he had broken.

Emma showed up at Isabella's cottage at noon, letting herself in when Isabella didn't answer the door.

"Go away," Isabella said from the couch, still in her pajamas, surrounded by a bunch of wadded-up tissues, like some heartbroken girl in a bad 80s movie.

"Not a chance." Emma sat down in the armchair across from her. "Look, I'm the one who wouldn't stop calling during this whole mess. The least you can do is let me make sure you're not drowning in it alone."

"I'm fine."

"You look like hell."

Isabella laughed. "Thanks. That helps."

Emma was quiet for a moment. "For what it's worth, I'm furious with my dad. What he did - not telling you about the loan guarantee, about the letter to the county - that was totally wrong. You have every right to be angry."

"But—"

"But nothing. There's no but. He was wrong. Although I will say, and this isn't an excuse, but my dad's been managing crises alone for so long, he forgot how to ask for help or how to give help without taking over completely."

Isabella pulled a fresh tissue from the box. "He told me I'm too weak to handle island politics, that he was compensating for my weaknesses."

Emma winced. "Ouch. Yeah, that's… that's not good. That's pretty bad."

"And I told him that he controls everybody because he's too afraid to feel helpless." Isabella's voice broke. "I told him about the Paris job interview, which I've been keeping secret for two weeks."

"The what now?"

Isabella explained about Rousseau International's offer, about the Thursday meeting she still had scheduled, and about how she'd used it as ammunition to hurt Thomas the same way he'd hurt her.

Emma was quiet. "Do you want the Paris job?"

"No." The answer came immediately, with certainty Isabella hadn't expected. "I want the inn. I want this community. I want your dad. It doesn't matter what I want. We destroyed each other yester-day, and it's just too broken to fix."

"Oh, that's crap." Emma's tone was sharp. "You two destroyed each other because you're both terri-fied. He's terrified of losing you again, so he tried to control the outcome, and you were terrified of trusting him, so you created an exit strategy. Neither of you was really being honest about what you needed or what you were afraid of."

"So what? We talk about our feelings, and every-thing's going to be magically better?"

"No. You talk about your feelings, and then you do the actual hard work of changing how you respond to things. Look, I don't know if you two can fix this. Maybe it is too broken, but if you're going to walk away, at least walk away knowing that you tried everything. Don't leave because you're scared. Leave because it genuinely doesn't work."

After Emma left, Isabella sat in her cottage for a long time in silence. Finally, she picked up her phone and sent three text messages.

To Claire Rousseau's assistant: *I need to cancel Thursday's meeting. I've decided not to pursue the posi-tion. Thank you for the opportunity.*

To Maggie: *Can we talk? I need advice.*

To Thomas, she typed and deleted at least a

dozen messages before finally settling on: *We should talk, but not yet. I need time to think.*

His response came immediately. *Take all the time you need. I'm not going anywhere.*

Thomas arrived at the inn before dawn, needing some quiet and physical work to try to calm the chaos in his mind. He'd spent the night replaying the fight and then hearing Isabella's accusations echo in the darkness. *You manage, control, and decide for everyone else because you're so terrified of being helpless.*

She was right. He had been doing it for almost his whole life. With his father, he took control of the crisis, accepting Sarah's family's blackmail without exploring any alternatives. He made the decision alone, nearly ruining his entire life in the process. With Sarah, he never told her the truth about why he married her. He managed her illness by becoming both father to Emma and nurse to Sarah and made medical decisions without even asking her what she wanted. With Emma, he raised her with such strict control after Sarah died, managing her schedule and choices because he was terrified of failing her or losing her.

And now with Isabella, he was guaranteeing her loan, vouching for her project, and using his connections, all without asking if that's what she wanted. Protection had always been his love language, but somewhere along the way, that protection had become control.

He was deep in the crawlspace, checking the foundation moisture barriers, when his phone rang. It was Robert Henderson.

"Hey Thomas, heard about the situation with Ms. Montgomery and wanted to check in."

Thomas crawled out of the crawlspace and brushed off the dust. "News travels fast."

"Always has on this island." Robert's voice was gentle. "Look, for what it's worth, the review board is speeding up her permit. She should have the approval by the end of the week."

"That's good. She deserves good news."

"Thomas," Robert paused briefly. "What you did - you know, guaranteeing her loan and vouching for the project—that came from a good place. I understand that. But you can't protect people from their own lives. Sometimes, the best you can do is stand beside them as they face a challenge, not fix all their problems for them."

"Yeah, I know that now," Thomas said as he sat on the porch steps.

"Do you? Because I've watched you do this for decades with Sarah, with Emma, with clients who needed guidance and not management, I understand your approach. You're a good man with good intentions, but that isn't an excuse for taking away someone else's choices."

"So how do I fix it?" Thomas asked quietly.

"Well, you start by being honest about why you do it. Not with Isabella, but with yourself. What are you really afraid of?"

After Robert hung up, Thomas sat on the porch steps for a long time, watching the sun rise over the marsh. What was he really afraid of? Probably being helpless again, watching someone he loved struggle, and being unable to fix it. The paralyzing terror he felt when his father's business collapsed, when Sarah got her diagnosis, or when Emma cried herself to sleep after her mother died. He'd spent his entire adult life trying not to feel that helpless ever again, and in doing so, he'd hurt people he was trying to protect.

Isabella met Maggie at the club for lunch, grateful that they found a table in the corner away from everyone who always wanted to listen to gossip.

"So," Maggie said, "Emma called me, gave me the basics, and now I want to hear your version."

Isabella told her everything. The loan guarantee,

the fight, the Paris offer, the way they had just evis-
cerated each other right there in the dining room. By
the end, she was crying again, and Maggie was
handing her a linen napkin.

"Well, that's quite a mess you two have created."

"I know."

"Do you love him?"

"Yes."

"Do you want that Paris job?"

"No, and I've already declined it."

"Then why haven't you told him that?"

Isabella twisted the napkin in her hands.
"Because I'm scared. He left me once. He just made
decisions for me again. Now, what if he does it again
and again? What if I trust him and then he destroys
me?"

Maggie was quiet for a moment. "Sugar, let me
tell you something about Thomas Langley. I've
known him since he was barely old enough to shave.
I've watched him raise that daughter alone after his
wife died. I've seen how he treats people, how he
builds things, and how he loves." She leaned forward.
"His fatal flaw is thinking he has to carry every
burden alone. It comes from raising Emma after
Sarah died. No one to share the weight. He had to
shoulder everything himself. That doesn't make him

a bad man. It makes him a man who needs to learn a different way of loving."

"But he keeps—"

"I know, making decisions for you. Yeah, he does, and that's wrong." Maggie's voice was firm. "But Isabella, you keep creating an escape route instead of just committing, and that's also wrong. You're both damaged in ways that make you hurt each other. The question is whether you're going to do the actual work of healing those wounds or you're going to just let old patterns destroy something that could be beautiful."

"I don't know if I'm even brave enough."

"Well, then you've already lost him, because love, and I mean real lasting love, requires a lot more courage than anything else. It requires showing up even when you're terrified and trusting even after you've been hurt. It requires vulnerability that feels like you might die."

Isabella thought about that for the rest of the afternoon, about whether she had enough trust and bravery to ever risk her heart again.

Thomas sat across from Emma in his little kitchen, nursing coffee he didn't want, while his daughter studied him with her concerned eyes.

"You look rough, Dad."

"Well, thanks. You're doing wonders for my self-esteem."

"I'm serious. When was the last time you really ate a proper meal or got some sleep?"

"I'm fine."

"No, you're not. You're not fine." Emma clinked her mug against the counter. "You're miserable because you screwed up and you don't know how to fix it with Isabella."

"There's nothing to fix. She's probably taking that Paris job and moving on. She'll be eating expensive pastries with some French guy named Pierre on a small sidewalk, staring at the Eiffel Tower in a few weeks, moving on to the life she was meant to have if I hadn't derailed hers years ago."

"Oh, for the love of—" Emma stood up. "Dad, stop. Just stop with this. Yeah, you screwed up. You made decisions for her without asking, again. Treated her like she needed managing instead of a partner, and that was wrong."

"I know. I've said that."

"I'm not finished." Emma's voice was steely. "You

screwed up, but so did she. She kept that major job offer a secret. She was so busy protecting herself from being potentially hurt that she didn't even give the relationship a real chance."

Thomas looked up, surprised by her defending him.

"You're both human," Emma said. "You both have trauma that causes you to react in unhealthy ways. You control because you're scared of feeling helpless. She runs because she's scared of being abandoned, and neither of you are villains. You're just two wounded people who said some ugly things to each other."

"So what do I do?"

Emma sat back down and reached across the counter to take his hand. "You do what Mom would have told you to do. You stop trying to fix things from a distance. You show up, you tell her the whole truth, you admit you were wrong and explain why you did it, and then you let her decide what happens next."

"What if she chooses Paris?"

"Well, then you accept it and move on. But at least you know you were honest. At least you know you gave her the real you, not the version that has to be perfect or in control."

After Emma left, Thomas sat at the kitchen table for a long time, thinking about Sarah—how he'd never told her the truth about why he married her, and how he managed her illness without always asking what she wanted. He tried to do the very best things for her, and maybe she went through treatments she wouldn't have chosen herself. He couldn't do that again. He couldn't let Isabella leave without knowing the whole truth.

He pulled out his phone and typed: *I need to tell you the real reason I do this - not the version that makes me look better, but the actual truth. When you're ready to hear it, I'm prepared to tell it.*

Isabella's response came about an hour later: *Saturday evening, at the inn, after the workers leave.*

Luella found Isabella in the kitchen on Thursday afternoon, supposedly looking at the equipment layout, but she was actually staring at a commercial oven without really seeing it.

"Child, you look like death warmed over."

Isabella turned, managing a weak smile. "Well, gee, thanks, Luella. That's very comforting."

"Wasn't meant to be comforting. Was meant to be

true." Luella sat on a stool. "Heard about your fight with Thomas. The whole island's heard about it, actually. Y'all sure didn't keep it quiet. That man's been walking around looking like his dog died."

"I do not want to talk about Thomas."

"Well, I guess that's too bad, because I've got some things to say and you're going to listen." Luella's tone showed that there was no argument to be had. "You interviewed for a job in Paris." It wasn't a question.

Isabella shouldn't have been surprised. Nothing stayed secret on the island. "Well, I guess I did over the phone a couple of weeks ago, but I canceled the in-person meeting."

"Because you don't want it?"

"Because I want *this*," Isabella said, gesturing around the kitchen. "I want the inn. I want to build something here."

"But you kept it secret from Thomas? Just in case? Is that your pattern, sugar? When things get hard, you start planning a way to leave before anybody can leave you first?"

"And how would you know?"

"I've been observing people for seventy-five years. You learn to recognize patterns. Listen, I think you've probably been on the run your whole life, especially after Thomas left you. You didn't get any explanation or anything, and I'm sure that shook you to your core. That's why you never stay long enough to build roots. Roots make you vulnerable."

"Like you said, Thomas left me once. Thirty years ago. Just left. No explanation, really, no closure. And even though he apologized and explained, he did the same thing again this week. He made decisions without me and treated me like I couldn't handle the truth. So why should I trust him not to leave again?"

"Because he ain't leaving, child. He's standing right there, right here in this inn every day, working himself half to death because he can't fix what he broke and he doesn't know what else to do." Luella leaned forward. "You're already gone, aren't you? You're physically here, but emotionally, you've got one foot out the door, protecting yourself and not committing fully. It's just another way of running."

"Then I guess I don't know how to stop," Isabella said.

"You choose. You stop by choosing to stay even when you're scared. You stop by telling him the truth, that you're terrified, but you want to try anyway. You stop by actually committing instead of thinking of ways to leave." Luella stood. "Love ain't safe, honey. Real love requires risk in everything. The question is whether you're brave enough to take that risk or if you're going to let fear make you leave before anyone can hurt you. Then you're going to spend your whole life alone."

After Luella left, Isabella sat in the kitchen for a long time, thinking about whether or not she actually had the courage to stay and stick it out.

CHAPTER 20

Isabella spent Saturday morning with Daphne doing a final walk-through. The Christmas decorations were being delivered on Monday. Of course, it was period-appropriate greenery, some simple candles, and elegant touches that would make the inn feel festive without overwhelming it.

"Everything looks perfect," Daphne said, checking off the items on her tablet. "The opening is going to be amazing."

"If there still is an opening," Isabella murmured, still wallowing in her sadness.

"Oh my goodness, there will be." Daphne's voice was firm. "You and Thomas will figure this out. Even if you don't, even if you end up hating each other, this inn is still going to succeed because you're brilliant at what you do, and this place is extraordinary."

By evening, the workers had all left, and the inn stood quiet. Isabella waited in the library, the room where so much of their partnership had been built. Watching through the window as Thomas's truck pulled into the driveway, she rehearsed what she wanted to say a dozen times, but as she watched him walk toward the entrance, all her prepared words evaporated.

He looked terrible - drawn, exhausted, older than he had just days ago - but when he saw her through the window, his expression shifted into something that looked terrified and hopeful all at once. This was it. This was the conversation that would either save them or wreck them.

Isabella took a deep breath and went to open the door.

Thomas stood in the doorway of the library. For a moment, neither of them moved. They just looked at each other across the space.

"Hey," Isabella said finally, her voice barely above a whisper.

"Hey." He stepped inside and closed the door. "Thanks for agreeing to talk."

"I almost didn't. I'm still so angry with you, Thomas, and I feel hurt and confused. I don't know how we could ever come back from this."

"I know." He moved to the window and looked

out at the grounds. "I've spent the past five days thinking about why I did what I did, and not the surface reason of protecting you, and helping you, and using my connections, but the real reason."

Isabella waited, her heart pounding.

He turned to face her. "I'm terrified of being helpless. I have been that way my whole life, ever since my father's crisis at least. When his business collapsed, and he faced bankruptcy - and potentially jail time - I felt powerless. I was twenty-two years old, you know, about to graduate, planning a future with you, and suddenly everything was falling apart, and I couldn't fix it."

He sat in one of the leather chairs. "Sarah's family offered me one way to fix it, a terrible way that cost me you, but a way, and I took that because doing something - even something that destroyed my own happiness - felt better than doing nothing, felt better than being helpless."

She remained standing, listening.

"Then Sarah got sick, and I spent seven years watching her decline, trying everything, controlling every aspect of her treatment and Emma's care in our household, and desperately believing that if I just managed it all perfectly, I could keep her alive, but I couldn't. She died anyway. I felt helpless all over again. That soul-crushing terror of watching someone you love suffer, and then being unable to fix it."

"Thomas—"

"Please, let me finish." He looked up at her. "I've spent fifteen years since then being with Emma alone, building my business, helping clients, serving on boards, and through all of it, I've been doing the same thing - controlling the outcomes, managing situations, making decisions for other people. Because at least then I'm doing something, and I'm not helpless."

He stood and paced to the bookshelf, tracing his fingers along the restored wood.

"Then you came back into my life. You - the woman I had loved and lost, whom I'd made decisions for once before - and then Grayson threatened your project, and when you called me scared and asking for help, every instinct I have screamed at me to fix it. Screamed at me to protect you, and to use everything in my power to make it disappear so you didn't have to suffer through it."

"So you guaranteed my loan without telling me."

"So I guaranteed your loan without telling you," he confirmed. "I told myself I was protecting you from unnecessary stress, that you needed to focus on the opening and not worry about your finances, and that I was being helpful and loving and supportive."

He turned to face her. "But you know, Robert Henderson asked me a question that I couldn't stop thinking about. He asked me what I was terrified of. And I'm afraid that if I don't control the outcome, people I love will be destroyed by circumstances that I could have prevented. I'm afraid of watching you struggle when I have the power to make it easier. And most of all," his voice dropped to barely audible. "I'm afraid that if I'm just honest and vulnerable and not in control, you'll see that I'm not strong enough, that I'm just a man who's terrified all the time and trying desperately to hide it."

The admission hung in the air between them. It was the most honest thing she'd ever heard him say before.

"You hurt me," she said, her voice shaking, "and not because you helped. I understand you were trying to help, but because you didn't trust me enough to tell me the truth, you made decisions about my business, my loan, and my professional reputation without even including me. You treated me like I was too fragile or too incapable to handle it."

"I know."

"And it felt exactly like when you left me all those years ago, when you decided for both of us that that was the best thing without giving me any say, when you decided because you assumed you knew better."

"You're right. I did the same thing, and I can't promise I won't struggle with the same instincts again, because apparently they're deeply ingrained. But I can promise to fight them, to catch myself when I start trying to control instead of support you, to ask instead of deciding for you, and to be honest instead of protective."

"How do I know you mean it?" Isabella asked. "How do I know you won't just do this again the next time things get difficult?"

"You don't." The words were simple. "You can't know. All I can do is show you through my actions over time. If you're not willing to take that risk, if you can't trust me after what I've done, then I understand. I'll finish the work here as soon as possible, turn over all the documentation, and step away so you can run your inn without me undermining your authority."

But the thought of Thomas leaving - of never seeing him in the halls of the inn again - made Isabella's chest constrict painfully.

"I canceled the Paris interview," she said abruptly.

His head snapped up. "What?"

"Tuesday, after our fight, I sent an email declining the position." She wrapped her arms around herself. "Because I don't want it. I never really wanted it. I wanted an escape route in case this" - she gestured between them - "in case we didn't work out. In case you hurt me again. In case I needed to run."

She moved to the window, staring out over the grounds. "Luella told me I've been running my whole life - through multiple corporate positions, through different cities, through different relation-ships - never staying anywhere long enough to build real roots because roots make you vulnerable." She turned to face him. "And you were right about me, too, in that fight. I do create exit strategies instead of committing completely. I keep one foot out the door so nobody can abandon me because I'm already halfway gone. It's my pattern. My way of protecting myself."

"Isabella…"

"Listen. I interviewed for that job on the phone because–"

"It was your dream."

"Not because it was my dream," she interrupted, "but because Grayson's threats terrified me. Because I realized just how vulnerable I actually am here - finan-cially, professionally, and emotionally. Because I've put everything into this inn, into this community, and now into you. And that level of commitment is terrifying when you've spent your whole life protecting yourself. My biggest fear was that I did need you to help me fix this, and I don't like to need other people." She met his eyes. "I kept it a secret because I was ashamed. Because I knew it meant I wasn't fully committed to us, and I wasn't fully trusting you. I was already planning my escape before you could hurt me first. And when you confronted me about it, I used it as a weapon. Threw it at you to hurt you the same way you had hurt me."

"We both hurt each other," Thomas said quietly.

"Yes, we did. Badly. And I don't know if we can come back from this. I don't know if two people with our particular damage can manage to build something healthy together, or if we're going to keep triggering each other's worst patterns."

He crossed the room slowly and stopped a few feet from her. "I love you, Isabella. I've loved you for thirty years. Even when I was married to someone else, I am embarrassed to say. Even when I tried to convince myself I had moved on. I don't want to lose you again."

"I love you, too," she whispered. "And that's what makes this so terrifying. Because loving you means trusting that you're not going to make decisions for me. And trusting you means risking that you'll hurt me again."

"And loving you means trusting that you're not going to run when things get hard. It means believing that you'll stay even when you're scared and that you won't keep one foot out the door waiting for an excuse to leave."

They looked at each other across that small distance, both of them afraid, both of them hurting, but both wanting desperately to bridge that gap.

"What if we can't change?" she asked. "What if these patterns are too deep? What if we try and fail and hurt each other even more?"

"Well, then at least we tried," Thomas said, his voice full of emotion. "At least we gave it everything we had. At least we were honest with each other. And which one would hurt more - to walk away now or to try and fail?"

She took a shaky breath. "I want to try. I want to do the work of learning to stay and trusting you. But I need you to promise me something."

"Anything."

"Promise me that if you start falling into old patterns or thinking you need to decide for me, that you'll catch yourself. That you'll tell me what you're thinking before acting on it."

"I promise."

"And I need you to promise that you'll start

telling me if you feel the need to run—that you're scared."

"I promise."

They stood in the library's darkness, the inn quiet around them.

"So what now?" she asked.

"Now we choose." He took a step closer. "We choose to try, and we choose to trust. And we know it's going to be hard work, but we're used to hard work. We're committed to doing that work together."

"Together," Isabella repeated. "As partners. Especially when it's difficult."

Thomas reached out slowly, giving her time to step back if she wanted. He cupped her face gently. "And I can't promise I'll be perfect, but I can promise I'll fight with everything I have. And I'll choose to be a partner to you. And I'll trust you to handle your own life, even when every instinct tells me to manage it for you."

She closed her eyes briefly. "I can't promise I won't get scared or have moments where I want to run, but I promise I'll fight it. That I'll choose this commitment."

"That's all I'm asking." His thumb traced her cheekbone.

"You know, we're probably going to fail a lot," she said, laughing.

"Probably. But we'll fail together. And we'll get back up and try again."

Isabella moved toward him first. She stepped into his arms, pressed her face against his chest, and allowed some tears to fall for the pain they'd caused each other and for the years they had spent apart. His arms came around her, immediately holding her close.

"I'm sorry for keeping the Paris interview a secret, and for using it to hurt you."

"I'm sorry too - for doing all the things that I did."

They stood together, holding each other as the library grew darker. Finally, Thomas pulled back slightly.

"Can I kiss you?"

"Please."

This kiss was different from before. Not tentative like their first kiss, and not comfortable like some of the ones that had followed, but like a kiss that held hope and second chances.

The week before the grand opening passed in a blur. Thomas and Isabella moved through the inn side by side, their partnership rebuilding every day. Every so often, Thomas would catch himself trying to decide without consulting her, but he caught himself every time.

The Christmas decorations arrived on Monday as planned: fresh magnolia garlands for the staircase banister, pine roping for the mantels, and simple white candles for every window. Daphne had chosen everything with historical accuracy in mind, creating holiday atmospheres that felt more Victorian than modern.

"It's perfect," Isabella said, standing in the entrance hall. "Elegant without being overdone."

"Luella wants to hang mistletoe," Thomas said, wrapping his arms around her waist from behind. "I told her that was her decision to make about her kitchen."

"And she told you it was going in the doorway between the dining room and parlor, whether you liked it or not, didn't she?"

"How did you know that?"

"Because I know Luella," Isabella said, laughing, "and because she told me this morning she was doing it specifically so we'd have to have an excuse to kiss at the opening."

"Subtle, as always."

"Are you nervous?" Thomas asked quietly.

"Terrified. What if nobody shows up? Or what if they come and hate it? Or what if Grayson shows up and makes a big scene?"

"Then we'll handle it together." He turned her to face him. "You've created something amazing here, Isabella, and people are going to want to see that."

"*We* created—" she corrected. "This inn exists because of both of us. I wouldn't have gotten here without you."

"Well, I wouldn't have wanted to get here with anyone else."

They kissed, soft and sweet, interrupted by Wade from the second floor, yelling about garland placement.

"Duty calls," Thomas said, touching her face once more before heading up the stairs.

Wednesday was the final staff training. Isabella had hired people carefully - people who understood the hospitality industry and appreciated the inn's history. The assistant manager she'd selected was Margaret Lee, who had twenty years of boutique hotel experience and a passion for historic properties.

"The key," Isabella told her staff in the dining

room, "is making the guests feel like they're experiencing history rather than just observing it. We don't want this to feel like a museum, so every interaction we have with them should reinforce that they're in a special place, but don't make them feel like they can't touch anything or relax here."

She walked through service standards, showed them the guest rooms with their carefully curated period details, and introduced them to Luella, who would oversee all food service.

"Miss Luella is the heart of this operation," Isabella said. "If she tells you something about how the kitchen runs, you listen to her. She's forgotten more about Lowcountry hospitality than most of us will ever know."

Luella, pretending to be utterly unaffected by the compliment, just humphed and returned to looking at her opening night menu.

Thomas appeared midday to conduct the safety orientation, explain fire exits, emergency procedures, and the systems that kept the old building functioning safely. This was what partnership looked like - not just one person running everything, but two people bringing their different strengths.

After the staff left full of enthusiasm and ready for Saturday's opening, Isabella found Thomas on the back porch looking at the gardens.

"Penny for your thoughts?"

He smiled. "Just thinking about how different this feels from when I started back in May. This was just another project. Now it's—" he gestured, "so much more."

"It's home," Isabella said.

"Yeah." He pulled her close. "It's home."

Thursday brought final inspections of the fire marshal, health department, and building inspector. Isabella and Thomas had walked through with each official, documentation in hand, answering questions with confidence. Every inspection passed with flying colors.

"This is exceptional work," the fire marshal said, examining the sprinkler system. "You've updated everything necessary. Not easy to do in a building this old."

When everything was done, Isabella looked at Thomas. "We did it."

"We did it," he repeated.

Then they were kissing, celebrating, and laughing with relief and joy.

"Two more days," Thomas said. "Two more days and we open the doors to this place."

Friday was for final touches. Emma arrived from Atlanta to help with last-minute details, with her marketing materials displayed in the lobby and social media posts already generating interest.

"The reservation system is working. Already showing bookings through February," she said, looking at her laptop. "And the holiday season is completely sold out."

"Sold out?" Isabella's eyes widened. "Really? Already?"

"People want to experience this place. Isabella, you've created something really special. Plus, I have to say my marketing is pretty amazing," Emma said, grinning.

"Humble as always," Thomas said.

Maggie stopped by Friday afternoon to review the placement of the historical society's informational materials, but really to check on Isabella and Thomas.

"You two look happy," she said. "Actually happy, not just pretending for show."

"Well, we're working on it," Isabella said. "Some days are easier than others."

"Well, that's real life, sugar. Anybody who tells you relationships are easy all the time is either lying or hasn't been in one long enough."

Maggie squeezed her hand. "I'm proud of you. Both of you. Not just for restoring this beautiful old building, but for doing the hard work of restoring your relationship with each other."

CHAPTER 21

The day of the grand opening arrived with clear, cold weather - perfect for a Lowcountry winter. Isabella met Thomas on the front porch of the inn.

"Big day," he said, smiling.

"Huge day," she said. "Are you ready?"

"With you, always."

As they walked inside, Emma smiled. "There's the woman of the hour," she said, waving Isabella over. "The photographer wants some shots of you in front of the inn before guests arrive. Natural light showing the building at its best."

Isabella spent the next hour being positioned and repositioned, feeling quite self-conscious but trusting Emma's vision. The photographer also wanted pictures of Thomas with his crew and gathered them on the porch, then took photos of Luella in her spotless kitchen.

"These are going to be great for the website," Emma said, reviewing the images on the camera. "Historic elegance meets modern hospitality, exactly the branding we want."

By three o'clock, everything was ready. The inn was glowing with candlelight and greenery, with fires burning in every fireplace, and the scent of pine, cinnamon, and wood smoke floating through the air. Guest rooms stood prepared for the first-night visitors - three couples who'd booked the inaugural weekend, paying premium rates for the privilege of being first.

The staff gathered for one final huddle. Isabella addressed them in the entrance hall, with Thomas beside her, both dressed for the elegant evening - Isabella in a deep green velvet dress and Thomas in a dark suit that made him look devastatingly handsome.

"Thank you," Isabella said, her voice catching a bit. "Thank you for believing in this project and for bringing your skills and passion to make it succeed. Tonight we're not just opening an inn, we're reviving a piece of this island's history. We're creating a place where people can come, connect, and make new memories. That is sacred work, and I'm honored to do it with all of you."

The staff applauded, clearly moved. Luella stepped forward, her expression stern but her eyes bright.

"This whole building's been standing here for one hundred fifty-three years," she said, "and I've been working here forty-three of those years. I've seen owners come and go, seen some renovations succeed and fail, seen this place at its best and at its worst." She looked at Thomas and Isabella. "But I've never seen anybody put as much heart into restoring it as you two have. You didn't just fix this building - you understood its soul. And it's going to make this inn special again."

Isabella felt the tears threatening to fall and blinked them back as Thomas squeezed her hand.

"All right," Margaret Lee, the new assistant manager, said. "Doors open in thirty minutes. Let's show this island what we've built."

The next hour was organized chaos as guests began arriving at five - island residents who'd been invited, local dignitaries, and members of the historical society, even the architectural review board. Maggie arrived early, elegant in navy silk, greeting everyone with the social grace of someone who'd been doing this her entire life, and she probably had.

"You should be proud," she told Isabella. "This is really extraordinary."

Vivian Pierce arrived with her usual entourage, and Isabella steeled herself for criticism, but for once, Vivian surprised her.

"Isabella," she said, extending her hand. "I must acknowledge that you've done exceptional work here. The restoration is historically accurate. It was a difficult balance to achieve that and make it livable." She paused. "I may have underestimated your capabilities."

It was as close to an apology as Vivian Pierce was likely to offer. Isabella accepted it graciously.

"Thank you. That means a great deal coming from someone with your knowledge of the island."

Even Grayson Williams made an appearance, though his stay was very brief. He congratulated Isabella with the practiced charm that didn't quite reach his eyes and acknowledged Thomas with a curt nod before departing.

"He knows he lost," Thomas said quietly. "That's got to sting."

"Good," Isabella said without sympathy.

By 6 p.m., the inn was full of people laughing, talking, admiring the restoration, and eating Luella's fantastic food. Musicians played period-appropriate holiday music in the parlor. Christmas decorations glowed in the candlelight.

Robert Henderson found them in the library, where they'd retreated briefly for a moment of quiet.

"Congratulations," he said. "This is some of the best restoration work I've seen in fifty years. Thomas, your father would be proud."

"Thanks, Robert. That means everything."

"And, Ms. Montgomery, you've created something special here. Not just a hotel, but a genuine connection to the island's past. I'm glad you chose to stay."

After he left, Thomas pulled Isabella close.

"How are you holding up?"

"Overwhelmed, happy, terrified that it's all going to fall apart," she laughed. "Normal opening night feelings, I think."

"It's not going to fall apart. Look at what you've built. This is real. This is success."

Emma appeared in the doorway. "Sorry to interrupt the lovebirds, but people are asking when you're going to give an official welcome speech. Luella says dinner service is ready whenever you are."

Isabella took a deep breath. "Now or never."

"Now," Thomas said firmly. "Definitely now."

They returned to the entrance hall, where

Margaret had gathered the guests. The crowd quieted as Isabella stepped forward, Thomas behind her.

"Thank you all for being here tonight," Isabella began. "When I first saw this inn last May, it was in severe disrepair, but I could see its bones - the incredible craftsmanship, the history, the potential to be something truly special again." She looked at Thomas. "I couldn't have brought this vision to life alone. Thomas Langley and his exceptional team understood exactly what the building needed. They treated every detail with reverence and preserved what could be saved, restored what couldn't. This inn exists because of collaboration - between past and present, between preservation and progress, between vision and execution."

Applause rippled through the crowd.

"But this inn isn't just ours. It belongs to this island, to this community that celebrated here over the past one hundred fifty-three years, and tonight we're honored to return it to you - restored, renewed, and ready to serve its purpose again as a gathering place."

More applause.

Thomas stepped forward. "Many of you have known me your whole lives. You knew my father and watched me grow up here. You supported my business over the years. This island has been my home for almost fifty years, but this project - " he gestured around the inn - "this has been the most meaningful work of my career. Not just because the building is beautiful, but because it represents partnership in its truest form. Isabella and I built this together, combining our strengths, and neither of us could have achieved it alone. The Wexley Inn is open," Thomas said. "Welcome home."

The applause was thunderous.

Luella announced that dinner was served, and the crowd moved toward the dining room, where long tables had been set with period linens and candlelight, laden with Lowcountry specialties.

Isabella and Thomas moved through the crowd, accepting congratulations and answering questions.

"We did it," she whispered to Thomas during a brief moment alone.

"We did it," Thomas said.

Hours later, after the guests had departed, the staff had cleaned up, the overnight guests had retired to their rooms, and the fires had burned to embers, Thomas and Isabella stood on the front porch.

"How does success feel?" he asked.

"Exhausting, exhilarating, and surreal." She leaned against him. "How about you?"

"Same, plus grateful and hopeful." He turned to

face her. "I love you, Isabella Montgomery. Thank you for giving us this second chance."

"I love you too." She touched his face gently.

They kissed on the porch of the inn they'd restored together. The building was witnessing this moment just as it had witnessed one hundred fifty-plus years of other moments - celebrations and sorrows, beginnings and endings.

Some foundations, it turned out, could bear weight again.

Some love stories, with enough courage, honesty, and work, could really have second chances.

The Wexley Inn stood restored, ready for its next chapter, just like them.

Six Months Later

Isabella sat on the veranda of The Wexley Inn on a warm June evening with her laptop open to some boring financial reports. They did show steady profitability, which was great. She also read reviews praising the character and comforts of her new inn while answering emails from guests requesting reservations.

The inn had exceeded all projections. Word of mouth had spread throughout the Lowcountry and beyond. Travel magazines had featured it. The Historical Society had used it for events, and Emma's consultancy was thriving, with the inn as her showcase project.

Thomas emerged from inside carrying two glasses of sweet tea and settled into the rocking chair beside her. He'd moved into Isabella's cottage, his own sold to a young couple who'd fallen in love with it just as Isabella had fallen in love with him. Isabella had moved into the inn so she could be there for the day-to-day operations.

"Busy day?" he asked.

"We're fully booked through September. We're already taking November reservations," Isabella said, closing her laptop. "How'd that consultation go for the Beaufort property?"

"Good, really good, actually. The owners want to move forward with restoration. I told them that it would require some input on the hospitality side from you, designing the spaces that work. Our first official joint project outside of the inn. Well, if you want it," Thomas reached for her hand. "I'm not trying to volunteer you for anything without asking."

"I want it," Isabella said. "Working together on the inn was… well, let's just say it was the best professional collaboration of my life, and I'd love to do it again."

"Equal partners?"

"Always equal partners," Isabella said, smiling.

Luella appeared in the doorway. "Dinner service is finishing up. Tonight's guests are all settled in, so

I'm going to head to my cottage. You two don't do anything I wouldn't do."

"Well, that leaves us a lot of options," Thomas said dryly.

Luella laughed and headed down the porch steps toward her cottage, waving without turning around.

"She's pleased with herself," Isabella said.

"She's been pleased with herself since we got back together. Keeps reminding me she knew it would work out," Thomas said, pulling Isabella from her chair onto his lap.

"She's insufferable about being right."

"She was right, though. Annoyingly so," he said, laughing.

They sat together as the June evening deepened, watching fireflies emerge from the marsh grass and listening to the sounds of the inn settling in for the night.

"I've been thinking," Thomas said carefully, "about us. About the future."

Isabella's heart rate picked up slightly. "What about it?"

"I want to marry you," he said, directly. "Not right now, necessarily, but whenever you're ready. But I want you to know that that's where I'm headed. That I'm not going to keep you guessing on my intentions. That I am all in on us, on this, on building a life together."

She was quiet for a moment. Then she smiled against his shoulder.

"I want to marry you, too, when we're both ready, when we've had time to prove that we can do this. But yes. Eventually, definitely, yes."

"Yeah?"

"Yeah." She pulled back to look at him. "You're my partner, Thomas - in business and in life - and I can't imagine doing this with anybody else. I want to grow old together, sitting in rocking chairs on the front porch of this old inn, listening to the sounds of the Lowcountry."

"Good." He kissed her softly. "Because I'm not going anywhere. No matter what challenges we face, I'm staying, and we're facing them together."

"Together," she agreed.

They sat on the veranda as the stars emerged, the inn quiet around them. Some things were worth fighting for, some patterns worth breaking, and some love was worth the risk of vulnerability and staying even when you were scared.

The Wexley Inn had taught them that, and they would carry those lessons forward to whatever came next. New projects, new challenges, new chapters of a story that had started thirty years ago and was just now finding its true beginning.

Did you know I have a private Facebook reader group with over 25,000 members? We have a ton of fun in there every day, so if you'd like to engage with me personally and meet other great people, join us at https://www.facebook.com/groups/RachelReaders.

www.ingramcontent.com/pod-product-compliance
Lightning Source LLC
Chambersburg PA
CBHW021401310726
48971CB00005B/1160